About the author

Tony Edwards lives with his wife Greta in a 16th century house in Surrey and drives a 1950's Bentley, the inspiration for his first novel *Wilson Lacigam's Bentley*. *The Elders* is his fourth novel and was inspired by a new social time bomb – the fact that there are more *over-sixties* than *under sixteens* in the UK today.

THE ELDERS

*To John
With Best Wishes
Tony*

DEDICATION

To our faithful friends
Vicky, Melly, Jacob, Mo,
Trubshaw, Barny, Sam
Bella & Bertie

Tony Edwards

THE ELDERS

AUSTIN & MACAULEY

Copyright © Tony Edwards

The right of Tony Edwards to be identified as author of this work has been asserted by him in accordance with section 77 and 78 of the Copyright, Designs and Patents Act 1988.

All rights reserved. No part of this publication may be reproduced, stored in a retrieval system, or transmitted in any form or by any means, electronic, mechanical, photocopying, recording, or otherwise, without the prior permission of the publishers.

Any person who commits any unauthorized act in relation to this publication may be liable to criminal prosecution and civil claims for damages.

A CIP catalogue record for this title is
available from the British Library.

ISBN 978 1 84963 099 3

www.austinmacauley.com

First Published (2011)
Austin & Macauley Publishers Ltd.
25 Canada Square
Canary Wharf
London
E14 5LB

Printed & Bound in Great Britain

Chapter One

An acute sense of unease turned-up with the morning post on Mr Cornfield's sixtieth birthday. It hung heavily in the air like a gathering storm; a rumbling, grumbling warning of darker days ahead with the whispered hint of indignities to follow.

But Mr Cornfield ignored it, carefully brushed the lapels of his brown tweed jacket, tweaked the knot on a favourite paisley tie and set off for work as usual, leaving three birthday cards unopened on the kitchen table in a silent snub to old age and retirement.

Hands clenched into angry fists, punched deep into his raincoat pockets, shoulders hunched against a chill, October wind, Mr Cornfield kicked an erratic path through the fallen leaves on Friday Street, incensed at the unfairness of it all. Legalised fraud, he called it, and repeated it several times, out loud, as if he might be talking to somebody else, before he reached the sub-post office where a small group of regulars waited in a huddle on the narrow stretch of pavement outside.

'Late night, eh Gerry?'

Mr Cornfield, who preferred to be called Gerald, greeted the first of the morning's worn out clichés with a weak but polite smile and a gentle nod while he fumbled with a bunch of door keys.

'Anyone we know, is she?'

From somewhere in the back of his throat a bogus, joyless chuckle struggled to reach his lips; a fake, fragile sound as contrived as the rakish wink and subtle twist of the head which denied the unhappy truth; Gerald Cornfield had gone to bed early, alone, as always. But he'd stayed awake until after two in the morning, brooding over the dual standards and double dealing which gave women a state pension at sixty but kept men like him waiting another five years; thirteen hundred work-filled days for a Gerald while a Geraldine could be pocketing thousands of pounds in retirement. It was totally unjust, downright sexist and a complete rip-off.

He eased the front door open, sweeping small bundles of post across the floor, carefully lifted a carousel of greetings cards to one side, and led the way into the tiny Surrey shop. In a moment he'd turned off the alarm and taken up his usual position behind the counter, staring at the navy blue roller blind which would soon rise like a curtain at the theatre, leaving him centre stage, ready for the day's performance. Curtain-up was always at nine, on the dot, and he hadn't missed a performance since he moved to Pixley Green six years earlier. But it was a dwindling audience and Mr Cornfield had long since seen the writing on the wall.

Snail Mail, some of them called it. A letter with a first class stamp still took a day or more to crawl to the next village but, with the click of a mouse, e-mails reached the other side of the world in seconds. And it was the same with pensions and benefits. Most of the locals had them paid directly into their bank accounts; no waiting, no queues, no delays. The sub-post office was a declining market place.

Mr Cornfield slipped off his jacket, folded it neatly across the back of the chair behind him and gently jerked the wooden toggle which sent the navy blue roller blind spinning smoothly up to the wooden beam across the top of the counter. He politely covered his mouth with his hand while he cleared his throat, before addressing the queue in front of him.

'I thought you should all know that I'll be closing down shortly.' He hesitated for a moment, fixed his eyes on the second hand of the clock over the front door. 'Not right away you understand, but as soon as I can make suitable arrangements.' There was another brief pause while he took a deep breath and puffed himself up to his full five feet ten inches. 'Time to move on,' he continued as jauntily as he could manage. 'New decade, new horizons; that sort of thing.'

There were no sad faces, no gasps of amazement. Feet shuffled, people examined the contents of their pockets, others stared at the floor, but nobody looked up or spoke. Eventually the lady from the dry cleaners stepped forward and quietly placed a small brown parcel on the weighing machine in front of him, to the right.

'Canada,' she said. 'How much?'

OK, it broke the silence but it wasn't what Mr Cornfield wanted to hear; needed to hear.

Eddie Bates was right; they didn't give a sod. But what had become of common courtesy, good manners, thanks for past services rendered, good wishes, the usual polite condolences? There was none of that from this lot. Nothing.

A public convenience, Eddie often called it. Not it in the lavatory sense, of course, he simply meant that people didn't really care who ran the sub-post office, just so long as *somebody* ran it. Ideally somebody like Gerald Cornfield who could always lay his hands on a step ladder or a screw driver, and things to lever open windows for people who'd locked themselves out, or perhaps even locked themselves in, like Mrs Davies and her elderly mother. Twice they'd done it, just before Christmas last year.

Pixley Green post office was a convenient local confessional where Mr Cornfield always listened, priest-like, dispassionate, unflinching, to intimate details of the neighbourhood's births, deaths, marriages and divorces. And then there were the operations; whispered accounts of hysterectomies, vasectomies, appendectomies and some lesser-known 'ectomies' which were definitely not for the squeamish. He could write a book on it; probably would one day.

A fluorescent tube above the counter shone, white and spiteful, through his neatly-parted silver hair and gave an unnaturally pallid tinge to his ruddy complexion. But at least the unforgiving light allowed him to read the small print on the growing piles of tedious official documents without his glasses, and helped to distinguish the 3's from the 8's and the 5's from the 6's in the benefits books.

On the other side of the road Eddie Bates' white Mercedes pulled out from a row of parked cars in front of the café with three short, sharp blasts of the horn, intended for nobody in particular.

Mr Cornfield returned the casual wave and watched the car speed off in the general direction of the supermarket. Eddies' Eatery had probably run out of bread or beans; something like that. It seemed to happen quite often around lunchtime when things got busy.

He carefully tore twelve second class stamps from the sheet and passed them across the counter with change from a five pound note, wondering what he'd have for dinner. Betsy would have made him something special for his birthday. Probably a cake too; a small, silly cake with blue icing and just the one candle, the way she always did. But not for the past three years. Not since that cesspit of a hospital let loose its germs during a routine hip operation. They made their so-called "Superbug" sound more like a comic book hero who might possibly save the world rather than a filthy little microbe lurking in the dirt, intent on destroying it, and Betsy.

Betsy had been a good wife, the best, and he missed her in little ways he'd never expected. She was a mine of information and always knew silly things like whether it was the music of Mahler or Delius in that final scene in *Death in Venice*, or who was married to George Burns, and the answer to other niggling questions which sometimes crossed your mind unexpectedly at half past eleven at night, when people like Eddie Bates just looked blank and shook their head or asked if you meant George Burns the poet or something equally daft. And, at the end of a long day, there was no one to plump up the cushions and share a bottle of wine. A jar or two at the pub with Eddie was fine but it wasn't the same thing, not the same thing at all. Eddie didn't really understand.

Not that Mr Cornfield wasn't grateful to him for being a good friend, he was. But Eddie didn't miss Deirdre the way he missed Betsy. In fact Eddie had never really missed Deirdre at all, not for a moment, since the day she ran off to Spain with the manager of the opticians. Eddie said he needed his eyes tested and sent him a "Get-Well-Soon" card when he heard they were getting married. Eddie didn't take life too seriously. No point, he often said with a solemn shake of the head, nobody gets out of it alive.

Mr Cornfield liked that. He admired the slightly cavalier, devil-may-care approach to life but never quite got the hang of it himself. He worried too much, which was probably why his hair was grey while Eddie's was still black as coal, if a bit thin on top. Deirdre used to say he reminded her of Sean Connery in the early "Bond" movies but, apart from the eyebrows, Mr Cornfield couldn't see it. Eddie didn't have the height; more like "Del Boy" than 007.

A flurry of leaves whirled in from the street ahead of a young woman with an empty pushchair and a small child clinging, crab-like, to the hem of her mother's plastic raincoat, thumb in mouth, instantly drawn to the greetings cards on a rack to the left of the door.

The woman emptied a blue canvas shopping bag across the counter in a casual search for the benefits book while, behind her, sticky fingers dawdled across the wedding anniversary wishes, vandalising the gold and silver with chocolate smears.

Mr Cornfield stiffened, looked past the woman, over to the card rack. 'Could you, um...?' He nodded and pointed towards the child.

The woman turned slowly, sighed, and grudgingly took her daughter's hand. 'The man doesn't want you to look at his precious cards,' she muttered sarcastically. Then louder and with a hint of hostility. 'They're for grumpy old people who've been married for centuries.'

He felt his pulse begin to race, dabbed the perspiration from his forehead, but managed to speak quietly and deliberately, remembering his position. 'That's right,' he said, almost in a whisper. 'Anniversary cards are for married couples; those curious folk who don't expect free housing and cash handouts when they decide to have children.'

'That's *their* problem,' she sneered. 'I'm entitled.' The cash on the counter was quickly scooped up, notes stuffed into a leather purse, coins thrown carelessly into the shopping bag with the benefits book. 'Silly old fart,' she called out as she slammed the door behind her.

And she was quite right of course; it *was* "their problem" and she *was* "entitled". But it wasn't just the upside-down welfare system, which picked up the tab for pregnant teenagers with one hand and short-changed elderly pensioners with the other, that rankled. It was the word *before* the "O" word which turned it into an insult.

If he'd been completely honest, Mr Cornfield would have told you that he didn't mind being called "old". What upset him was the way people put "grumpy", "dirty", "silly", or worse in front of it. He'd always strived to be amiable, well-scrubbed and, hopefully, a little bit wiser than when he was a lad, but one generation's "wise old man" was a new generation's "silly old fart". Nothing clever about growing old; merely a question of staying alive for rather too long.

Shortly after four fifteen, a tidal wave of maroon school blazers crashed off the bus in front of the hairdressers and sent a babbling torrent to deluge the newsagents then gushed noisily on, down towards the record shop. A smaller stream trickled across the road and quietly seeped into the sub-post office.

Mr Cornfield waited for them to shut the door. 'Can I help you gentleman?' he shouted above the chattering.

'Just looking at stuff thanks.' A boy with spiky ginger hair fiddled self-consciously with an earring while he span the carousel round to the "Purple Ronnie" cards. He tugged the school tie from his neck and stuffed it untidily into his jacket pocket. 'How much are these?' he asked with the croaky adolescent squawk of oncoming puberty, spinning the carousel as fast as he could.

Mr Cornfield rat-tatted the glass screen with a ball point pen. 'Would you mind not doing that?' he called out.

'It's sposed to spin round,' the boy shouted back, turning away from the counter. 'Anyway, how much?'

'Two pounds fifty.'

'I'll take it.' The boy dragged the carousel towards the door. 'Charge it to my account,' he screeched, barely able to control the juvenile laughter. Five boys squeezed through the door almost as one; a giggling, maroon lump of adolescent insolence which raced-off down the road leaving the carousel leaning heavily against the shop window, half a dozen cards strewn across the floor.

'Deserve a good hiding, they do,' an elderly woman grumbled through pursed lips. 'A damned good hiding.' She zipped-up the front of a green anorak protectively and gripped the handles of a bulging carrier bag with both hands, in front of her. 'You just can't trust the little blighters.'

Mr Cornfield rubbed his eyes wearily and stepped out from behind the counter to inspect the damage; one of the wire racks badly bent and a few cards missing.

Stolen, that was the word, the right word. And would the police be interested? Not in the least. If you could interest a copper who wasn't too busy checking road fund licences, he'd shrug his shoulders and say there was nothing to be done. A childish prank, he'd say. In Gerald Cornfield's day you'd have got a clip round the ear and a good telling-off for a "childish prank". But not anymore.

He reminded himself that Scorpios were supposed to be having a good day, especially if it was their birthday. The morning horoscope promised that people close to him would be helpful and cooperative and Pluto's energy was going to ensure that things went his way in the afternoon. Well it hadn't, and there wasn't much of the afternoon left. Pluto had obviously lost the plot.

'Fancy a quick sharpener?' Eddie Bates poked his head around the door, raincoat collar up around his ears, and downed an imaginary pint with a gloved hand. 'I'll be up the road.'

Mr Cornfield smiled for the first time that day. 'Bloody good idea,' he said without hesitation. 'See you in ten minutes.'

* * *

It hit you directly you stepped down into the bar; etched on the tobacco-stained walls, oozing from the treacly brown paintwork, written in the furrowed brow of a scar-faced terrier who bared white needle teeth if you so much as looked at him. "Men only", it said, and meant it. You could even smell it in the spilled beer and crisp packets. The Crow; not just a man's pub but an *old* man's pub, where another round of drinks diluted the problems of the day and abject failure could be seen as success through the bottom of a glass.

Gerald and Betsy never went there. They weren't really pub people anyway and preferred a glass of wine at home by the fire to a pint in a smoke-filled bar. But it was different now Betsy had gone. The Crow had somehow become Gerald's local and he welcomed a quiet drink with Eddie and some of the lads. Not so much friends as familiar faces, people who knew your name and would raise a glass to your health from the other side of the room. People who'd be there tomorrow and the next day to refocus a hostile world into a friendly pub perspective.

Eddie Bates leaned back against the bar, elbows on the brass rail around the edge, beige raincoat hanging loose, and chatted to half a dozen people across the room, more or less at the same time. Quick-fire comments rather than joined-up conversation, but delivered with the ease of a Wimbledon champion back-handing a volley of tennis balls across the centre court.

'And how many official portraits of Her Majesty has our favourite postmaster off-loaded today then?' he called out as Gerald crossed the room towards the bar.

Gerald shrugged. 'Laid end to end, they might just reach the post box, which is where they'll stay if the postal strike goes ahead.'

'Not another bloody strike?' Eddie emptied his glass and slapped it down resolutely on the bar. 'What do the lazy bastards want this time?'

Gerald slowly shook his head and permitted himself a long, deep sigh as he reached for a bar stool.

'One large Scotch coming up,' Eddie insisted, with a reassuring slap on the arm. 'You look as if you need it.'

'I think perhaps I do.' Gerald paused to loosen his tie, undo the top button of his shirt. 'You were right you know,' he said in a forlorn voice. 'I must have told fifty people I'm closing down and not one of them so much as raised an eyebrow.'

Eddie fixed him with a resolute stare, nodded. 'Sod 'em,' he said. 'Sod the lot of 'em.' He waved a twenty pound note at the barman who leaned, motionless, against the till, a tea towel slung haphazardly across his shoulder. 'Two Red Labels Ron, my old son; when you've got a moment, that is. And make them large ones.'

'I haven't got a clue what I'll do next?' said Gerald. 'For money, I mean. Shifting supermarket trolleys and stacking shelves isn't me at all, and I really don't think I've got the energy for office cleaning.'

Eddie slipped his change into a jacket pocket and eased a large whisky along the bar. 'Then set your sights a bit higher old mate.'

'Higher? At my age?' He stared dolefully into the glass. 'Who's going to employ a silly old sod of sixty?'

'Sixty's nothing these days. Crikey, they made Churchill prime minister for the second time when he was seventy-seven. That gives you another seventeen years to get yourself sorted.' Eddie raised his glass. 'And, before I forget, happy birthday my old son.'

'Good of you to remember.' Gerald forced a tired smile and sipped his drink. 'And you're dead right of course. Blokes of our age may have lost their youth but they've got a lifetime of valuable experience. That must count for something, wouldn't you say?'

'Bloody right it does mate,' Eddie assured him at once. 'It counts for everything.'

Gerald stroked his chin thoughtfully. 'I'll tell you what,' he said with a mild flicker of excitement. 'I bet there are people who'd be happy to pay a few quid for a bit of sound, rational advice from men with our experience of life.'

Eddie appeared slightly puzzled. 'Advice about what exactly?' he asked cautiously, not wanting to dampen Gerald's new found enthusiasm.

'Oh I don't know. Lots of things.' Gerald shifted about on the bar stool, trying to get his thoughts into some kind of logical order. 'Take you for example,' he said after due consideration. 'Twice divorced; you must have a world of advice to offer.'

Eddie stared at him from under thick eyebrows. 'Best advice I can offer is not to get married unless there's a Z in the month. And only then if it happens to be a leap year.' He waited for Gerald's polite chuckle. 'How much do you think they'd pay me for that?'

'I think you may have missed the point,' he said, edging a little closer. 'After two failed marriages you know how *not* to mess it up. You could advise other people how to *stay* married.'

'Me give advice? That would be like asking a politician to tell the truth. It's not part of the vocabulary.'

'You underestimate yourself. Who better to point out life's little stumbling blocks than a man who's tripped over them a few times. You know where they are and how to avoid them.'

Eddie stared at his empty glass. 'And how about you mastermind; what would be your specialist subject?'

'Bereavement I suppose.' Gerald paused to order another round of drinks before going on. 'Not that I'm very good at it,' he said, searching the ceiling while he blinked a tear from his eye. 'But I could always offer a sympathetic word or two and a friendly shoulder to cry on.'

'Sorry old mate, it's all been done.' Eddie wrapped his arm around his friend's shoulder and gently squeezed. 'You can pick up the phone and talk about bereavement with the The Samaritans, day or night. And lots of blokes drop in on Relate, or whatever they call themselves now, before they finally throttle their Mrs.'

'OK let's forget about death and divorce,' Gerald said quickly. 'But there must be a million and one other situations where people need advice.'

Eddie nodded. 'But they probably go to the Citizen's Advice Bureau.'

Gerald's attention strayed across to the other side of the bar and the spirit bottles hanging, upside down, in a row in front of him. Half full or half empty? A matter of opinion but, for him, today, right now, definitely half empty. Upside down and nearing the end, just like his life. He watched in silence while Eddie rummaged through his inside pocket, found a well-chewed pencil, and carefully wrote something on the back of a beer mat. He propped it up against the pump handle.

'How does that grab you?' Eddie asked proudly, leaning back to admire his handiwork.

Gerald gave a modest snort of disapproval. 'Rent-a-Pensioner.'

He said it two or three times but it didn't seem to improve with the repetition. 'Perhaps it sounds a tiny bit exploitive, if you'll forgive the expression,' he suggested politely. 'Anyway, what's it mean?'

'It means what you were saying; advice from the old folk but with a commercial angle to it, so to speak.' Eddie twisted around and nodded towards a short man with a belly that tested his shirt buttons, sitting at the corner table. 'Take old Reg Charlton over there? Been a pensioner for a while now but not so long ago he was a top sales rep. Talk about ice to the Eskimos; he could sell red tape to Brussels.'

'And who do you think would want to rent Reg?' Gerald asked.

Eddie leaned forward, hand over his mouth, and spoke in the secretive half whisper he always used when he wanted things to sound more important. 'Big companies with massive sales teams,' he confided. 'They'd pay hundred quid or more an hour to learn Reg's trade secrets.'

'Do you really think so?' said Gerald, unconvinced. 'I mean what's Reg got to offer that you won't find in half a dozen manuals?'

'The little tricks of the trade. Those unwritten rules.' Eddie's eyes narrowed. 'Reg could reveal things you won't find in any sales manual.'

'Such as?'

Eddie shrugged dismissively. 'How do I know? I'm not a bloody salesman.'

Gerald, who couldn't abide indecision, quickly finished his drink and stood up. 'Well, there's one way to find out,' he said, carefully buttoning his jacket. He smoothed down the neatly parted hair with palm of his hand and started towards the corner table.

'What are you having Reg?' Eddie called across the room. 'This one's on me.'

'Just a half thanks.' The other man raised a beer glass. 'Got to be off in a minute.'

Reg Charlton sat perfectly still, arms draped carelessly across the back of the chair, and stared blankly at his knees while Gerald probed for unwritten rules, things that weren't to be found in any books or manuals, and the all-important tricks of the trade. Towards the end of the conversation Reg became slightly more animated and prodded the air in front of him with his finger, seemingly emphasising an important bit. Then he whispered something in Gerald's ear, quickly downed his beer, got up and left, pausing only briefly to give Eddie a thumbs-up as he closed the pub door behind him.

Eddie waited for Gerald to rearrange himself on the bar stool before he spoke. 'Was I right or what?' he asked with the supreme confidence of someone who thinks they already know the answer.

'Or what,' said Gerald.

'No tricks of the trade?'

'Not one. You'd be wasting your money renting Reg Charlton for more than a couple of minutes.'

Eddie Bates sucked his teeth. 'OK, so what *did* he say?'

'Actually I wrote it down.' Gerald took a slip of paper from his top pocket and held it up to the light. 'According to Reg, tricks of the trade count for nothing. He says if you don't have the right temperament for the job you might as well forget it.' Gerald reached for his glasses, squinted at the last scribbled line. 'Apparently it's not *how* to be a salesman that matters, it's *who* should be a salesman.'

'Anyone can be a bloody salesman,' Eddie grunted. 'You just knock on doors and refuse to take no for an answer.'

'That's not quite how Reg sees it,' said Gerald, hoping he didn't sound too dogmatic. 'Reg says anyone can knock on doors but it doesn't mean they've got the right temperament to be a salesman.'

'Temperament... shmemperament... so now he's a philosopher?'

But Gerald wasn't in the mood for an argument. He clasped his hands tightly together, settled his elbows on the bar and stared at the half empty row of spirit bottles in front of him. They began to look altogether more full as an idea wandered slowly and cautiously into his mind.

'Tell me this,' he called out with a sudden and unexpected flush of passion. 'What's the most valuable commodity in life but also the most difficult to find?'

Eddie shrugged. 'Rich widow?'

Gerald gave him an impatient smile, paused to sip his drink. 'The answer, Eddie, is wisdom but the question is where will you find wisdom today?'

'Google,' Eddie said at once. 'Internet's full of the stuff.'

Gerald shook his head. 'The internet's full of information. Wisdom, on the other hand, is knowing how to use it.'

'And who's going to tell you that?'

'Us. We could do it for a fee.'

Eddie raised a cynical eyebrow but decided it might be safest to say nothing, at least for the moment.

'Think about it,' Gerald went on with barely a pause for breath. 'Even the most primitive cultures looked to their elders for wisdom and guidance. We oldies may be reviled rather than revered, written-off as silly old farts, but we could probably change all that.'

Finely-tuned antennae in the highly-developed finance sector of Eddie Bates' brain had started to receive positive cash signals as he recognised the subtle vibrations of a potentially good idea.

'I suppose most people would be in the market for a bit of wisdom from time to time,' he said. 'Question is, would they be prepared to pay for it?'

'Don't see why not. It's in short enough supply in this day and age,' said Gerald. 'Trouble is you can't just grab a handful of wise words, index them under W for Wisdom and expect a computer to solve all your problems. It has to be tailor-made for different people in different situations.'

Eddie peered across the rim of his whisky glass. 'Tell me something,' he said, hunching forward. 'What exactly did our Reginald whisper in your ear just before he left?'

'I'm not sure it's a terribly original notion,' Gerald sighed. 'He said wisdom was nature's compensation for a lifetime of mistakes.'

'He might have a point,' said Eddie.

'Perhaps.' Gerald carefully folded Reg's notes and wedged them between some credit cards in a black leather wallet. 'We've all got a lifetime of mistakes behind us so, if he's right about the compensation bit, we could set ourselves up in the wisdom business.'

'How, exactly, would you see that working then?' Eddie asked casually, trying to put some kind of cash value on the idea.

Gerald thought for a moment. 'I'm not absolutely sure,' he said, gently stroking his chin. 'But there must be a way to market something as rare and valuable as wisdom.'

'Dead right.' Eddie held his beer mat at arm's length. 'And to start with we'll need a company; Rent-a-Pensioner Limited, for example.'

'The name's not quite right, is it?' Gerald muttered through tightly-stretched lips. 'Sounds a bit like an over-sixties call-girl racket.' He paused and glanced around the bar at the others; a dozen or so men, old men with regrets but, like Reg, with their share of wisdom, their compensation. 'Maybe the name should reflect the concept of wisdom and guidance from society's elders? Older & Wiser, perhaps. And Limited if you think that's important.'

Eddie grinned. 'That's not bad,' he said, leaning forward to land a playful but painful punch on Gerald's upper arm. 'Not bad at all.'

But Gerald wasn't completely sure. While it was beginning to look as if Pluto hadn't completely lost the plot after all, and Scorpio might, at last, be having its promised good day, he was acutely aware that he'd nearly finished his fourth large whisky. Or was it his fifth, he'd lost count?

'Tell me something Eddie,' he whispered. 'Do you think we may have had a drop too much to drink?'

'Absolutely not,' Eddie said, signalling to the barman for another round. 'Crikey, we haven't been here five minutes.'

Mr Cornfield buttoned-up his shirt collar and straightened the knot in his paisley tie. 'That's what I thought,' he said with a satisfied smile, then drank a silent toast to Betsy and wished himself a very happy sixtieth birthday.

Chapter Two

Nobody ever said Penelope Black was better qualified than any of the others who answered the advertisement in the Pixley News & Mail. But there were more important reasons why they finally chose her for the job.

For a start she was a middle-aged woman and probably better suited to working with older men than some of the young girls who said silly things like "bear with me" when they answered the telephone, instead of asking if you'd hold the line for a moment. But the deciding factor was that she was happily married with three grown sons who'd all flown the nest, so there'd be no sick children at home with chicken pox, hangovers from nights on the tiles, boyfriend problems, or unexpected pregnancies to keep her away from work.

The final interview, like all the others, took place in Gerald Cornfield's kitchen at Pycroft Cottage; he and Eddie either end of a long pine breakfast table, Mrs Black, dressed comfortably in brown corduroy slacks and a chunky man's sweater, in the middle, facing the Aga. The job as secretary/PA was hers if she still wanted it, they told her. Only there wasn't a job, not quite yet anyway, so would she mind holding on for a week or so, just until the endowment policy money came through?

Mrs Black was disappointed. She gripped a ballpoint pen like a dagger and clicked the tip in and out with her thumb while she thought about it, her full, round face blank and expressionless. 'You advertised for someone to start right away,' she reminded them.

'Circumstances beyond our control,' Gerald said at once, trying to lighten the mood. 'Anyway, perhaps we could somehow compensate you for the delay.'

The clicking stopped abruptly. Mrs Black pushed the sleeves of her sweater up beyond fleshy elbows. 'Ten per cent,' she said looking at each man in turn.

'Ten per cent?' Gerald repeated, wondering if she might be talking about an increase in the advertised salary or, perhaps, asking for an advance on her first month's pay cheque. But he was wrong.

'Ten per cent of the company,' she announced with all the confidence of a seasoned entrepreneur. 'And a directorship,' she quickly added, as if it went without saying. 'No point in equity without authority, I always say.'

Mrs Black's sudden and unexpected demands, coupled with her apparent grasp of what Gerald regarded as high finance, came as a bit of a shock. He turned to Eddie for a response.

Eddie frowned, more in confusion than anger, and sucked his teeth. 'Do you realise what ten per cent equity could be worth one day if this little company takes off?'

Mrs Black remained tight-lipped and defiant. 'One day, some day. That isn't today though, is it?' she said curtly. 'And right now, at this very minute, we're talking about ten per cent of absolutely nothing.'

Gerald smiled nervously, sensing an argument. 'We could probably run to a few M&S vouchers, from time to time. And there might possibly be a Christmas bonus as well.'

Mrs Black ignored him, clicked the top of her ballpoint pen faster than before.

'Five per cent,' said Eddie, rising to his feet and bringing the bartering to a close. 'And you can forget the directorship.'

'I deserve more,' Mrs Black declared flatly.

Eddie reached for the coffee pot. 'Five per cent's a whole lot more than we planned to give you, or anybody else.' He paused, wondering if this smug woman was worth all the hassle. 'Take it or leave it.'

Mrs Black slid her cup and saucer across the table towards him and waited until he'd poured the coffee. 'Five per cent then,' she said quietly. 'But I'd prefer the title PA to secretary/PA.'

'Done.' Eddie smiled, passed the biscuits. 'It's a deal Penny love.'

'One more thing.' Mrs Black prodded her tightly-permed, grey hair with chubby fingers and spoke in an altogether softer, less demanding voice. 'I'd rather you didn't abbreviate my name to Penny.'

Eddie's smile broadened. 'Understandable,' he chuckled. 'Penny Blacks... old and rare, with sticky backsides and perforated edges.'

Mrs Black wasn't amused. She looked straight ahead, unsmiling.

At a little after half past eleven Gerald saw her to the front door and waited until the white Volvo Estate disappeared round the corner at the far end of Friday Street, taking with it the large, furry dog which peered, motionless but menacing, through a huffed-up window in the back. He returned to the kitchen wearing an anxious frown.

'Do you remember Mrs Black mentioning a dog?' he asked, flopping down wearily on the kitchen chair. 'Only it looks like she carts one of those Old English thingies around with her.'

'Dogs weren't discussed,' Eddie said through a mouthful of biscuit. 'Not that I remember anyway.'

'Nor me.'

Gerald didn't like dogs, never had, not since his aunt Helen's Poodle bit his leg on the beach at Brighton when he was four. On a cold day you could still see the scar; a pale pink half circle like a cartoon smile, just below the ankle bone.

The dog hairs on Penelope's cord slacks were a bit of a give-away but he'd somehow pictured a small pooch, curled-up safely at home in a wicker basket, not a chauffeur-driven fur ball being ferried about in the back seat of a car like a Mafia hit man.

And Penelope wasn't altogether honest about Winston when she turned up for work two weeks later. The problem wasn't that the dog had a mind of its own but that he didn't have a mind at all, at least not one capable of understanding simple instructions like "sit", "stay" and "get off the table". But it wasn't his fault; Penelope must have said so a dozen times during her first few days with Older & Wiser.

The root of the problem was Winston's highly developed intelligence and low boredom threshold, she insisted. He'd pine terribly if she left him at home or in the back of the car and it just wasn't fair to keep him locked up somewhere like a criminal. Besides, by mid afternoon on day three, Winston seemed to have made himself quite at home in the modest back room tucked away behind the post office, now pretentiously referred to as 'the office'.

So problem solved, apart from the hole near the fence in the yard beyond; a bomb crater of a hole, excavated in a moment and abandoned as quickly.

Gerald's overstretched bank account also had a hole; an unplanned but temporary hole which would be plugged when the much-delayed cheque from the insurance company finally arrived. But the bank didn't like 'unplanned' lending; it ranked with unauthorised, unsecured, unconditional and, above all, unprofitable. For over three years they'd tried to persuade Gerald to borrow money he didn't want or need but now, finally, he needed it, they wanted it back.

Overdrafts, Eddie Bates would assure you, are like umbrellas. Banks hand them out when the sun shines and snatch them back at the first sign of rain. A sad farewell, then, to a white Mercedes, traded-in for an altogether more sensible VW and sufficient funds to pay off Gerald's 'unplanned' borrowing. Eddie seized the moment and told them where they could deposit their loan.

And so to wisdom, the sweet nectar of an autumn generation, waiting to be harvested like honey from the bees. Half a dozen recruits to begin with, perhaps, six of the best, maybe even more. Neatly packaged advice for people with problems; a priceless commodity for an utterly foolish world. All so perfectly simple.

But why did otherwise intelligent men become complete buffoons when you asked them for the smallest droplet of wisdom? Why the same hackneyed expressions like "Live life to the full", "Never say die", and, one of the daftest, "Money can't buy happiness"? Eddie's little aptitude test had revealed an unexpected but fundamental flaw in the mature adult male.

Gerald said it was embarrassment; people didn't like to blow their own trumpets, show you the full spectrum of their wisdom. It made them seem big headed and quite a few men were naturally modest.

Not being one of life's naturally modest men, Eddie wasn't so sure. Maybe they were a bit short on wisdom. Possibly it wasn't needed anymore, not in this day and age. Fair enough, perhaps, a few thousand years ago in the Bible. Consider Kings 1, Chapter 3, Verse 27. Perfectly OK for Solomon to decide which of two women was the real mother of a disputed baby by offering to slice it in half. Today that sort of wisdom would get you five years for assault with a deadly weapon and, besides, a DNA test would sort the whole thing out in a moment. Science, it seemed, might one day make wisdom redundant; perhaps it already had.

By the following Tuesday there were three wise men on the books, if you included Reg Charlton. But you couldn't really count Gerald and Eddie because they were management. Realistically, then, just the one. Which is when Gerald Cornfield had a great idea.

An advertisement in the classified columns of The Times. Just a couple of lines, inexpensive, straight to the point and carefully targeted.

WANTED. Men over 60 to pass-on the lessons they have learned from the University of Life. Contact Older & Wiser Limited, it said, followed by the telephone number.

Sorry, said the classified advertising man, but it infringed Gender Discrimination Legislation. And then there was another issue about advertising for a specific age group. This was highly discriminatory too. Not to put too fine a point on it, the advertisement was illegal.

Gerald had never "infringed" anything in his life, not knowingly anyway. And he'd never discriminated against anyone. He slowly crumpled his great idea into a ball and tossed it into the waste bin; a few chosen words, twenty-one in all, manifestly intended to degrade and humiliate the entire female population, calculated to alienate and offend anyone and everyone under sixty. A dastardly act, a felony, perhaps even the small beginnings of a life of crime, narrowly averted only by the diligence of a classified advertising manager.

'Absolute bollocks,' snorted Eddie Bates reassuringly. He peered over the top of Penelope's computer. 'Pardon my French but did you feel sidelined by the advert?'

She hammered the keyboard with vicious fingers for a moment until she'd reached the end of the paragraph then stopped abruptly and looked up. 'Yes, actually, I did.'

'Because you're not a man?' Eddie asked in a matter-of-fact way. 'Or because you're not sixty?'

'Because women everywhere would feel excluded,' she snapped back loudly then, realising she may have over-stepped the line between resolute and rude, took a more moderate tone. 'Perhaps you should consider referring to people rather than men?'

'Try telling that to the Women's Institute,' Eddie said. 'Pick up the phone and tell them they should consider referring to the People's Institute and see what they have to say about it.'

'That's quite different.' Penelope rose to her feet, incensed, but controlled. 'Coffee anyone?' she asked, as if it might have been the reason she'd stood up in the first place. She quickly slid open the louvered door which hid a tiny kitchen area; more of a cupboard, behind her desk.

'Black, no sugar,' said Eddie. 'But, if you don't mind me asking, why's it different?'

Penelope busied herself with the cups and saucers. 'Because the WI has been around for nearly a hundred years,' she said without turning round.

'And good luck to them.' Eddie forced a polite chuckle. 'I don't feel in the least left out because I've never wanted to be in. It's a club for women and, as far as I'm concerned, it can stay that way for the next hundred years.'

Winston's dribble trickled in a thin stream from the sides of his mouth to the floor with the first sighting of the biscuit tin. A few muffled, half barks, two ginger nuts snatched from Penelope's hand, carried, like a recent kill, to the back door mat.

Gerald waited until the last of the crumbs had been vacuumed up by the flabby black mouth before laying a sheet of blotting paper over the pool of dribble. Then he washed his hands thoroughly, took his coffee to a round oak table in the corner of the room and sat down.

'Why isn't there a Men's Institute?' he muttered to himself, more as a passing thought than a serious question.

'Same reason there's a Minister for Women but not for men,' Eddie said brusquely. 'They think we should take care of ourselves.'

'Then why not a Minister for Pensioners?' Gerald dunked a ginger nut into his coffee and stared thoughtfully at the floor. 'Surely old men and women deserve a parliamentary guardian?'

Winston gazed, unblinking, at the remains of Gerald's biscuit, droplets of dribble splatting to the floor in front of him.

'Do you ever feed this dog before you leave home in the morning?' said Gerald, gently edging him away with the side of his foot. 'He always seems to be hungry.'

Penelope huffed and shrugged her shoulders, span another biscuit in Winston's direction. 'Perhaps there should be a Minister for Animals,' she said icily. 'People don't always appreciate that dogs get peckish, just like the rest of us.'

Winston swallowed the third biscuit whole, wagged a stumpy tail in gratitude. He stood quietly facing the back door until Penelope opened it just wide enough to let a dog out and a blast of cold air in.

'Postcards,' Eddie babbled into his coffee. 'We could do it with postcards.'

'Do what with postcards?' said Gerald.

'The advert; we could put postcards in the window at the paper shop.'

Gerald stiffened. 'Along with all those second hand prams, three piece suites, and odd job men I suppose?'

'Why not? At least the paper shop isn't bothered about all this politically correct nonsense.'

'What makes you think that?'

'Well, for one thing, they employ Paper Boys and not Paper People.' Eddie slowly parted the beaded curtain which separated "the office" from the shop. 'Must be off,' he said jauntily. 'I'll be across at the café, removing that sexist menu board of mine from the wall.' He turned and grinned. 'Men You, geddit?'

Penelope dived into her shopping basket for her asthma inhaler. 'That man is the original chauvinist pig,' she gasped, in between puffs. 'Do you honestly think he's a wise man?'

'I think he's perceptive and shrewd,' said Gerald, choosing his words carefully. 'And they're qualities which go hand in hand with wisdom.'

'Perceptive and shrewd then,' she repeated, 'but not a wise man.'

Gerald slowly shook his head and turned towards the question. 'That's not what I said, but does it matter?'

'Not really. Just wanted to know what you thought.'

Gerald decided to let the subject drop. And, anyway, the well-dressed old gentleman who tapped impatiently on the front door with the handle of a rolled umbrella reminded him it was two o'clock and time to reopen the post office.

The parcel, about the size of a shoe box, was addressed to the passenger transport department at the county council offices and Major Edgar William Bevington, who presented his card so Gerald could fill-in the postal form on his behalf, wanted it Special Delivery.

'Maximum compensation in the event of loss is £2,500,' Gerald explained without looking up. 'Will that do?'

Major Bevington positioned a pair of narrow spectacles on a prominent but elegant nose and glanced quickly at the form. 'Nearly two thousand signatures on a petition. What do you suppose they might be worth?'

Gerald smiled. 'I'm not at all sure but £2,500 sounds more than generous; £1.25p a signature,' he said, trying to decide whether or not he'd ever seen the man before. 'Local signatures, are they?'

'Doubt it.'

'You're not from round here then?'

'I *am* from round here, so the correct answer to your question is, of course, No,' said Bevington importantly. 'Moved in more than a month ago but, if I hadn't, the correct answer to your question would have been Yes, I'm *not* from round here.'

'I suppose so,' Gerald mumbled without bothering to work out if the man was right or wrong.

'I obtained them on the London Underground,' Bevington continued. 'Circle Line; captive audience you see.'

Gerald stopped writing and squinted through the glass at the other man who was now examining the fluorescent marker pens on the opposite side of the shop. 'Not a local petition then?' he enquired.

'It most certainly is,' Bevington declared indignantly. 'We want the bus stop moved from outside my house.'

Gerald hesitated, wondering if he should pursue the conversation. 'May I ask why the bus stop outside your house would be a matter of concern for London underground passengers?'

'Don't suppose it is,' he said, slipping his receipt into a red leather purse and clicking it shut. 'People mostly sign petitions to get rid of you. Embarrassment you see.'

'You've done this sort of before then?' said Gerald.

'All the time. Protest and petition; isn't that what democracy's all about?' Bevington picked up his umbrella and made towards the door. 'Keep my card,' he said. 'Never know when I might be able to assist with a bit of lobbying for something or another eh?'

Gerald watched him cross the road to the newsagents, pausing briefly to talk to a uniformed chauffeur at the wheel of an old and slightly faded Alvis convertible. He returned in a moment with half a dozen folded newspapers under his arm, settled himself comfortably in the back seat, and was quickly driven away.

He reappeared a few days later in the Pixley News & Mail; top of page five, a lone figure in a pinstripe suit, broken glass scattered around him, arm extended, pointing to graffiti daubed across what remained of a bus shelter near the gates of an impressive country house. Vandalised for the third time, according to the headline over a story about Edgar Bevington's campaign to move the bus stop further up the road, opposite the police station. Two thousand people had apparently signed a petition supporting the move to a safer location.

Two thousand indifferent but embarrassed Circle Line passengers on the London underground, Gerald decided. Not exactly the spirit of a local petition but you couldn't help admiring the gall of the man who apparently called himself an Elderpreneur; easily missed, near the end of the article, no more than a passing comment about older people making a difference in society. Bevington had invited other Elderpreneurs to join his campaign.

Gerald took the visiting card from the notice board behind him and dialled the number.

'Bevington.' The voice was clipped.

'Cornfield. Pixley Green sub-post office. We met a few days ago.'

Silence.

'I've been reading about you... in the local paper.'

Silence.

'Hello. Are you still there?'

'What can I do for you?' Bevington grunted.

'Maybe this is not a convenient time,' said Gerald. 'Perhaps I should call back later?'

'Now will be fine.'

'Elderpreneur?' Gerald asked hesitantly. 'I wondered what exactly you meant by that.'

Bevington cleared his throat. 'What it sounds like; older people with an entrepreneurial spark.'

'Interesting,' said Gerald. 'Could we meet up some time to talk about it?'

'When did you have in mind?'

'No time like the present. How would this evening suit?'

'What time?'

'Shall we say seven?'

'No. We'll say eight thirty. Here.'

'OK if I bring my colleague Eddie Bates?' said Gerald.

Bevington gave a little grunt of consent and hung-up the phone before Gerald could thank him or check whether or not Lovelace Farm House was the beamed building near the converted barns on the far side of the common.

It was. Eddie Bates knew the house well. He'd been there two or three times when it was owned by an artist who'd painted a particularly flattering portrait of Deirdre; one of only a few things she'd taken with her when she left for Spain.

E.W. Bevington, resplendent in a maroon velvet smoking jacket, opened the front door wide and stared, unsmiling, at his guests. 'You're late,' he announced dispassionately, before turning back down a narrow hallway towards a dimly lit room at the far end.

The two men followed behind like shadows, past a gallery of framed photographs of their host, dressed in the uniform of a British army officer, the smell of wax polish and expensive cigars hanging heavy in the air.

'What's your poison?' The voice boomed from the centre of the room where Bevington stood to attention beside an ornate round table, head up, chest out, hand hovering in readiness over a selection of decanters and half a dozen assorted bottles.

'Scotch and soda,' said Eddie, flopping down untidily on a well-worn leather couch to the right of a log fire. 'No ice,' he added quickly.

Gerald stood awkwardly near the door, hands behind his back, waiting for an invitation to sit but none came. 'It's a beautiful house,' he said, more out of politeness than genuine interest or admiration. 'Eighteenth century, I'd guess.'

'Guess again,' said Bevington brusquely. 'It's actually sixteen fifties, that sort of period.' He tilted his head forward and peered at

Gerald with the superior look of a high court judge about to pass sentence. 'You haven't told me what you'd like to drink.'

Gerald tugged nervously at his shirt cuffs. 'Dry sherry please.' He stepped forward to receive the glass which Bevington promptly placed, temporarily out of reach, on a small side table at the other end of the leather couch, and gestured to him to sit.

'Warm in here,' Eddie said, stretching out his legs and loosening a bold, printed tie; red with a yellow palm tree.

Bevington sipped a gin and tonic and stood with his back to the fire. 'I'm afraid I feel the cold rather badly. Spent too long in the tropics; thins the blood.' He brushed some imagined specks from the lapels of his velvet jacket and thrust his hand into his pocket. 'Now what exactly can I do for you?' he said with a conspicuous twitch of his upper lip.

Eddie flung his right arm casually over the side of the couch and settled back leaving Gerald to do the talking.

'I was wondering,' said Gerald, pausing to search his pockets for a sheet of notes. '*We* were wondering,' he began again, 'whether your Elderpreneur campaign might be not be akin to our own plans.'

'Which are?' Bevington asked. He threw back his shoulders and took a sideways glance at himself in a large gilt framed mirror above the mantelpiece then quickly turned to face the fire, running the flat of his hand over neat, obedient hair; surprisingly dark hair for a man of his age, but with the dull, lifeless hint of artificial colouring.

'We plan to market wisdom,' Gerald declared with a self-conscious laugh. 'Sounds odd, I know, but it's really a fine idea.'

'Wisdom?' Bevington grunted at his reflection. 'Common sense, sound judgement, logic, reason, good thinking, that sort of thing?'

'Exactly,' said Eddie.

Bevington slapped the side of his belly in a nostalgic, ritual check for his military pistol; a phantom weapon long since abandoned. 'But there isn't enough wisdom around to fill a sherry glass,' he said, 'never mind sustain a business.'

'We rather thought there might be,' Gerald replied hesitantly.

'Show me then,' said Bevington. 'Let me see your wisdom.'

'It's not quite *ours* exactly.' Gerald quickly referred to his notes. 'You see we're trying to recruit a group of mature, adult men to provide a consensus view. Elders if you like.'

'Men who've been there, done that, bought the T-towel,' Eddie added.

'T-shirt,' Gerald interrupted quietly. 'It's bought the T-shirt.'

Eddie shrugged, waved away Gerald's nit-picking.

'And do you count yourselves among them?' Bevington wanted to know.

Gerald hesitated for a moment, looked to Eddie for a response. 'I think we probably do,' he said.

'We're the founder members,' Eddie grinned.

E.W. Bevington straightened up and stood perfectly still. 'Then perhaps you'd apply your wisdom to a small conundrum,' he said. 'Man in sixties, comfortably off, nice house, reasonable lifestyle, widower. Woman in late thirties, attractive, divorced. She'd like to move-in with the man. He's not so sure. What should he do?'

'Take a look in the mirror.' Eddie presented Bevington with his empty glass before going on. 'Then he should take a look at his bank balance and ask himself which will be more attractive to a women who's young enough to be his daughter. Wrinkles or wallet?'

Bevington passed the whisky bottle and soda siphon. 'Please help yourself,' he said. He paused to throw a log on the fire and stood for a moment in silence, watching the flames. 'Let's just say he's unsure why she's attracted to him.'

'In that case he should ask himself if he might not be better off with someone who's happy with his wrinkles; someone nearer his own age.'

'But suppose the woman loves him, despite his wrinkles?' said Bevington.

Eddie shook his head slowly and gulped back his drink. 'Then this woman's not only a gold digger, she's also a bloody liar.'

'But she *might* love him,' Gerald interrupted. 'Why not?'

'Easy way to find out,' said Eddie. 'This chap of yours should say he wants to marry her but must first divorce a vindictive wife. Explain that he'll have to sell the house and move into a flat, cut back on overheads, tighten the old belt. Tell her he's willing to hand everything over to his wife to be free.'

Bevington paused, closed his eyes, scratched his chin. 'I suppose that *could* possibly change her mind,' he said after a moment.

'But we don't know that for sure,' Gerald quickly added, trying to introduce a note of optimism. 'It might not.'

'Of course it would.' Eddie leaned forward, rested his elbows on his knees, and spoke in his secretive half whisper. 'She'd be off in a flash,' he said. 'And that's not just wisdom, it's human nature.'

'Completely obvious,' Bevington agreed. 'Obvious, that is, until you consider her personal wealth; some three or four million I believe, possibly even more.'

Eddie frowned. 'You didn't mention she was rich.'

'You didn't ask,' said Bevington. 'But it underlines a fundamental rule, that true wisdom flows only from a knowledge of *all* the facts.'

Eddie's face slowly softened into a smile. 'Does this devoted millionairess of yours actually exist?'

'Only in my imagination,' said Bevington. 'A harmless fiction.'

Eddie nodded. 'Thought not,' he said smugly. 'Which underlines the other fundamental rule, the one about wrinkled old men only being pursued by rich young ladies in their dreams.'

From somewhere in the hall a clock chimed nine. Bevington checked first his wristwatch then the phantom pistol before recharging his glass. 'Right then,' he announced in an officious voice which left no doubt that the previous conversation was now terminated. 'Let's talk about Elderpreneurs, the great unemployable. Originally shunned by companies because of their maverick, disruptive, entrepreneurial spirit; unwanted today because of their advancing years. Only one thing to do, create your own employment, start your own business.'

'And is that what you've done?' Gerald enquired politely. 'Started your own business.'

Bevington didn't answer. Instead he crossed the room to a leather-topped desk and took a grey box file from one of the lower drawers.

'Business plans from Elderpreneurs,' he said, handing the file to Gerald. 'I've already arranged funding for two of them.'

'You're a financier?' Gerald asked.

'Not a bit of it.' Bevington took up his previous position in front of the fire. 'I'm a middle man,' he said. 'I look for people with good ideas, find people with the cash to fund them, and introduce one to the other in return for a small equity in the new business.'

Gerald clicked open the file and gazed at a bundle of manila envelopes, each with a few words written in red on the front. Full Bloom Cosmetics was scrawled in untidy handwriting across the first. 'Make-up company?' said Gerald.

'More of a cover-up company. Cosmetics for the mature woman; a totally new concept in beauty care.'

Gerald casually flicked through the bundle. 'And the others?'

Bevington's reply sounded particularly well-rehearsed. 'Products and services from Elderpreneurial companies,' he declared with a satisfied smile. 'Run and staffed *by* our generation, *for* our generation.'

An envelope near the bottom of the pile had already caught Gerald's eye. It was marked 6T+ with the words *"Styled for the mature woman"* written in blue pencil across the corner. 'Sounds very innovative,' he said, holding it up for everyone to see. 'But isn't it, perhaps, a bit too specialised?'

'No more specialised than catering for the teenage market but with much greater potential,' Bevington snorted. 'The over-sixties already outnumber the under-sixteens in this country. What's more, we're bigger spenders.'

'But aren't we also lining-up to join that big corporation in the sky?' Eddie interrupted. 'Must surely be, if I may use the phrase, a dying market?'

'Definitely not.' Bevington's eyes narrowed as he tried to remember the exact figures. 'The number of over eighties will increase by nearly a half in the next twenty years,' he said. 'From two and a half to three and a half million. It's a fast-expanding market.'

Eddie folded his arms and slipped back into the couch. 'You make it sound as if the oldies might become a powerful market force.'

'And we will,' said Bevington. 'We *were*, after all, the generation which started the youth revolution and invented teenagers back in the nineteen fifties. Fifty years on we're reinventing old age.'

'Never thought of myself as a revolutionary,' Eddie muttered through a less than dignified yawn. 'Always gone with the flow myself.'

Bevington went back to the desk and picked up a small, faded, black and white photograph in a silver frame; a young man hugging a guitar, unsmiling, wearing corduroy jeans and a chunky crew-necked sweater. 'Me before joining-up in nineteen fifty-six,' he sighed. 'That's when it all changed; when the limbo years between childhood and manhood suddenly became your teens.'

'So how do you reinvent old age?' Gerald asked as he closed the file and placed it on the small table beside him. 'Surely it's just a matter of time, and you can't hold back time.'

'No need to hold back time,' said Bevington. 'We'll simply live longer.' He hesitated for a moment. 'And that's both good news and bad news.'

Gerald shrugged. 'What's the bad news?'

'If we live longer we'll create a greater burden for the welfare state. We'll be seen as a tax on the young.'

'Not a lot anyone can do about that,' said Eddie.

'We'll have to do something,' Bevington snapped back. 'What's more, we'd better do it quickly because there's a new generation out there wondering if we're going to live for ever.'

'Sod 'em,' said Eddie. 'We've paid our dues.'

'Of course we have but when there's more of us than them, the whole system will fall apart.' Bevington moved away from the fire, picked up the box file with one hand and, like a preacher with a bible, solemnly raised it above his head. 'New ventures like these will help to create an independent older generation, free from the begrudging charity of a mealy-mouthed welfare system.'

Gerald slipped his notes back into the inside pocket of his jacket and placed his hands together tidily on his lap. 'I wondered what you thought about our idea?' he asked almost apologetically.

'Not bad,' Bevington replied with a twitch of his upper lip. 'Needs a bit of work but it's got potential.'

The faint rattle of cups and saucers turned everyone's attention towards the door and the tall, slim, attractive woman with bubbly red hair who floated gracefully across the room on a cloud of expensive perfume and smiled as she placed a tray on a round table by the window. 'I thought your guests might like some coffee darling,' she said softly.

Bevington stood swiftly to attention, rapped on the table with a clenched fist. 'Gentlemen. I'd like to introduce my wife Katrina?'

Eddie Bates decided that wrinkled old men might sometimes be pursued by wealthy young ladies after all. The burning question was why?

Chapter Three

'Are you the chap I should be talking to?'

Mr Cornfield looked up at the young man who impatiently tapped a ballpoint pen on the post office counter, and instantly recognised the strained, uneasy smile of yet another newspaper reporter.

'That depends on what it's about,' he answered, busying himself with some random papers which he shuffled into a neat pile in front of him. But he guessed it would be about Albert Henshaw and his walking stick.

The press had made him sound like some kind of geriatric guerrilla leader, a "Senior Citizen Chez Guevara", they called him, and what began as a relatively unimportant local story had been picked up by a national newspaper; which was when all the fuss started.

Albert Henshaw wanted only a few wise words of advice about self-defence for the elderly when he filled-in his application form, stapled the requisite cheque for ten pounds to one corner, and dropped it off at Pixley Green sub-post office three weeks before Christmas. Half a dozen elderly gentlemen duly took their places around Edgar Bevington's magnificent dining table and unanimously agreed that a frail old man needed a weapon of self-defence. But that, of course, would be illegal, unless it could be seen to have another, non-violent, practical purpose. A stout walking stick seemed like a wise option for Albert Henshaw.

The charges brought against Albert and his new walking stick when, on Christmas Eve while taking the dog for a walk, he fractured the arm of the young assailant who'd demanded his wallet, were quickly dropped.

Almost overnight he became something of a local hero. But the emphasis of the story was beginning to change and the young man on the other side of the counter seemed more interested in the people behind the organisation known as Older & Wiser.

'With the benefit of hindsight,' he asked, choosing his words with obvious care, 'was it wisdom or foolishness to advise an elderly gentleman to fight back against a street mugger?'

Gerald Cornfield stopped what he was doing and squared up to the question. 'I think events support the view that it was wisdom,' he said firmly. 'Unfortunately this is neither the time nor the place to discuss it. Later, perhaps, when we close.'

'No problem.' The other man turned to go but then hesitated at the door. 'I wonder,' he said, as if he'd just remembered something important. 'Would you say you were wiser than the average man?'

'Certainly not,' Gerald snapped back at once, having answered the same question four or five times in the previous twenty-four hours. 'But it's a fair bet that the combined wisdom of six moderately intelligent adults might be greater than one.'

The reporter nodded unconvincingly, closed the door behind him and crossed the road to the café, pausing for a cursory glance at the menu before settling himself at a table near the window. He wiped the condensation from two latticed panes and starred back towards the sub-post office, a mobile phone intermittently pressed against the side of his face, waiting for Eddie Bates to return.

Gerald could have told him if he'd asked. Eddie was at the gym; week three of his new fitness regime to tone the muscles, trim the waist and, they'd assured him, turn back the clock ten years. He'd be gone for the rest of the afternoon.

But while Eddie Bates had been working long and hard to shed a few pounds, Edgar William Bevington had, quite effortlessly, slimmed-down his name. 'Just call me E.W.,' he'd insisted. 'Shorter, simpler,' he reckoned. 'Easier to remember as well.'

Pretentious nonsense Gerald called it. *Eee-Double-Yoo* was three syllables while *Ed-Gar* was only two so it was neither shorter nor simpler. Difficult enough to remember someone's first two names without having to put their initials together like some kind of schoolboy code. And suppose everyone did it? There'd be no more Geralds and Eddies, just an army of Gs and Es.

Gerald pondered the thought as his afternoon cup of tea appeared on the counter beside him; three thirty on the dot, two digestive biscuits in the saucer. And just beyond the doorway behind him, Winston, unmoving, a steady dribble cascading from his mouth to a small pool at his feet, like a pre-cast water feature set in an ornamental pond.

'One of those is for Winston,' Penelope announced from the back room as Gerald dunked the remains of his second biscuit into his tea.

'Why give it to me then?' he shrugged.

'I'm trying to help you bond with the dog. There's no point in me giving him biscuits if it's you he hates.'

Gerald hadn't realised that Winston harboured such emotions. He quickly turned away, barely able to disguise his contempt for the fickleness of a dog whose friendship could apparently be bought for a digestive biscuit.

Winston stared back at him for a moment, hot air huffing from a half open-mouth, thin black lips set in a mocking smile, or was it a full blown snarl? Gerald wasn't sure.

A man with a cumbersome black bag hanging from his shoulder squeezed through the front door and stood quietly to one side, hands clasped in front of him, while Gerald explained the new postage rates to an elderly lady with a small package for "a very dear friend" in Bexhill-on-Sea. He waited until she had counted her change.

'I'm meant to be meeting our reporter here,' he said, slipping the bag from his shoulder to the floor with a sigh of relief.

Gerald nodded towards the café and the figure seated at the window. 'Would that be him over there?'

The other man gave a thumbs-up and made towards the door. 'OK if I leave my cameras here for a moment while I nip over and get him?' he said.

'Up to you,' Gerald replied half-heartedly. 'I've already told your colleague, I won't be free until half past five.'

'Not a problem,' he called out as he sauntered across the road to the café. 'It won't take a moment.'

And he was right, it didn't take a moment. It took from half past four to nearly quarter past five.

Just a couple of quick pictures, only a few more questions, they assured him, and all so slickly orchestrated that Gerald barely realised what was happening. But then they were gone, thanking him for his time and leaving him to worry about what he'd said and how it might look in print.

The message sprayed, black, across the sub-post office window the following morning was as unambiguous as it was ungrammatical, the middle "e" noticeably absent from the word Arshole. Someone, it appeared, didn't like the article in the down-market tabloid newspaper and, after reading it himself, Gerald wasn't too keen either.

Yes, of course, he remembered saying old people must find ways to defend themselves against yobs and hoodlums and he'd been happy to confirm that Older & Wiser advised Albert Henshaw to carry a walking stick for protection, but that hardly warranted the unfortunate and somewhat sensational headline.

OLDIES DECLARE
'WALKING STICK' WAR
ON YOUNG THUGS

Casual readers would, surely, visualise an army of stick-waving pensioners beating-up rowdy teenagers on the street corners of Surrey? But the picture in the newspaper was of a less than menacing Gerald Cornfield, sub-post master, unarmed, standing uncertainly at the front door of Pixley Green post office, its faded red facia sign clearly visible just above his head.

The telephone calls started shortly before midday; four in quick succession, all much the same; oafish, juvenile voices struggling to string a sentence together, threats of the physically impossible liberally sprinkled with the "F" word, rarely used as the verb it was intended to be. Then dozens of calls that rang out just the once and stopped abruptly like a swatted fly before anyone could reach the phone.

To begin with, at least, Gerald wasn't too concerned. Not a matter for the police, he told himself as he set about cleaning the graffiti from the window with a rag and some turpentine. But the half brick which shattered the glass panel in the front door later in the day was another matter altogether. It could have injured someone, possibly fatally. Gerald decided it was time for action.

The call to Pixley Green police station was answered by a recorded announcement from a call centre somewhere else which invited him to dial the extension number he required – if he knew it. Gerald, who objected to dealing with disembodied voices, didn't know it, nor did he want to leave a message for a member of staff so there was no point in pressing the star key either. He pressed zero to speak to an operator and was transferred to a pleasant enough young lady who explained that other, more serious incidents meant it was unlikely that anybody would be available to drop by that day. Gerald thanked her, quietly replaced the receiver, and promised himself to pursue matters another time. Then he quickly swept-up the broken glass, called a glazier to deal with the front door and tried his very best to put the events of the day behind him.

But the steady stream of telephone calls to Pixley Green post office that afternoon were not all outbursts from the verbally challenged and, at just after five o'clock, Penelope Black produced a neatly-typed list of men and women who'd phoned to offer their congratulations and support; more than a dozen of them, including five asking for application forms.

The first of the letters arrived the following morning. Nearly thirty to begin with; people in trouble, despairing, frightened, searching for answers to their problems. And by Friday evening, when six weary old men gathered around E.W.'s highly-polished, mahogany dining table for their weekly meeting, the final tally was heading into the late sixties.

Gerald glanced at the agenda. Was it really only the fourth meeting of Older & Wiser? That's what is said on the top of the page but it seemed as if he'd always known the close camaraderie of the men now seated around the table with him; knights without armour or weapons but united in the pursuit of wisdom and common sense.

E.W. tapped the side of his teacup with a spoon bringing two or three different conversations to an abrupt halt and focussing the meeting on the business of the evening. He began by reading some of the more urgent letters.

Gerald found himself staring at a small vein on Eddie's forehead which swelled slightly as his face reddened with anger at the injustice of some of the stories; most from elderly people, threatened by officialdom, harassed and intimidated by neighbours, tricked by conmen, robbed and assaulted by street gangs, exploited and abused by relatives; many neglected or ignored by a failing health service and most too frail to fight back; too frightened or confused to complain.

What they needed was reassurance and a bit of a helping hand from a society which seemed to have turned its back on them.

At the point when Eddie's vein looked ready to burst, he reached for one of the letters, removed the small safety pin which fastened two dog-eared five pound notes to the corner of the page, and glanced quickly at the details.

'The bastards,' he muttered, lips now rigid with rage. 'The bloody bastards.'

E.W. scowled, gave a little sigh. 'Are you planning to share your thoughts with us or may I continue?'

Eddie's eyes burned. 'This woman's been attacked and robbed, twice, outside her local supermarket. Both times in full view of other shoppers who apparently stood by and did nothing,' he said, giving the letter a swipe with the back of his hand before he tossed it across the table in disgust.

'What's your point?' E.W. asked impatiently.

'Just this; a few words of wisdom from us won't stop stuff like this happening.'

'I assume she's informed the police,' Gerald said at once, looking round the table for reactions.

Eddie Bates nodded. 'And a fat lot of good it did her too.'

'Perhaps,' said E.W. with a wry smile, 'we should advise her to carry a walking stick, like Albert Henshaw?'

'At eighty-three there's a fair chance she's already got one,' Eddie snapped back. 'Probably needs it to stand up straight, never mind waving it about in self-defence.'

'And that,' E.W. continued drily, 'demonstrates that wisdom should not only be logical but also practical.'

'Perhaps we should all give it some thought over the weekend,' said Gerald in an attempt to lift the cloud that seemed to have descended over the table. 'Try to come up with some positive advice.'

E.W. shook his head. 'What's needed here is positive action, not woolly-headed advice.'

'He's talking about retribution.' The voice, soft and lilting, with a silky tinge of Irish, came from the open doorway. Katrina Bevington, wild red hair tied back in an unruly tangle, tight blue denims hugging her thighs, leaned casually, one hand on the brass door knob the other carrying a small bundle of papers. 'Kids today need their arses kicked not anti-social behaviour orders,' she said, as she turned and swaggered out of the room, disappearing into the relative darkness of the hallway.

Gerald smiled nervously. 'What exactly does she mean?'

'She means punishment,' E.W. explained. 'The most effective and proven cure for crime.'

'Absolutely,' Eddie agreed. 'Kick their bloody arses.'

But Gerald began to feel uneasy. In just a few moments the conversation had turned from dispensing wisdom to administering justice and kicking arses.

'Surely that would be illegal?' he suggested, looking to the others for support.

E.W. spoke directly to the portrait of the Duke of Wellington hanging on the wall opposite. 'My dear Gerald,' he began in a slightly condescending voice. 'It may be illegal but, in the current climate, it's increasingly inevitable.'

Eddie nodded his support.

Gerald looked bemused, gently dabbed his brow with a crisp, white handkerchief.

E.W. paid no attention to either of them and continued with barely a pause for breath. 'If our judges won't, or perhaps can't, dish out a few dollops of justice in the courts, we'll have to serve it up in the streets.'

Gerald didn't like the sound of that. 'By what authority?' he called out with the sudden anxiety of someone who's just discovered they're on the wrong bus, headed in completely the wrong direction. He paused for a moment to compose himself. 'What I mean to say,' he continued in a more restrained voice, 'is how can you rationalise handing out your own private justice?'

'The same way you've justified handing out your own home-spun wisdom,' said E.W., snorting air down his nostrils like an enraged bull. 'Because it's badly needed but largely unavailable in this day and age.'

Gerald ran his finger nervously around the inside of his shirt collar. 'I'm sorry but offering a bit of sound advice is one thing. Setting-up some sort of spurious criminal justice system is quite another.'

E.W. adjusted the narrow spectacles, perched precariously near the end of his nose, and glanced casually around the room. 'Quite so,' he said. 'The criminal justice system we've got will have to do for now.'

Eddie shrugged. 'So what are you saying?'

'Just that the punishment should fit the crime.' E.W. focused, once more on the portrait of the Iron Duke, checked an absent holster for the phantom pistol. 'Why is it that prison overcrowding means that violent criminals are released from jail early, and drug-taking, knife-wielding muggers are given just a few hours community service, but there always seems to be a vacant cell for pensioners who refuse to pay their rates? If the likes of you and I hold back a paltry fifteen quid in council tax, the feet won't touch the ground and we'll be banged-up before you can say "Senior Citizen".'

'It does seem a bit unfair,' Gerald agreed, nodding his head thoughtfully.

E.W. scowled. 'Unfair?' he roared. 'It's bloody outrageous. And, by God, it's got to bloody well stop.'

The room fell suddenly silent.

E.W. took a few deep breaths and sat down, arms folded defiantly across his chest.

Eddie Bates was the first to speak. 'I take it you've already given this a bit of thought then,' he said. 'Sorted it out in your mind, so to speak.'

'Correct,' E.W. answered curtly. 'I've given it a great deal of thought.'

Eddie leaned back, stretched out his legs. 'So?' he said, hands clasped behind his head, gazing solemnly at the ceiling. 'What's to be done?'

'I wonder if this could, perhaps, be scheduled for a future meeting,' Gerald interrupted, trying to change the subject and bring the meeting back to the agenda before them.

'I'll deal with it now if I may,' said E.W. firmly. 'No time like the present.' He stood up and, without apology or explanation, left the room.

Reg Charlton, who'd said nothing all evening, unbuttoned his waistcoat with a huge sigh of relief. 'Maybe he's organising some sandwiches or something,' he said, scratching his belly.

'Probably gone to the toilet,' Gerald decided, having given the matter due consideration. 'Didn't want to make a fuss about it.'

Eddie rolled his eyes. 'For all we know he could have gone to bed or down the bloody pub.'

Katrina Bevington stepped out from somewhere in the shadows as if by magic, wearing a tight, white T-shirt with some words printed across the front. She paused in the centre of the room, head up, slender hands pressed firmly into her waist, and thrust out her chest. Wisdom on Line, it said in bold red letters set in a curve around her breasts.

And below, in smaller letters, a website address for Older & Wiser.

Like the M25, the worldwide web was somewhere Gerald had never wanted to go; an overcrowded super-highway which he'd hoped to avoid as he travelled life's more tranquil byways. But here it was, staring him in the face, bold and brazen, in bright red letters across Katrina Bevington's ample bosom. This was the internet, the future, and there was no going back. Gerald Cornfield was unexpectedly and unavoidably part of the Dot Com revolution.

'May we have your comments gentlemen?' E.W. called out from the open doorway.

'What about old people around here?' Gerald heard himself ask after a brief moment of adjustment. 'Most don't have computers.'

'No problem whatsoever,' E.W. said slowly and with the patronising tone of a school master with a class of half-wits. 'The locals will still be able to pick up a form from the post office. But now the whole country can call for a bit of home spun wisdom and advice, on-line.' He looked around for signs of enthusiasm but saw only blank faces. 'With a website,' he continued in the same slow, superior voice, 'we'll maybe transform a back-room business into a viable company.'

Eddie stared back, unconvinced. 'How do you send cash down a computer?' he asked.

'Credit cards,' said E.W. flatly. 'I've already approached both Visa and Mastercard and I'm considering a third option.'

Eddie grimaced at the prospect. 'I prefer readies; coin of the realm,' he said with a laddish wink. 'More convenient all round.'

E.W. instinctively turned his back on the less than subtle suggestion of petty tax evasion. Such trivial deception was the product of small minds, unworthy of men of vision with the bigger picture in focus. He decided it was time to get to the point; face the facts.

'I think we're all agreed on one thing,' he declared, looking at each of them in turn. 'The majority of the requests for wisdom are from people looking for justice and the protection denied them by a negligent and unreliable police force.'

The suggestion brought nods of agreement from the others but, noticeably, not from Gerald Cornfield who stared, in silence, at the agenda in front of him.

'Please forgive me; I'm sure I've probably missed something,' he said, forcing a polite smile. 'The thing is there doesn't appear to be an item about justice and law enforcement set down for this evening's meeting so why on earth are we talking about it?'

E.W. waved away the interruption with a dismissive flick of the hand. 'It comes under Any Other Business,' he muttered, his voice barely audible.

Gerald hesitated, acutely aware that the others didn't seem to share his concerns. 'I'll admit the police may seem a trifle unreliable these days,' he continued cautiously. 'Negligent in some ways, you might say. But I really don't see what we can do about it other than complain to the appropriate authorities.'

The response was immediate but it came from Katrina Bevington.

'When the NHS adds your name to the bottom of a very long list for hip replacements, you have two options,' she said, swaggering slowly towards the table. 'You can hobble around in pain for eighteen months, possibly for the rest of your life, or you can go private. Your decision.' Katrina Bevington smiled and pulled up a chair next to Gerald. 'A complaint to the appropriate authorities, as you so sweetly put it, would be like posting a letter in the dustbin.'

She took his hand, squeezed, kissed him gently on the cheek. 'We're simply giving some thought to a bit of private law and order.'

'Vigilantes,' Gerald said at once. He made a cursory examination of his fingernails, avoiding eye contact.

'Will you listen to yourself,' she giggled girlishly. 'Anyone would think we'd signed-up Charles Bronson for Death Wish a hundred and eighty-two, or whatever number they've reached in the movies.'

'He's dead,' said Eddie, expressionless. 'Charles Bronson... He died a few years back... Alzheimer's I think; something like that.'

Katrina smiled ruefully, shook her head. 'Oh my goodness, what a pity,' she said. 'And there was I hoping he'd give us a hand; perhaps pop-off a few villains in between films.'

E.W. rattled the spoon in his cup. 'Children, children, settle down now; we still have one or two things to discuss.'

Gerald scratched the back of his head the way he always did when life became complicated. 'I don't approve of this private law and order thing,' he sighed. 'You said yourself, it's against the law?'

'On the contrary, I'd prefer to see it as a welcome supplement to the law,' said E.W. 'No need to trouble the local constabulary.'

Gerald glanced at his watch. 'Crikey, is that the time?' He slipped his fountain pen back into his jacket pocket, tidied his papers. 'I'll have to be off in a short while,' he whispered and started to leave.

'If I might crave your indulgence for just a moment longer.' E.W. gave a little nod to his wife and settled back in his chair.

Katrina smiled with emerald green eyes that sparkled with excitement as she left the table and crossed the room to a panelled door. She opened it and stepped quickly to one side, like a ring master introducing a star act to a circus audience.

'May I introduce Rupert Clark-Hall,' she said. 'He's what you might call a law enforcement executive.'

A young man in a navy blazer and grey flannels, brushed blonde, cherubic curls from a lightly suntanned face and paused momentarily in the doorway to adjust the light blue diagonal stripes of an Eton tie.

Katrina patted his bottom. 'He's much better looking than Charles Bronson, don't you think? Taller too.'

Gerald Cornfield wasn't at all sure what Charles Bronson looked like but he'd already decided that Rupert, whatever his name was, seemed rather too pleased with himself.

Chapter Four

A pale pink rose had started to appear in Mr Cornfield's dreams; gossamer petals carefully displayed on delicate folds of white satin and, above it, magically embroidered in a crescent of lacy, pink and silver letters, the words Full Bloom Cosmetics.

But, in the cold light of day, not so much a dream as a potential nightmare which he'd happily wandered into, eyes wide open, full of confidence and brimming with naive enthusiasm.

The daunting truth was that, for the first time in more than ten years, Gerald Cornfield had a mortgage. And most of the borrowed money was now invested in Full Bloom Cosmetics, with the rest shared more or less equally between 6T+ Fashions, and Vintage Years, the slightly contrived name for a wine importing business. Twenty-five thousand pounds at five point nine per cent interest over a five-year term.

It sounded more like a prison sentence than a mortgage but Gerald found a crumb of comfort in the promise that income from the three companies would probably cover his mortgage repayments and, with a bit of luck, produce a small profit besides. At least that's what E.W. told him when he set the whole thing up a few days earlier.

And, anyway, he wasn't alone; Eddie Bates and some of the others had also dipped their intrepid toes into the chilly waters of commercial investment and joined the ranks of E.W's Elderpreneurs.

In fact, after a few straight Scotches, a bit of fingernail chewing, and a quick tally of the likely number of Saturdays left in his life, it was Eddie who'd led the way and jumped-in, feet first, with an investment of "one hundred K".

Eddie went to unnecessary lengths to tell everyone that "one hundred K" was city-slicker talk for a hundred thousand pounds, although Gerald failed to understand why, and the somewhat sketchy explanation which followed made no sense whatsoever; something to do with K standing for Kilo.

But Eddie was right about one thing; there were probably less than a thousand weekends ahead of them. And that sobering calculation was the sort of thing to put life swiftly into perspective for two sexagenarians whose only investments, until then, amounted to a couple of blocks of premium bonds and the residue from an endowment policy, on short-term deposit with Saga.

The way Gerald Cornfield saw it, life hadn't so much passed him by as taken a detour and avoided him altogether. But E.W. had given him the chance to change all that; make up for lost time. And while taking out a new mortgage at sixty was, undoubtedly, a trifle unsettling, he felt sure he'd soon get used to it, maybe even start to enjoy being an Elderpreneur.

Rupert Clark-Hall was another matter entirely. Much to Gerald's displeasure, he turned-up regularly at E.W.'s Friday meetings but sat quietly in the corner of the room, reading his newspaper. He showed little or no interest in the proceedings, contributed even less, and invariably left a little before everybody else with an eloquent "adieu gentlemen", accompanied by a foppish wave and a short, sharp nod of the head.

It seemed unlikely that Katrina's so-called law enforcement executive would be capable of *enforcing* anything; more a man of leisure, dressed for inactivity; a white silk handkerchief neatly arranged in the top pocket of the navy cashmere jacket, grey flannels with razor sharp creases, and a crisp white shirt. It never varied, almost a uniform, and always with the dark blue tie with light blue diagonal stripes.

The news that E.W. had retained Rupert to promote peace and quiet in the neighbourhood came as a bit of a surprise to the others, especially as his fees were to be met by a small levy on each of the various Elderpreneur companies. And that included Older & Wiser.

'He'll be minding our Ps and Qs, so to speak,' E.W. announced at a Friday meeting towards the end of February.

As so it was that Rupert Clark-Hall finally vacated his seat in the corner of the room, folded-up his newspaper and joined the rest of them at the table; immediately opposite Gerald Cornfield, on Katrina Bevington's right and with his back to the Duke of Wellington.

'What are your plans?' Gerald asked, even before he'd sat down.

Rupert looked up slowly, fixed him with steel blue eyes. 'It might, perhaps, be best if my activities were on a strictly need-to-know basis,' he said quietly, almost apologetically. 'Less worrisome for everyone.'

Katrina laughed suddenly. 'Rupert doesn't want to burden us with too many boring details, that's all.'

'But I'd really like to know,' said Gerald, sounding more adamant than usual. 'If we're funding Rupert's work, I think we should all know what he's doing.'

Rupert rolled a pencil slowly between his thumb and forefinger and glanced at each of the others in turn. 'Very well then,' he replied after a very deliberate pause, his manner easy and full of confidence. 'I'm prepared to tell you what I do, but not how or when I do it.'

'Fair enough,' Eddie said, nibbling the skin around his thumbnail. 'Tell us what you do.'

The pencil snapped in two with a dull crack. Rupert placed the pieces on the table. 'My brief is unambiguous,' he said, looking straight at Gerald. 'I'm to maintain peace and quiet, suppress rowdiness and disorder and try to discourage criminal behaviour.'

E.W. nodded his tacit approval.

'That's not *what* you do,' said Gerald. 'It's *why* you do it.'

The steel blue eyes fixed him again only this time with a look of resentment. 'What are you doing tomorrow evening Mr Cornfield?' Rupert asked.

Gerald shrugged. 'Nothing very much.'

'In that case we'll pick you up at seven thirty for a demonstration.'

But E.W.'s Alvis arrived half an hour early, at exactly seven, and Katrina was at the wheel.

'I'm afraid the demonstration's going to start slightly earlier than originally scheduled,' E.W. confided from the back seat. 'Rupert likes to get his timing just right. Something to do with cinema times I gather.'

The front passenger door swung open and Katrina patted the beige leather seat beside her. 'Sit here,' she said with a playful wink. 'I'll look after you; make sure you don't miss anything.'

Gerald tried not to stare at Katrina's outfit; black leather jeans, skin tight and tucked-in to black patent boots, topped by an immodest white blouse which displayed rather too much cleavage for Gerald's taste. 'We're not going to a party or anything?' he asked, buttoning his yellow cardigan. 'Only I'm not really dressed for that sort of thing.'

'Definitely not,' E.W. grunted. 'We're merely observers this evening.'

The car sped noisily away from Friday Street, turned left in the general direction of the town centre, through two sets of traffic lights, neither convincingly green, and along the lower road to the car park at the bottom of the hill where Katrina quickly reversed into a small space in the far corner, looking out on the high street.

Gerald closed his window to the smell of stir-fried vegetables, drifting across the road from the Chinese takeaway, just along from the cinema, now bustling with late arrivals for the evening performance. And further down the road, towards the traffic lights, The Jolly Farmer spilled half a dozen baggy-jeaned youths on to the street. Zipped and hooded, hands buried in blouson tops, they stood for a moment, motionless, heads bowed, staring at their feet. One spat resolutely at the pavement; some of the others joined in. The tallest lit a cigarette, flicked the spent match at a passer-by. A few shuffled off, in a huddle, towards the cinema. The rest followed.

'Debussy I think,' said E.W. 'Clair de lune, if you can lay your hands on it.'

Katrina obliged, slid the CD into place and slowly increased the volume until E.W. raised his finger approvingly.

'Perfect,' he whispered. 'Just perfect.' He took the handkerchief from his top pocket, wiped his glasses and settled back as if he'd just tuned-in to his favourite TV programme.

'Is Rupert meeting us here?' Gerald wanted to know.

E.W. shook his head slowly but decisively. Katrina fiddled with her hair in the car mirror but neither of them spoke.

'Those kids,' Gerald said peering through the windscreen. 'They don't look old enough to drink in a pub.'

Katrina rolled her eyes. 'But aren't you just the gullible one Gerald?' she sighed. 'Of course they're not old enough; probably got chucked out before they even reached the bar.'

'What must their parents think?' said Gerald.

'Their parents don't *think*; that's the trouble,' Katrina said sourly. 'That's always assuming the parents are in the plural, and not just the one of them, with rock 'n roll for religion and reality TV for moral guidance.'

Gerald wiped away some condensation from the windscreen. 'If I'm not mistaken they're headed this way,' he whispered, 'making towards the car park.'

'It's the predatory instinct,' said E.W., sounding a bit like a consultant psychiatrist. 'Busy cinemas mean full car parks and easy pickings from vulnerable cars; wildebeest at the waterhole while the jackals close in.'

Gerald laughed shakily, unsettled by E.W.'s apparent acceptance of what might happen next. 'Shouldn't we call the police?'

'And tell them what?' E.W. scoffed. 'There's some dubious looking kids in the high street? They'd probably book me for wasting police time.'

The picture of slouching insolence on the opposite side of the road became temporarily obscured with the arrival of a large black van which shuddered to a stop across the car park entrance; hazard warning lights flashing in the gloom. The driver jumped out and hastened across the road to the Chinese takeaway.

'He's blocked us in,' Gerald cried out in amazement.

E.W. hunched forward, placed a reassuring hand on Gerald's shoulder. 'Hold your horses. It'll be gone in a moment.'

But Gerald had already started to make a note of the registration number and the company name, displayed in gold letters across the side of the van. Zenith Electrics, it said. And just below, in smaller writing, Tops in TV & Radio.

A sudden outburst of manic, pubescent laughter punctuated the relative calm of the evening as the jackals circled the van. And then, in an instant, one of them opened the nearside door and climbed across to the driver's seat.

Katrina grabbed Gerald's knee and squeezed. 'Would you look at that,' she whispered. 'The silly man's left his van unlocked.'

'Looks like he left the keys in the ignition too,' E.W. added, as three hooded youths crammed into the front of the van and sped off down the high street.

Katrina started the car, eased slowly forward and out through the gate, following at a discreet distance behind the van as it steered an erratic path towards the canal.

'Pound to a penny they're making for the waste ground near the old boat yard,' said E.W.

Gerald looked back anxiously at the empty road behind him. 'I don't see any sign of Rupert. Are you sure he's coming?'

'Definitely,' E.W. said firmly. 'You can rely on it.'

The black van bounced down a muddy track and on through a broken-down perimeter fence where it came to an abrupt halt beside a dilapidated shed a few yards from the edge of the canal; discarded prams, fridges and rusty bikes scattered around in twisted piles.

Katrina stopped the car at the fence, checked her make-up in the rear-view mirror, clicked her headlights to full beam and stepped confidently out of the car. She stood perfectly still, eyes fixed straight ahead, as three youths turned towards her, blinking in the sudden glare of the lights.

'Can I help you darling?' one of them called out while the other two wrestled with the back door of the van. 'Lost yer way?'

Katrina folded her arms and leaned back casually against the front of the Alvis. 'I think that's possibly my van you're trying to break into,' she called back. 'Perhaps you took it by mistake.'

'Mistake?' one of them shrieked. 'We don't make mistakes.'

She shook her head. 'Wrong sweetie, you made a big mistake this evening; take my word for it.'

A dog barked in the darkness, somewhere far beyond the trees on the other side of the canal and then, for a fleeting moment, complete silence and a fragile calm before the rear doors of the van burst open with a resounding crash and two men in black tracksuits leaped out on an unsuspecting prey.

Katrina stepped to one side, away from the headlights, turned towards Gerald and smiled. 'Sorry, I must be in your way,' she called out.

But it was already over; finished as quickly as it had started. Three pathetic rag dolls bundled effortlessly into the back of Rupert Clark-Hall's Trojan horse and quickly gone.

A trickle of perspiration found its way into Gerald's eye. He wiped it away with an open hand and straightened himself up. 'Where are they taking them?' he asked, peering into the gloom beyond the headlights. 'I mean, what's going to happen to them now?'

'What do they deserve?' E.W. asked quietly.

'I don't know. I think that was more than enough, wasn't it?'

E.W. smiled. 'Maybe. Maybe not. Why don't we leave it to Rupert and his chums to decide eh? It's their show after all.'

Katrina slid back into the driving seat and ran scarlet fingernails through her hair with a sigh. 'But didn't I tell them they'd made a mistake?' she said, turning slightly as she backed the car slowly up to the road. 'They just wouldn't listen to a bit of common sense.'

'One of them wasn't moving,' Gerald whispered. 'As if he might perhaps be dead.' He hesitated, waiting for a reaction, but none came. 'He wasn't was he; dead I mean? He had blood around his mouth.'

E.W. shook his head. 'Theft doesn't carry a death sentence in a civilised society,' he said, settling himself for the drive back. 'On the other hand stealing a van should have serious consequences or there'd be no deterrent.'

Gerald felt uncomfortable. He wondered what Betsy would have made of it all; how she'd have felt about him being implicated in a violent assault and possible kidnapping. The nearest Gerald had ever come to violence was when he'd seriously considered biffing one of the local town councillors for calling the Queen an old relic, then decided against it when someone mentioned the offending councillor's well-documented success as an amateur boxer. Discretion, he persuaded himself, was the better part of valour and, besides, everyone was entitled to their opinion, weren't they? Violence simply wasn't in Gerald Cornfield's genes, and that certainly didn't make him a coward. But the possibility loitered in a small, dark corner of his mind which he rarely visited.

'Surely leaving the van unlocked with the keys in the ignition was unfair?' he protested. 'Bit of a set-up; placed temptation in their way, so to speak.'

'Come on now, temptation's everywhere,' said E.W. 'The only difference is that we delivered the temptation with its own built-in punishment. Now that's what I call justice.'

Gerald held his head. 'But we should have done the right thing,' he said, sounding suddenly forlorn. 'We should have called the police.'

'And they'd have handed out an ASBO or, maybe, given them a bit of a telling off,' E.W. snapped back with a sarcastic laugh. 'That's always assuming they'd come out in the first place.'

'Think of it this way,' Katrina quickly cut in, hoping to lighten the mood. 'If they hadn't stolen Rupert's decoy van, they'd have probably robbed half a dozen cars instead. Some would say we've made a valuable contribution to crime prevention.'

'But they won't fall for it twice,' Gerald insisted. 'Next time they'll check what's in the back before doing anything.'

Katrina turned down the volume on the CD player as the Alvis swung into Friday Street and slowly came to a halt outside Pycroft Cottage. 'After tonight, Gerald, there may not be a next time,' she said with a sinister finality. 'The lesson won't be forgotten in a hurry, and that's absolutely guaranteed.'

Gerald decided this was an argument he couldn't hope to win and, in ways he preferred not to think too much about, perhaps didn't even want to win. The Bevington's views on crime and punishment were odious, unacceptable and completely distorted. Their barbaric ideas demonstrated a primitive logic which Gerald could never endorse and, for the time being at least, he'd decided to ignore. But something else, more important, worried him greatly.

'Where do we stand if Rupert and his chums get themselves arrested?' Gerald asked with an anxious glance at each of them in turn as he stepped from the car. 'Those kids will almost certainly identify them.'

E.W. leaned forward and spoke in an intimate whisper. 'They won't be able to identify anyone until they've served their sentence. And after that... well, let's just say I doubt if they'd bloody well dare.'

Katrina grinned, blew a kiss through the open window and accelerated away with two short, sharp blasts of the horn, Debussy at full volume.

Chapter Five

The essence of old world charm clung to Rupert Clark-Hall like a spicy, gentleman's cologne. It seeped slowly but steadily from the very centre of his being with every practised mannerism and movement; each gesture a modern-day manifestation of the courtesy and consideration, graciousness and gallantry of a bygone era.

And Penelope Black was a sucker for Rupert's schmaltz.

She positively basked in his attentiveness, wallowed in his compliments, luxuriated in the delusion that he meant every well-chosen, insincere word. But the coquettish smile and girlish giggles when, on alternate Friday afternoons, she handed over a cheque for his operating expenses, were enough to turn an Old English Sheepdog off his digestive biscuits.

The amounts varied; usually just forty or fifty pounds but sometimes as much as a hundred. And never an invoice, just a scrap of paper with a word or two in Rupert's illegible handwriting.

'It's not always prudent to be specific about such things,' he told her when, with apologies, she reluctantly broached the subject. 'Put it down as travelling expenses or something. Entertaining, maybe.'

The following day he sent her roses and a lyrical message of thanks. Mrs Black never mentioned Rupert's expenses again.

But Gerald wasn't happy. It felt as if Older & Wiser had joined the corporate equivalent of the European Union; having its hard-earned cash siphoned-off to fund dubious projects it didn't support, hadn't voted for, wouldn't benefit from, and which were not only constitutionally illegal, but probably criminal too. And, like so many EEC initiatives, there seemed to be no effective veto.

He tried desperately to put sponsored lawlessness from his mind but his thoughts always drifted back to his twenty-five thousand pound mortgage which helped to fund it, and the very real possibility of rising interest rates. All things considered, Rupert

Clark-Hall simply wasn't worth the money or the worry, and it was high time somebody said so.

But whispers of alien abductions in Pixley Green put a new and unexpected complexion on Gerald's concerns; a reddish blue complexion, to be precise.

Two youths, missing since Saturday evening, turned up on the Monday afternoon with absolutely no memory of their lost days. And, if rumours were to be believed, they weren't the first, either. The talk was that maybe eight or nine young lads had mysteriously vanished and then reappeared a couple of days later, unable to remember where they'd been and why their skin was now a rather unbecoming but very regal shade of purple. Probably some sort of vegetable dye, a local GP suggested. Difficult to wash off right away but odds-on to fade with time.

The disappearances sounded like an elaborate hoax and understandably flippant newspaper reports of teenage abductions by alien beings weren't taken seriously by anyone. "Purple Youths – was it Little Green Men?" suggested a local newspaper headline. But Gerald fancied it might have more to do with the light blue stripes on a dark blue Eton tie.

Accessory before and after the fact; the words jangled in his brain like nails in a jam jar. Wasn't it the phrase they always used in courtroom dramas when people who suspected criminal behaviour failed to report it to the police? Crimes like kidnap, actual bodily harm, assault with a spray can, maybe, tinting with intent.

Eddie Bates thought it was a prank; a bit like the mysterious crop circles which suddenly appeared in one of the local fields a few years earlier. Nobody ever explained how they got there and, by the following week, nobody cared. But he listened on the extension when Gerald made the call.

Rupert was evasive and neatly side-stepped any suggestion of his personal involvement. If a handful of kids had no recollection of any offence against them, they couldn't possibly testify to a crime, so the question of prosecution was academic.

No harm done then, apart from the temporary embarrassment of an all-over purple skin tone.

He remained coolly detached from the finer detail but remarked that purple people, like branded cattle, would be easy to identify. And he thought the choice of colour apt; synonymous with bruising, a recognisable symptom of bodily injury and, accordingly, of physical defeat. Purple people were marked men with dented pride; a shortfall in self-esteem, he called it. All highly appropriate in the circumstances.

So when three grinning youths vanished on the day they received Anti-Social Behaviour Orders for rolling a convoy of wheelie bins into a busy road junction, Gerald Cornfield wasn't surprised. But when they turned-up wearing only a bin liner each to cover their purple modesty, he decided things had gone too far.

A week later, and in the face of mounting pressure, Rupert reluctantly agreed to explain himself to the Friday meeting.

But he was tight-lipped and uncooperative. He called it simply The Shed although, from the scant description, it sounded more like a barn, somewhere in the vicinity of Dorking. The location remained intentionally vague but the purpose was clear.

'Just think of it as a rehab centre,' he said blandly. 'Somewhere for delinquents to spend a short time reflecting on their disruptive, anti-social behaviour, in the company of like-minded louts.'

The numbers varied but usually no more than three or four at a time, and each dunked unceremoniously in purple dye immediately on arrival.

Katrina Bevington wore a satisfied smile. 'You're an evil little man Rupert Clark-Hall,' she said, planting a playful kiss on his cheek. 'How could you be so horrible to vulnerable little lads? Painting them the colour of winter pansies and all; so degrading.'

Rupert rocked back on his chair, shrugged his shoulders. 'And it's meant to be degrading,' he sighed. 'If the kids regard ASBOs as a badge of honour, a more humiliating retribution is obviously necessary... in my humble opinion.'

But Rupert didn't have a *humble* opinion, or anything else that could reasonably be described as humble; not in Gerald Cornfield's opinion anyway. Rupert wasn't humble, he was arrogant and Gerald said as much when the opportunity arose.

'We should have been told,' he protested, glancing around him for support. 'You can't just take a bunch of people off the streets and cover them in paint. We could all go to jail.'

Rupert looked pained. 'Or we might win the lottery, although both scenarios seem rather unlikely.' He tugged at his shirt cuffs, pulled them just below the sleeves of his jacket, and stood up. 'Let me give you some facts and figures,' he said quietly as he stepped over to the fireplace. 'Six out of ten cases of violent attack by teenagers never go to court and the yob is let off with nothing more than a warning. Only one in fifty teenagers convicted of a violent attack is ever locked-up and nearly half of those convicted re-offend within the year.'

'And painting them purple's going to stop all that, is it?' Gerald interrupted.

Rupert turned his back on the question and stared down at the open fire, hands clasped firmly behind his back. 'Try to understand,' he continued. 'Crimes committed by young offenders have already reached epidemic proportions; up by nearly twenty per cent in the past year, according to official figures. Did you know that?' he asked, the voice slower and more patient but noticeably louder. 'Right now, tonight, standards are being set for the next generation of street criminals. If we do nothing to reverse the trend we'll have a country so overrun by feral youth that law and order will be little more than a distant memory. We'll never reclaim our streets.'

'But it's not our job to reclaim the streets,' Gerald huffed. 'We should leave it to the police; let them deal with it.'

Rupert turned slowly around. 'But they *are* dealing with it Mr Cornfield,' he said, with a look of mild irritation. 'They're handing out on-the-spot fines which don't get paid, cautions and warnings which are totally ignored, and ASBOs which have become the yob equivalent of an OBE.' He paused, flashed a cynical smile as he unbuttoned the front of his jacket. 'Unfortunately our prisons are full of imported criminals so there's no room – not even for us.'

Eddie Bates swallowed the remains of his coffee and pushed his cup and saucer to one side with a sweep of his right hand. He fixed Rupert with narrowed eyes. 'Something's still bothering me,' he said. 'How come none of these kids remember anything?'

Rupert nodded. 'Good question, Mr Bates; one which I've been expecting and will, of course, be delighted to answer.' He reached for his inside pocket and a small, silver pistol which he pointed directly at E.W. 'Stand-up please,' he said quietly. 'It's time for you to leave us.'

E.W. looked surprised but managed a cautious smile. 'Sorry,' he said, twisting round in his chair. 'You've lost me. What am I meant to do now?'

'You're meant to stand-up,' Rupert answered wearily. 'But if you insist on remaining seated, so be it.'

He fired three shots and E.W. slumped to the floor, hands clutching his throat, blood seeping through his fingers. The front of his shirt turned a deep burgundy red.

And silence.

Just for a moment, a unique unholy stillness which permeated every corner of the room. But then screams, wretched screams, Katrina's pitiful cries of anguish as she fell to her knees at her husband's side.

Rupert took the white silk handkerchief from his top pocket, let it fall gently into her lap. 'Wipe your hands,' he said dispassionately. 'You'll get blood everywhere.'

Gerald felt sick, a cold sweat on his brow, his body shaking. He tried to speak but words dissolved into a meaningless, snivelling whimper.

'What you all feel at this moment is abject fear,' Rupert declared in a hushed whisper. He moved closer to the table, pointed the pistol at Gerald's head. 'The feeling's unpleasant, degrading and, above all, it enslaves you to the most powerful of human instincts – survival. And when you fear death, I control your life.'

Eddie stood up uncertainly, arms slightly raised, the palms of his hands forward in a gesture of quiet submission, and prayed he wasn't about to upset the madman standing opposite him. 'OK, you've made your point,' he said as calmly as he could manage, carefully avoiding eye contact. 'Are you going to tell us what this is all about?'

'It's a very simple answer to your question, Mr Bates; the one about purple kids not remembering anything.' He dragged a chair towards him, set his foot on one of the rungs, leaned forward, elbow resting on his knee. 'You can't have failed to notice how witnesses to murder very often develop severe amnesia after the event,' he said through a stifled yawn. 'In fact a whole generation seems to lose its memory whenever so-called gang culture does a bit of shooting or stabbing.'

'And you'd like us to forget what happened here this evening too?' Eddie asked, wondering if he might have been better off saying nothing at all.

'On the contrary,' Rupert said without hesitation. 'I want you to remember every detail of my little demonstration.'

Katrina Bevington's sudden burst of spluttered laughter was unexpected. 'Would it be alright if I got up now?' she giggled. 'My knees are killing me.'

'My apologies.' Rupert offered his hand, helped her to her feet. 'I talk too much.'

E.W. raised himself slowly on one elbow, examined the burgundy stain on his shirt front. 'It's ruined of course,' he said. 'This stuff doesn't wash out.' He grabbed the edge of the table and pulled himself up, brushed down the front of his jacket with the flat of his hand and made towards the drinks table. 'I should think you could all use a very large drink,' he called out.

Rupert checked his watch, smiled apologetically. 'So sorry E.W., not for me, I'm afraid. Got to be off.' He slipped the silver pistol back into his inside pocket, buttoned his jacket. 'May I leave it to you to explain in more detail?'

'No, you may not,' E.W. grunted as he poured the brandy. 'It's your show; you explain it.'

Gerald felt as if he's been on a roller coaster; distinctly queasy and more than a little bit dizzy. His ashen face looked strained and his hands trembled but an uncharacteristic sense of rage was beginning to bubble-up inside him. For the first time in his life that he could remember, Mr Cornfield was undeniably angry and he wanted everybody to know it.

'For Christ's sake,' he yelled, slamming a clenched fist down on the table. 'Could you two make up your bloody mind and get on with it?'

'I'll second that.' Eddie gave his friend a supportive slap on the back. 'We don't have all night.'

Rupert Clark-Hall shrugged, reached for a brandy. 'It's nothing more than basic psychology,' he said, emptying his glass in one gulp.

'When it's time to release our inmates from The Shed, we find a good reason to shoot one of them dead, as a warning to the others. He isn't one of them, of course, he's one of us. And he isn't dead but, to the inexperienced eye, he certainly looks that way.'

'You lot assumed I was a gonna,' E.W. chimed-in from the comfort of a fat, fireside chair. 'Probably frightened the shit out of you too.'

Eddie nodded half heartedly. 'That's for sure. But is it enough to stop these kids going to the police?'

'I'd say so.' Rupert ruffled an impatient hand through cherubic curls and poured himself another brandy. 'We know who they are and where they live. They, on the other hand, don't have a clue where they've been or who took them there. All they know for sure is that we shoot people who don't do as they're told.'

But Gerald wasn't impressed. 'What exactly are they told?' he asked.

Rupert swirled his brandy around the glass, pondered the question for a moment. 'They're told to behave themselves,' he said flatly. 'We encourage them to mend their tedious ways, to stop being a pain in the public's arse. But, most importantly, we warn them to keep their obnoxious, mucky, little mouths firmly shut.'

'Or what?' Gerald sneered.

'Or accept the consequences.'

'Which are?'

Rupert shook his head. 'Too many questions Mr Cornfield,' he said. 'And high time I was on my way.'

'So you'd shoot them?' Gerald looked suddenly smug. 'Would you?'

'Threats are meaningless,' Rupert snapped back, 'unless, of course, they're carried out.'

Gerald laughed, smoothed down his neatly-parted silver hair. 'Blank bullets, tomato sauce blood, a pretend sort of a shooting, like tonight? Not much of a threat when they discover the whole thing's just a silly charade.'

'And, of course, you're absolutely right,' said Rupert. 'If pretend shootings don't put them on the straight and narrow, we'll have to make things more realistic; real bullets, real blood and, with regret, real death.'

'Murder.'

'Not at all,' Rupert protested. 'Execution; just the one should do the trick, prove we mean business.' He finished his drink, placed the glass down carefully on the table. 'But I'm quite sure it won't come to that,' he said unconvincingly. 'Well, fairly sure, anyway.'

Chapter Six

Pixley Green sub-post office quietly closed its doors for the very last time without ceremony or regret. There were no wails of protest, no petitions of support, and no last minute reprieve from the Royal Mail.

It stood empty and abandoned for most of March, shabby interior stripped bare for all to see, a sad, shamed relic from another time; humbled, humiliated and, above all, redundant. Apart from postal orders and road fund licence renewal, which had long-since been discontinued, everything it once offered a grateful public now seemed to be readily available from somewhere else.

But a small crowd gathered outside less than a month later when a man dressed as a mobile phone cut the tape to reopen the tiny premises as Cool Communications. A giant text message, emblazoned on a plastic screen which windowed his face like a space helmet, announced that there would be twenty-five per cent off the entire stock of state-of-the-art communications products during the first week of trading. "Help Yourself To Unbeatable Bargains", proclaimed the red and white banner over the door.

And they did. Burglars emptied the shop the very same night leaving Gerald wondering how he'd managed six relatively crime-free years as a sub-post master.

But he was already beginning to regret moving the office to the larger of his two spare bedrooms at Pycroft Cottage. It marked the start of a new set of problems.

To begin with, Penelope Black didn't think it was seemly; a married woman spending all day in a bedroom with another man, sometimes two men if Eddie Bates had nothing better to do. It just wasn't right. And then there was Winston. He wasn't good with stairs and didn't like heights; one of the reasons why she and her husband had moved to a bungalow a few years earlier.

The dining room, with its long oak table, seemed to offer a convenient and infinitely more appropriate option and, after shifting six matching oak chairs to one side, Mrs Black set her things down with an impatient sigh but without further complaint.

Unfortunately, rearranging the dining room was only the beginning and, by the following weekend, Mrs Black's programme of improvements had focused on the lounge. A comfy floral couch was shunted away from the coffee table, back towards the French doors which lead out to the patio. It gave the room more space, she argued; made it look so much bigger. Then came the business with the hand-painted tea plates displayed on the mantle shelf; all quickly relegated to the cupboard under the stairs. Victorian dust catchers, she insisted with clinical authority; bad for the sinuses. And, besides, they clashed horribly with the carpet.

But Mr Cornfield's inherently forgiving, tolerant nature was tested to the limits when his favourite slippers turned-up in the rubbish bin.

They were, he was prepared to concede, very old slippers and, yes, possibly a trifle faded, worn-out even, but they were comfortable slippers and the idea that they made the place look untidy was utterly preposterous.

The root of the problem was blindingly obvious; Penelope Black had nowhere near enough work to do. And that, in turn, was a measure of the dwindling demand for Older & Wiser's low-budget wisdom.

Mr Cornfield leant back in his chair. A contemplative frown creased his brow as he stared hard at the ceiling and pondered again the company's recent business activity. As always, it seemed to boil down to a few visits from a handful of elderly people looking for someone else, anyone else really, to make the important decisions in their lives. It was, of course, an abdication of personal responsibility but Mr Cornfield had long since realised that people in search of wisdom were looking for a few carefully selected words to endorse what they'd already decided was the truth.

Two or three sceptical pensioners had, quite rightly in his opinion, questioned the wisdom of handing over their homes to a bunch of fast-talking, financial whiz kids with so-called equity release plans. Then there were the usual squabbles among relatives, particularly brothers and sisters, and a few petty but potentially expensive boundary disputes between warring neighbours, often as emotionally charged as confrontations with vindictive daughters-in-law over access to grandchildren. And that was about it... except for the steady flow of people who seemed to have lost faith in the police and were searching for ways to protect themselves from real or, sometimes, imagined dangers.

But it's a sorry fact that the wisest words of Solomon himself are about as much help as a swimming manual to a drowning man when defenceless, vulnerable people feel threatened and altogether too frightened to venture out after dark.

What people really wanted was positive action, not pious advice. And, if necessary, they were prepared to pay for it.

Gerald Cornfield sighed deeply and faced the facts. He hated to admit it but it rather looked as if E.W. might be right; wisdom and enlightenment were no match for the epidemic of violent crime which seemed to have infected the neighbourhood. And even if the local thugs and muggers only managed to put you in hospital for a few days, the resident superbugs would very likely finish you off before you could say senile dementia.

Street violence or hospital viruses; if one didn't get you, the other probably would.

But the police weren't patrolling the streets, stopping drunken yobs from kicking your brains out. They lurked in lay-bys, booking unsuspecting motorists for speeding when a quick glance at the official statistics proved that twice as many people were killed in hospital beds as on the roads. They might just as well have walked the wards of the cottage hospital, handing out ASBOs to negligent nurses and nicking C-Diff and MRSA viruses for GBH as waste their time penalising drivers for doing 32 miles an hour.

Mr Cornfield gazed out across the garden to the bird table where a gang of sparrows pecked nervously at the last of the daily serving of pinmeal before they took-off in an abrupt and undignified flurry of feathers, banished by two hot-headed starlings. And, in the tree above the twittering and bickering, a lone robin puffed out his chest and waited, biding his time until the hostilities ended and he could take his turn at the table.

'Pecking order,' Mr Cornfield whispered to himself dismissively. 'Survival of the bloody fiercest, more like.' The wholly inequitable laws of nature appalled him. Where were justice, fair play, compassion in the overall scheme of things? Mother bloody Nature was a callous, heartless bitch; a tyrant who preached intimidation and oppression.

He rattled the handle on the French doors to scare off the bully boys from the bird table, but they stood their ground, daring and defiant, beaks held impudently high, feathers fluffed. A pigeon, indifferent to the commotion, waddled importantly across the flowerbed, raking through the fall-out from the feast above.

Only the robin seemed concerned and quickly disappeared into the camouflage of the next door neighbour's willow.

Gerald remembered how Betsy sometimes tried to redress the imbalance of nature with a bombardment of sprouting potatoes or onions and shallots from the kitchen window in a gesture of solidarity with the smaller birds. But it never really helped; Betsy's rotting vegetables were indiscriminate missiles and shooed-off the oppressed with the oppressors.

Best not to get too involved, Gerald had always told her. Let the birds sort things out among themselves. But now he wasn't so sure.

Three short, sharp barks pierced the quiet of the afternoon as Winston bounded across the lawn towards a gnarled, old apple tree which leaned, wearily, against the roof of the garden shed.

Gerald glanced at his watch; three o'clock on the dot. Winston was, if nothing else, regular in his habits. Even the birds seemed familiar with his daily routine and took off, on cue, the moment Mrs Black opened the kitchen door.

Soon she'd rattle the lid of the biscuit tin, bringing Winston racing back to the house, fur flying, feet filthy, mouth soggy with saliva.

Gerald wondered how long the aging apple tree could survive Winston's twice daily saturations. The next door neighbour's new cat, a relatively small animal by comparison, had bleached a random network of stains across the lawn in just a few weeks so the tree seemed unlikely to survive beyond summer.

He'd half turned away from the window when the jagged mouth of a mechanical digger jerked suddenly into view just above the fence at the far end of the garden. It crashed to the ground in three or four well-aimed, shuddering blows which shook the house and then, almost as quickly as it arrived, was carried off on the back of a low loader which had reversed into the narrow lane separating Pycroft Cottage from a small stretch of farmland opposite.

The farmer usually cleared the ditches on the perimeter of the field at least once a year but this was somehow different, more of a concerted assault in the area of the five bar gate. Gerald reached the fence only slightly ahead of Mrs Black and peered across at the wanton vandalism.

'They've smashed down the gate, posts and all,' Gerald said at once. 'Why in the world would anyone want to do that?'

Mrs Black surveyed the damage from the slightly elevated platform of an upturned plastic bucket and slowly shook her head. 'I don't like the look of it,' she confided in a hushed whisper, gripping the top of the fence to steady herself. 'That's not good at all.'

'Of course it's not good,' Gerald snapped back. 'Somebody's pulverised the gate.'

Mrs Black stepped down from the bucket and brushed the front of her skirt with the cuff of a thick, woollen cardigan. 'Looks to me like travellers.'

'But they've gone.'

'For the moment,' she said with a new pessimism in her voice. 'But they'll be back.'

Gerald shrugged his shoulders. 'Now what exactly makes you think that?'

'Classic Pikey routine. Get rid of the gate then come back an hour or so later and take over the field.'

'But they can't do that, it's private land.'

'They'll say they found an empty field, with open access.'

'And I'll say I saw them smash down the gate.'

Mrs Black shook her head again and sighed. 'They'll swear it wasn't them. They'll insist it was like this when they arrived and that somebody else must have done it. It's always someone else with Pikeys.'

Gerald's pulse began to race. 'I'll bloody well call the police,' he muttered to himself as he headed back towards the kitchen. 'They'll know what to do.'

The telephone conversation was brief, the advice clear and concise; in no circumstances should anyone confront the travellers. And if and when they ever turned up, the police were to be informed at once. But, no, unfortunately the police couldn't just evict them from the site so it was probably as well to blockade the entrance before they arrived; a tractor or a car would be ideal.

Mr Cornfield's pale blue Austin Allegro was less than ideal but would have to do. It had been confined to the garage for nearly two months waiting for spare parts; something to do with the clutch and a master cylinder. He wasn't technically minded and left such matters to a retired mechanic who lived at the corner bungalow and serviced cars for a few close neighbours, when the mood took him. Unfortunately the mood hadn't taken him for quite some time and although the spare parts had finally turned-up, Mr Cornfield's Allegro remained undriveable. It would have to be pushed into position.

Mrs Black settled herself at the wheel, tucked the hem of her skirt between her knees, and released the handbrake while Mr Cornfield leaned his full weight against the front of the car, both hands on the bonnet, and eased it backwards from the garage into the road. A gradual slope down to the end of Friday Street built up momentum for a sharp left turn and the short run up to the beginning of the lane where they came to a complete standstill.

'It's no good,' Mr Cornfield wheezed. 'We'll never get it up the kerb and into the lane.'

'Perhaps you'll have more energy if you rest awhile?' said Mrs Black.

He shook his head, unable to speak.

Mrs Black smiled from the comfort of the driver's seat. 'Why not just leave it here?' she suggested. 'It *is*, after all, blocking the entrance to the lane.'

Mr Cornfield closed his eyes, nodded wearily and waited, hand on chest, for his racing heart to slow down. 'You're probably right,' he panted. 'It might do the trick.'

But it didn't. At exactly seven o'clock, after unceremoniously shunting an Austin Allegro to one side, a procession of caravans and lorries rumbled triumphantly across the field like tanks into occupied territory, followed by half a dozen wide-eyed ponies and an assortment of scraggy dogs who quickly flushed out any former inhabitants from their cosy hedgerow hideaways. A flurry of birds made for the tree tops; a lone, protesting cat retreated indignantly through the fence to the safety of its own back garden. And then, one by one and with a lot of screaming and shouting, the invaders silenced their engines.

Mr Cornfield watched from his bedroom window as a blaze in the centre of the field lit up the evening sky, sending showers of fiery sparks in all directions and a rancid, black pillar of smoke in an upward spiral to the heavens. Small children prodded the flames with sticks and then disappeared back into the shadows of the encampment where loud, discordant voices violated the calm of the neighbourhood.

Soon after nine o'clock a cacophony of horns sounded a greeting to still more rogue vehicles; maybe five or six, which reversed neatly into spaces seemingly allocated to them in a brazen planning programme which ignored the rest of society.

The police promised to take a look at the situation just as soon as an officer was available; probably tomorrow.

Mr Cornfield rose early the next morning but had barely started his breakfast before the police turned-up, just ahead of BBC Radio 4's seven o'clock news; two uniformed officers, a man and a woman, who stood solemnly, side by side, and suggested it might be best if they came in. They removed their caps, wedged them under their left arms and loitered awkwardly in the hallway while Mr Cornfield arranged two more chairs at the kitchen table. PC Bolton took out a notebook and pencil and waited for WPC Jennings to respond to a shrill but muffled voice, which squawked urgently from a small black box attached to her breast pocket, before they both sat down.

'Have you spoken to the travellers yet?' Mr Cornfield asked.

PC Bolton shuffled his chair closer to the table. 'We haven't approached them yet sir, no,' he answered cautiously. 'It's obviously important for us to speak to the owner of the property first.'

'It belongs to the local farmer,' said Mr Cornfield. 'Lives at the old house, along from the three barns near the roundabout.'

PC Bolton nodded. 'And we shall be going there just as soon as we've finished here.' He turned a page of his notebook, hesitated for a moment before he continued. 'You are, I believe, the owner of a blue Austin Allegro, sir, registration number...'

'That's right,' Mr Cornfield interrupted, looking slightly irritated. 'I parked it just around the corner to block access to the lane.'

'Then you'll probably be aware that you're not displaying a road fund licence sir?'

'But the car's broken down, waiting for repairs.'

PC Bolton looked up from his notes. 'Any motor vehicle must be properly taxed before it's allowed on the road.'

'I realise that but I was hoping to stop the travellers occupying the field.'

'Perhaps you have the vehicle's MOT certificate to hand?' PC Bolton asked, with a casual glance at his watch.

'It's having an MOT when it goes in for the clutch repair and service.'

PC Bolton rose slowly and deliberately from his chair and stood to attention. He slipped his notebook and pencil into his jacket pocket and said something about not pursuing Mr Cornfield's offence – at least not for the moment. 'But,' he added in a more sinister tone, 'I suggest you apply for a new road fund licence at the soonest.'

Mr Cornfield shook his head in disbelief. 'And what about that load of traveller trash in the field behind me? Have you bothered to check their road fund licences?'

'While their vehicles remain parked on private land sir, they would not be committing an offence.'

'But it's not their private land to park on in the first place.'

PC Bolton remained aloof. 'That's something we shall need to discuss with the farmer sir,' he declared firmly. 'It's unlikely, but possible, that he gave them permission.' He walked slowly towards the front door, followed by WPC Jennings, her head twisted awkwardly to one side, ear pressed tight against the small box squawking from her right breast. 'One last thing sir,' he said, turning back to face Mr Cornfield and drawing himself up to his full height. 'I'd be careful about using language likely to incite racial hatred… like traveller trash, for example; it's a criminal offence which carries a prison sentence.'

'I hadn't realised travellers were considered to be a race,' Mr Cornfield snapped back. 'More like a rabble.'

'I'm sure you'll be aware, sir, that many travellers originate from Ireland and might justifiably object to being described as trash or, indeed, rabble.'

The crackling voice from WPC Jennings' right breast sent them both scurrying down the front path to the waiting patrol car.

Mr Cornfield stood perfectly still at the front door until they'd turned right at the road junction, lights flashing, sirens blaring, and travelling altogether too fast towards the town centre.

'Someone on a double yellow line somewhere,' he muttered to himself as he slammed the door shut behind him.

Just half an hour earlier he'd been fairly optimistic that travellers could be evicted without too much fuss and bother but that notion had been completely shattered. The law, it seemed, turned a blind eye to trespassing travellers, while keeping the other eye peeled for motor cars with missing tax discs.

The next half an hour in Mr Cornfield's life remains curiously blurred. He says he has no clear recollection of showering, shaving, dressing or, most significantly, going round to confront the travellers in the field at the back of his house. Nature, it is said, sometimes deletes unpleasant memories or perhaps the blow to his head somehow erased the whole sorry incident from his mind; it's altogether unclear. He remembers only regaining consciousness, slumped against the fence in the lane, a sharp, stabbing pain across his cheek, blood stains on a pale blue shirt and only limited vision in his left eye.

Over the next few days there were half-hearted appeals for witnesses, but none came forward. And the travellers were adamant; they'd neither seen nor heard anything on the morning in question.

Mr Cornfield's swollen left eye went from black and scarlet to a vivid blue and then, after a week, mellowed to a pale, yellowish orange, with angry tinges of red around the edges. But the world was still very hazy and he'd started to wonder if his sight would ever return to normal.

It was Eddie Bates who first became slightly [and uncharacteristically] biblical about the whole thing at the Friday meeting, with talk of vengeance and an-eye-for-an-eye. And then Rupert Clark-Hall was sufficiently inspired to quote the Ten Commandments, particularly the one about not coveting other people's bits and pieces. But while Gerald became increasingly despondent and subdued, Rupert grew progressively more righteous, holy even, as he pondered one or two appropriate responses to the outrage.

'I think it might be best all round if we encouraged our travelling brethren to think about moving on, before they get too comfortable,' he announced after a moment of quiet contemplation. 'I'll probably invite a couple of my more presentable colleagues to toddle across for a diplomatic word or two on our behalf, make sure everyone fully understands how we feel. Clear the air, so to speak.'

There was immediate agreement to Rupert's somewhat imprecise suggestion, and no further questions.

And so it came to pass that three wise men from the East [of London] came to the place where the travellers dwelt, and walked among them, saying unto them; 'Bring to us your elders that we may speak with them.'

And there came forth a vile person who spake of vengeance and many were gathered behind him in anger and told the wise men to leave the land on which they stood, lest there should be a reckoning.

And the wise men listened to his words and knew that his heart was without goodness or mercy and that the spirit of violence was within him. For it is written that whosoever shall speak with loud and vicious tongues and maketh threats unto you has turned his face away from good.

But the wise men girded themselves and knew no fear and said unto him; 'Gather up your wives and your children and your animals and go from this place in peace lest ye shall know the wrath of men and their neighbours.'

And the vile person mocked them and asked of them; 'How shall I know this wrath and who shall dare to visit it upon me?'

And he that was of the greatest height among the three wise men did smite him thrice with his right hand so that he did fall to the ground and feel the pain of retribution upon his brow.

And the highest of them spake to them of a prophecy of fire and burning chariots, saying unto the people gathered there; 'Know that thee must keep a vigil while they brethren sleep lest ye shall all perish in a fire which shall consume thy place of rest when the sun is gone from the heavens.'

And the vile person knew that it was so and was sore afraid. And he gathered up his people and his animals and took them that day from the field to another place in Kent, which is East of Edenbridge.

And when they heard these things, the people and the owner of the field and the neighbours of he that owned the field, were well pleased and rejoiced, saying one to another; 'He that smiteth one of us has too been struck by the hand of justice and his tribe has been driven from our land.'

Rupert Clark-Hall handed two £50 notes to each of the three men, congratulated them on their negotiating skills and permitted himself a pious smile as he waved them off.

His fleeting visit to Pycroft Cottage, a few minutes later, had more to do with common courtesy than genuine concern but the bottle of "medicinal" whisky was well-intended and much appreciated.

'Would you have done it?' Gerald asked. 'I mean would you, could you, have burned them out, or was it just talk?'

Rupert lightly tapped the side of his nose with his finger, the way he always did when he wanted to shake-off a question. 'When the threat is real,' he whispered, 'there may be no need of the deed.'

'But will they be back?'

Rupert shrugged. 'I doubt it. They've seen we have our own rules and retribution and know we don't rely on the feeble protection of laughable laws and a totally pathetic police force.'

'Which means, of course, that some other quiet neighbourhood will now be infested by violent, anti-social, parasites, and all the rubbish they seem to cart around with them.'

'Not necessarily,' Rupert said with a sudden flush of pride. 'Not, for example, if they were to commission a bit of private law and order... for a suitable fee, of course.'

Gerald tried to look shocked but couldn't quite manage it, realising that what he felt wasn't shock but excitement; jubilation even. He set two glasses on the table and poured the whisky. 'To rules and retribution, whenever and wherever they're needed,' he said, fixing Rupert with his good eye as he raised his glass.

'Amen to that.' Rupert took a swig of his drink, reached into his pocket and quickly flipped a pound coin. 'Heads or tails? Call.'

Gerald hesitated. 'Heads I suppose,' he said falteringly.

'Heads it is. You win.'

'Win what?'

Rupert emptied his glass. 'Later, old chap,' he whispered, once again tapping the side of his nose. 'All in good time.'

Chapter Seven

Eddie Bates fell head over heels in love just before noon the following Saturday, shortly after falling off a ladder which had been resting at a precarious angle against the illuminated facia of Eddie's Eatery.

But this was no accident; it was fate. If he hadn't climbed quite so high, reached out quite so far to change the spot-lamp, stupidly stood on one leg and lost his balance, he'd never have been rushed to the cottage hospital and into the welcoming arms of the most adorable woman in the universe. This was destiny by celestial decree.

Torn ligaments in the left ankle; a small price to pay for a life-changing, preordained, rendezvous with staff nurse Holly Lockwood. And Eddie was adamant; it was divine intervention, kismet.

Staff Nurse Lockwood glanced at her patient with deep blue, compassionate eyes and told him he was a very lucky man. It could have been so much worse; fractured limbs, broken collar bone, perhaps even a broken neck. Fatal.

The most captivating female in the cosmos had an elfin face, short, boyish, black hair, and a wide, mischievous smile which said she refused to take life seriously. But until the magical moment she stepped purposefully into his life through the swing doors of Accident & Emergency, Eddie Bates had always been a big boobs, bleached hair, false eye lashes sort of a bloke; women who slapped-on their make-up with a palate knife and doused themselves in cheap, lingering, highly contagious perfumes which infected others like a virulent disease, contaminating anyone who came close.

Holly Lockwood definitely wasn't his type. What's more she failed the Gerry Marsden generation test. Never heard of him or Gerry & The Pacemakers, she said; sounded like a geriatric pop group with heart problems. And if she couldn't remember exactly what she was doing the day President Kennedy was assassinated, it was probably because she was struggling to become an embryo at the time. So, while Holly was almost certainly on the wrong side of forty, she was a bit too young for a sixty-something café proprietor.

But it didn't matter; not a jot. By two o'clock, when he was ready to leave the cottage hospital, Eddie Bates was totally committed. She was his soul mate, the object of his affection, the woman he would marry and spend the rest of his life.

And it was at this pivotal moment in Eddie's brief and altogether one-sided romance, the point when he'd planned to tell her how he felt, ask her out to dinner, that the gold band on her left hand came horribly into focus.

'Married?' he enquired casually.

She shook her head.

He glanced again at the ring, gave a little nod.

'Divorced,' she said. 'Nearly two years now.'

'Great.'

She stopped what she was doing, stared at him in astonishment. 'Great? What's great?'

'I just meant good that it's over and done with, in the past.'

Holly Lockwood fixed him with the deep blue eyes, now somehow darker, more serious than before. 'You ask a lot of questions,' she said flatly.

Eddie shrugged, squeezed an imbecilic grin across his face. 'Sorry, just making conversation.'

'Do you have far to go?' she asked him, checking his admission notes. 'Is someone with you?'

Eddie rose unsteadily to his feet, wedged the grey, tubular crutch under his left arm, mumbled into his shirt collar. 'I'll get a cab,' he said. 'It's only ten minutes.'

'Best not to put too much pressure on that leg. Try to stay off it for a while.' She turned and started towards the swing doors.

'I was wondering,' Eddie called after her. 'Would you be free for dinner this evening?'

She threw back one of the swing doors, held it open for him to pass. 'Sorry. I'm on duty this evening.'

'Ah, yes, of course.' He slid a bandaged left foot forward, tried to disguise the pained expression on his face. 'Some other time then?'

'Perhaps.' Staff Nurse Lockwood stepped back, fiddled with the name badge on her chest as her patient squeezed past and through the door to the reception area.

Eddie shuffled awkwardly on the spot, ransacked his brain for the right words but opted, finally, for a more direct approach instead. 'Perhaps won't do,' he said quietly but firmly. 'I need a yes or no.'

She slowly shook her head, smiled gently while she jotted down her mobile phone number on the back of a hospital appointment card. 'It might be best if you leave it for a couple of weeks,' she said, trying not to sound too bossy. 'Life's a little bit complicated at the moment.'

A sudden wave of excitement surged through his body like an electric current. It lit-up his eyes and sent a high voltage tingle to the very tips of his toes. He reached for her hand, almost kissed it, wavered for a fleeting, catastrophic moment, somehow changed his mind and shook it firmly instead; a cold, formal, unemotional handshake which wouldn't have been out of place at a summit of world leaders. Eddie Bates cursed himself for being so indecisive, clumsy and altogether out of practice in matters of romance.

'Right,' he said, quickly moving-on. 'That's a definite date then. Well, obviously not quite *definite* yet, but pretty well definite; *almost* definite, near as damn it, shall we say? So all settled; I'll call you, on your mobile, in a fortnight's time, two weeks from now, so to speak. That'll be a weekend, of course, a Saturday, just like today.' His disjointed ramblings echoed embarrassingly in his ears as he hobbled down the steps and into the waiting taxi. But he was fairly sure Holly Lockwood waved from one of the windows.

The twin torments of true love and torn ligaments conspired to keep him awake for most of that night and, while a large packet of frozen peas eased the burning pain in his ankle, there was no such poultice for an aching heart, no quick-fix remedy for the bitter sweet agony of love. And it was well into the early hours of Sunday morning when, mind still spinning with wild, unfamiliar emotions, body totally exhausted, he finally dozed off.

But, less than an hour later, the April sun barely in the heavens, he woke to the impatient warble of the bedside phone.

Gerald Cornfield apologised for not calling earlier but he'd only just heard about the accident. The plump girl at the newsagents reckoned he'd fallen off the roof. Must have been serious, she said. Carted him off in an ambulance, they did. Probably be laid-up for weeks.

Eddie's foot found a damp pack of soggy peas and kicked it out of bed. 'What time is it?' he yawned.

'Just gone eight,' said Gerald. 'I called the hospital first but they said you weren't there so I assume it's not too serious.'

Eddie swung both feet to the floor, ran the tips of his fingers over the swelling. 'It's my left ankle,' he said quietly. 'Torn ligaments. Doesn't look much but it's burning up; feels like braised leg of Bates.'

'Don't suppose you'll be at E.W.'s lunch today then.'

Eddie's mind went blank. 'Lunch?' he said, trying to visualise the weekend pages in his diary. 'Are you sure I know about it?'

'I sincerely hope so. It was you who insisted it should be a Sunday, when the café's shut.'

'Oh bugger,' Eddie muttered, suddenly remembering the last meeting and E.W.'s invitation. 'Forgot all about it.'

Gerald hesitated, took a deep breath. 'Actually there's something else; something more important.' He paused again, just for a moment, unsure. 'One of the Sunday papers. There's a bit of a story about people taking the law into their own hands.'

Eddie made a little grunting sound, cleared his throat, but didn't answer.

'Village vigilantes, they've called them. Three or four paragraphs, News of the World, page five. Some kid claims they beat him up; threatened to kill him.'

'Who is he then, this kid?' Eddie flopped back on the bed, closed his eyes to the steady, throbbing pain in his ankle. 'Where's he from?'

'It doesn't say. But Surrey police are apparently looking into it.'

'So is that it?'

'Not quite. Last paragraph mentions that one of the assailants was well-spoken.'

'Ah, that'll be the Prince of Wales, yob hunting, I shouldn't wonder.' Eddie sniggered to himself but then let out a sudden gasp of pain. 'Do you think we could do this later?' he said through tightly gritted teeth. 'I need to slap some frozen peas on the ankle.'

Eddie had hung-up before Gerald could answer. He hobbled awkwardly to the fridge, rummaged around for a second packet of frozen peas, settled, finally, for a handful of ice cubes in a plastic bag. The aching ankle was quickly becoming a pain in the arse and seemed intent on disrupting his entire life.

But Eddie Bates refused to be an invalid. He didn't *do* illness, ailments, aches, pains, sprains, fractures, infections, infirmity or afflictions and he certainly didn't do disabled and debilitated. So he made up his mind to do what he always did at times like this; grin and bear it, swallow a couple of painkillers with a large whisky, and pretended it wasn't happening.

Shoes were a different matter altogether; even his favourite suede moccasins flatly refused to accommodate a fat left foot. Slippers, velour mules with a fleece lining and most of the centre seam torn open, offered a practical solution. And so, with considerable reluctance and a growing sense of embarrassment, Eddie Bates settled for brown brogues and burgundy mules, one of each.

He stood perfectly still in front of two long wardrobe mirrors and spoke quietly to his reflection. 'What do you bloody well look like?' he said, stroking the stubble on his chin. 'Do you seriously think a woman like Holly Lockwood would give you a second glance? No chance mate. Forget it.'

Three paracetamol tablets had started to numb the pain, or perhaps it was the large whisky that was numbing the brain. He wasn't sure, didn't really care, but decided a shower, a shave and a cup of strong, black coffee might be a good idea before he returned Gerald's phone call.

Gerald, a naturally sympathetic individual, at once commiserated with him, asked if there was anything he needed. 'I don't suppose you'll be able to drive,' he said dolefully. 'Not for a while anyway.'

'Hadn't thought about it. Don't see why not; you only need one foot for an automatic.'

Gerald didn't bother to argue, quickly changed the subject before Eddie could go on about his driving skills. 'Have you decided what you're going to do about E.W's invitation?'

'I'll be there, of course. What time?'

Gerald was emphatic. 'It's twelve thirty for one, on the dot. E.W's unveiling something before lunch.'

'Katrina maybe?'

'In your dreams.'

'Funny you should say that because I've just met the woman of my dreams. I'd like you to be the first to know I'm in love.'

'Yeah, right.' Gerald gave a little laugh which said he'd heard it all before. 'Tell me about it later, over lunch.'

Eddie slowly replaced the receiver with a sigh and resisted a sudden and overwhelming urge to call Holly Lockwood. He wondered if she'd bothered to even mention him to any of *her* friends; whether she'd given him a moment's thought since waving goodbye from the hospital window. Perhaps she'd just filed him away in a fat, beige folder with his medical notes, indexed under D for deluded; the idea was far too depressing to contemplate. He resolved to banish such thoughts from his mind, pull himself together, and get a grip, before things got completely out of hand.

At exactly quarter past twelve, casual in a beige lightweight suit, perfectly coordinated with one brown brogue shoe, less so with a ripped, burgundy slipper, he eased himself into the driving seat of his car and headed for Lovelace Farm House and E.W.'s unveiling.

Debussy's velvet music floated effortlessly across the lawns at the back of the house where tall, slim Champagne flutes sparkled on a silver tray, centrepiece to a large round table on the terrace, bottles of chilled Dom Perignon in a huddle to one side. And E.W., relaxed on a plump, floral lounger, eyes closed to the midday sun, glass held limply aloft, demanding the attention of a solitary waiter.

Eddie stood for a moment at the open French doors, leaning heavily on the grey, tubular crutch, and glanced around for a familiar face. E.W., of course, and Katrina, dressed in flimsy, flowery chiffon, hovering nearby, but the others were new to him.

Half a dozen men, probably mid thirties, dressed alike in navy blazers and each wearing a maroon tie with some kind of silver wing pattern. They chatted together on the edge of the lawn; a relatively subdued conversation but punctuated by spasmodic bursts of raucous laughter.

Over to the left, partially hidden by a row of conifers, an old man on a ladder struggled with a long string of red and white triangular pennants, most of them already draped in curves from the eaves of a black timber barn, the remainder bundled together awkwardly in his arms. And supervising the work at a suitably neutral distance just clear of the barn doors, from where active involvement was completely out of the question, Gerald and Rupert sipped Champagne and pointed importantly with their fingers.

Somewhere in the house a clock chimed and then struck one. Eddie checked his watch, stared in disbelief at the hands, still showing twelve fifteen, and realised he was half an hour late.

E.W. opened his eyes, raised himself on an elbow and gave him a withering look, the sort responsible parents sometimes give badly behaved children. He grunted something to Katrina and turned quickly away with a dismissive flick of the wrist.

Katrina's unusually solemn expression gradually softened into a smile. She looked across to where Eddie was standing, took two flutes of Champagne from the tray and stepped lightly across the terrace. 'My goodness, it's the late Eddie Bates,' she called out for everyone to hear. 'We were about to send out a search party.'

'Watch stopped,' Eddie said flatly. 'Not sure when. Could have been yesterday for all I know.'

She sensed his embarrassment, gently kissed his cheek, handed him a glass. 'Sorry to hear about the ankle. Sounds painful.'

He nodded. 'A few of these should make life more bearable.' He took a gulp of Champagne, looked past her, towards the barn. 'What's happening over there?'

Katrina turned. 'Just a few flags to celebrate the unveiling.'

'Ah yes, the unveiling. I've been wondering what it might be.'

'It's what you might call a street cleaner,' she whispered secretively, the Irish lilt somehow more noticeable than usual. 'It clears away filth and generally tidies up the streets.'

'I thought the local council dealt with that sort of thing?'

'Oh they do but, like so many things these days, they don't seem to be able to cut the mustard; not fit for purpose, as they say.'

Eddie shook his head and chuckled quietly to himself. 'This is a wind-up, right?'

'Certainly not. This is deadly serious.' She flashed him a saucy wink then looked away and gave a little thumbs-up signal to the waiter.

The music stopped abruptly and E.W. rose to his feet. He straightened up, slapped the side of his belly in a routine check for the phantom pistol, took a deep breath. 'If you'd all like to join me over at the barn I have something to show you,' he announced with a flourish. 'That's always assuming Rupert's finished festooning the place with his little flags.'

Eddie reached for another glass of Champagne and prepared himself for the slow and painful walk to the other side of the lawn where they'd already started to gather in a haphazard line, in front of the barn doors.

Gerald sidled across and spoke in a hushed voice. 'You're late?' he said, sounding like a school master ticking-off a small boy. 'We were getting worried.'

'Don't you bloody start,' Eddie snapped back. 'I've had quite enough black looks and sarcasm this afternoon without you sticking your oar in.'

E.W. clapped his hands and called for quiet.

Rupert Clark-Hall stepped forward, slipped a padlock from the barn doors with the effortless artistry of a seasoned magician, and threw them open to the afternoon sun. A single shaft of light sliced through the gloom like a dazzling sword from the gods and fell across the bonnet of a transit van; a very ordinary, run-of-the-mill, bog standard, white van, vehicle of choice for a generation of plumbers and roofers.

But Rupert obviously didn't see it that way at all. 'I have the honour to present a remarkable addition to our armoury,' he announced with theatrical aplomb. 'Our very first VRU.'

There was a light ripple of applause, although nobody seemed quite sure why, followed by an embarrassing silence.

Eddie looked blank. 'What's a VRU?' he whispered.

Gerald shrugged. 'No idea, but I wouldn't mind betting the V stands for Van.'

'And the R for Ropey,' Eddie quickly added. 'Looks as though it's seen better days.'

The uncomfortable hush was shattered as Rupert revved the van to life and edged it out of the barn to a stretch of paving, close to the conifers. He opened the rear doors and stood back.

'Come and take a look,' he called out.

Gerald hesitated for a moment, chose his words carefully. 'I don't mean to sound too critical,' he began politely, 'but the van looks rather unremarkable from where I'm standing. Just like any other van, in fact.'

Rupert pressed both hands into his blazer pockets and somehow looked even more smug than usual. 'That *is* the general idea; unremarkable and very, very ordinary on the outside so we don't draw attention to the inside.'

The group moved, as one, to the back of the van and peered in. Two open-fronted cubicles had been constructed on each side of the vehicle, narrow booths with thick leather straps at top and bottom. And, facing them, running front to back through the middle of the van, a row of bench seats.

'It's a scaled-down Black Maria,' Rupert explained, in case there might be any doubts about its purpose. 'We have the capability to transport up to four prisoners at a time, each securely strapped in their own little cell.'

'Looks like a van-load of up-ended coffins with the lids off,' Eddie grunted. 'Not so much a Black Maria as a communal hearse.'

Rupert ignored the jibe, climbed into the back of the vehicle and a more exalted platform to emphasise the importance of his announcement. He spoke in short, clipped sentences which had more in common with a military briefing than an informal chat about bizarre uses for white vans.

'A six-man team will proceed by VRU to the point of action. They'll engage, overcome and apprehend hostiles. After containment, hostiles will be transported in individual cells to a prefixed destination.'

Eddie Bates lightly tapped the side of the van with the rubber tip of his crutch. 'VRU. What's it mean?'

'Violence Response Unit. It does what it says on the tin, respond to violence. We're talking about the wholesale removal of violent kids from the streets.'

Gerald felt a cold shiver through his body, remembering a black van, Zenith Electrics in gold letters on the side, parked invitingly in the high street; easy pickings for three young thieves who drove it off to the waste ground close to the canal. And then the retribution; bloody noses and broken bones, courtesy of two men in black tracksuits.

'Are you sure the timing's right?' he asked. 'What with today's newspaper reports, police investigations into teenage beatings by vigilantes. Won't the police be watching out for something like this?'

Rupert shook his head. 'These kids get away with terrorising entire neighbourhoods precisely because the police are nowhere to be seen. The only thing they'll be watching out for is themselves.'

Eddie shuffled closer. 'But Gerald's got a point hasn't he? What about identification, CCTV, number plates?'

'Masked faces, false plates.' Rupert took three different number plates from a hold-all. 'Plenty more where these came from. We'll change them every time.'

'And the six-man team?' Eddie asked, guessing he already knew the answer.

'Right behind you. A few colleagues. Ex-Paras.'

Eddie turned, smiled politely, gave a little nod. 'That just leaves one question then. Who's driving?'

Rupert jumped down from the van, placed a comforting arm around Gerald's shoulder, squeezed tightly.

'Not me?' Gerald gasped.

'But of course you,' said Rupert. 'You won the toss.'

Mr Cornfield didn't enjoy lunch. He'd somehow lost his appetite.

Chapter Eight

There was a black V-neck sweater in Gerald Cornfield's wardrobe which he never, ever wore. It was a surprise present from Betsy, bought in the January sales a month or so before she died. But three years on, the price tag was still stapled to a pristine sleeve.

The problem was Gerald's claustrophobia and the sudden panic that always gripped him when he pulled sweaters over his head; frantic moments of irrational fear when a tight web of suffocating wool seemed to cling to his face, weave itself into his hair, imprison him, slowly stifle the breath from his writhing body as he struggled to be free.

And a woollen mask which completely wrapped itself around the skull, leaving just three small holes for the eyes and mouth, aroused precisely the same frenzy of anxieties.

The traditional headwear of choice for IRA terrorists and B-movie bank robbers and now, it seemed, Violence Response Unit personnel, incarcerated Mr Cornfield's face like an instrument of torture. He could empathise with The Man in the Iron Mask, knew at once how he must have suffered, but pacified himself with the knowledge that it would only be for short spells at a time; while the action was underway. OK to wear dark glasses the rest of the time, Rupert had assured him at the preliminary briefing.

Tracksuits were a completely new experience for Gerald and he was pleasantly surprised by the instant feeling of freedom and comfort; no belts and buttons, no fiddly flies, and absolutely no need for a shirt and tie. He slipped it on, laced-up his very first pair of trainers and examined his profile in a mahogany-framed mirror. Not only comfortable but also moderately flattering; it rounded-off some of the body's more conspicuous lumps and bumps and gave a man of his advancing years an altogether more athletic silhouette.

Perhaps it was the colour. Betsy always said that black flattered the female form and gave men an air of sophistication and elegance.

But he wondered how she might have felt about a man in a black, woollen, balaclava mask.

Mr Cornfield gritted his teeth, shut his eyes tight to the torment to come, and pulled the fearsome sheath over his head in a single resolute movement. He paused, breathed deeply to regain composure, and told himself it was alright; no problems, nothing to worry about, everything as it should be.

Only it wasn't; he was trapped, head pounding, pulse racing, a prisoner in a ridiculous knitted bag. He gazed into the mirror at the grotesque, shapeless skull and two blank, alien eyes which peered back at him from shadowy sockets; a menacing, unfamiliar stare, unrecognisable and somehow separated from the man within. Perhaps that was the trick of it – a personality change, the ultimate disguise.

He ripped the mask from his face and threw it to the floor in a sudden wave of panic. It was a futile act of denial and he realised that the time had come to face-up to the phobia which had terrorised him for most of his adult life.

The small, silver car which skidded noisily to a halt outside Pycroft Cottage that evening gave three short, sharp blasts of its horn, as if the screeching tyres weren't enough to wake the entire neighbourhood. Mr Cornfield zipped-up the front of his tracksuit, smoothed down his hair with the palm of his hand, and trotted to the front gate with the easy stride of a seasoned athlete.

A young man in a black T-shirt, stretched like a second skin over bulging biceps, flung the passenger door open with a nod from a fiercely-shaved head. He revved the engine impatiently, left hand gripping the gear lever, while Mr Cornfield glanced around to see if there were any witnesses to his eight thirty departure. A curtain fluttered in the front window of the house immediately opposite, but that was to be expected. And, anyway, she had terrible eyesight and couldn't tell a policeman from the postman; not that anyone ever saw much of either these days.

The driver waited until his passenger had fastened his seat belt then slammed his foot down on the accelerator and raced towards the crossroads. 'Be there in twenty mins Gerry,' he said. 'Barring accidents.'

Mr Cornfield grimaced. 'Actually I'm known as Gerald.'

'Whatever. I'm Ben, but they call me Dizzy.'

'Dizzy?'

'After Benjamin Disraeli. Dizzy, geddit?'

Gerald looked surprised. 'Wasn't Disraeli a bit before your time?'

Dizzy shrugged. 'All the great politicians were a bit before my time. Even Churchill. These days we just get pillocks in Parliament.'

'Excuse me,' said Gerald with an indignant scowl. 'What about Margaret Thatcher?'

'She was OK I suppose. Not one of my heroes.'

'And who, exactly, *is* one of your heroes?'

'David Sterling,' Dizzy answered at once.

Gerald looked blank. 'I think perhaps you mean David Steel? Little chap. Liberal Party. Name sounds a bit like David Sterling.'

Dizzy stared back in disbelief. 'Never heard of David Sterling? You're having a laugh.'

'Sorry, no. I really don't have the slightest idea who David Sterling might be.'

'*Colonel Sir* David Sterling,' Dizzy corrected. He took a deep breath and spoke slowly and deliberately, as if he expected Gerald to commit the sequence of words to memory. 'Founder of the SAS. Born 1915, died 1995. Greatest soldier who ever lived. Six feet, six inches with his boots off. Affectionately known in the armed forces as the Phantom Major.'

'Ah yes.' Gerald was none the wiser but nodded importantly, hoping he hadn't offended his young companion. 'I think perhaps I may have heard of him. Great man.'

But Dizzy's mind was elsewhere. 'Bugger,' he yelled suddenly and braked hard. An angry chorus of horns and squealing tyres filled the night air as he swerved left off the main Dorking road, and accelerated away into the relative calm of a narrow country lane. 'Nearly missed the bloody turn-off again.' He pointed towards a group of farm buildings, silhouetted in the moonlight, beyond some open fields. 'It's over there,' he said. 'The Shed.'

Gerald gripped his seat belt with both hands as the car bounced and slithered along a muddy track, up towards a block of dilapidated stables, where it came to an abrupt halt.

'Here we are then,' said Dizzy. 'And under twenty minutes, door-to-door.'

Gerald glanced at his watch; ten minutes to nine. 'It looks completely deserted,' he said, peering through the rear window into the darkness. 'Are you sure this is the right...?'

But Dizzy was already out of the car and headed towards the largest of three ship-lapped outbuildings before Gerald could finish the question. He paused for a moment, beckoned, then quickly disappeared inside.

It might have been the dark desolation of the place or the thought of what might lay ahead that set Gerald's stomach churning. But it had more to do with a schoolboy sense of excitement and anticipation than fear. He hurried towards a shaft of light from the half-open door.

The baronial elegance which greeted him was unexpected and in marked contrast to the stark exterior. Two iron chandeliers, suspended like giant cartwheels from the rough-hewn crossbeams of a vaulted roof, lit a gallery of faded tapestries on the walls and sent shadows across the magnificent stone floor; mighty York slabs, shaped, smoothed, and mellowed by the feet of ages.

On the far side of the room, where a cluster of easy chairs faced a blazing log fire, Rupert Clark-Hall rose slowly to his feet and waved a brandy glass. 'Come and join us,' he called out. 'You're just in time for a therapeutic snifter before we go.'

The quarrelsome squeal of Gerald's trainers on the shiny stone floor set his teeth on edge as he crossed the room to the fireplace. He glanced quickly at the others, a few familiar faces from E.W.'s lunch party, and waited, perfectly still and mercifully silent, while Rupert poured a large Hennessy XO.

Dizzy pushed a chair forward, gestured for him to sit.

'Are we expecting someone else?' Gerald asked, nodding towards an unoccupied chair, closest to the fire.

Rupert slowly shook his head. 'It's Bookie's chair. Sort of tradition.'

The others stared solemnly at the floor.

'Bookie?' Gerald smiled, hoping they wouldn't think him too intrusive.

Rupert drained his glass, balanced it precariously on the arm of the chair. 'Colonel James Bookman. Stupid accident with a chute. Shouldn't have happened.' He casually flicked the glass, watched it shatter on the stone floor, smiled. 'The bastard's still with us, of course, in spirit.'

The others raised their glasses in a toast to their phantom guest. 'To Bookie,' they shouted at the rafters, as if he could hear them on some other celestial plane. 'Best of the best.'

Gerald felt uneasy, like a stranger at a funeral. He sipped his drink, stared silently at the tapestry above the fireplace, and waited until they'd all settled down again before he spoke.

'So this is The Shed,' he said, to nobody in particular. 'Very impressive.'

Rupert laughed. 'Sorry to disappoint you. The Shed's next door. Empty, but not for long. We're expecting a few special guests later on this evening.'

Gerald's stomach did a backwards summersault as the brutal reality of what was about to take place finally kicked-in. But he tried to sound unconcerned. 'How many guests are you expecting,' he asked nonchalantly. 'Where will they be coming from?'

'Three or four, if they're out in their usual force.' Rupert thrust his hands into black leather gloves, stretched them tight over his fingers, and made a fist. 'We'll pick them up just north of Pixley Green.'

A mobile phone trembled to life. Dizzy read the text message, gave a little thumbs-up. The others quickly finished their drinks and left through a door at the rear of the building to a discordant symphony of squeaky feet.

Rupert checked his watch. 'Overture and beginners please. Curtain up in twenty minutes.'

Gerald followed him to the open door, hesitated for a moment. 'It's all going to be OK, isn't it? Tonight I mean.'

Rupert grinned, handed him a map. 'Leave the worrying to me, old chap. You just concentrate on getting us there and back.'

The van was parked outside; engine running, lights on full beam, doors open, and Dizzy checking everyone into their positions. He slammed the rear doors shut and walked round to the front of the vehicle where Gerald was hunched over the map, staring at the area circled in red.

'Know where you're going, do you?' Dizzy asked. 'Don't want you dropping the lads off at the wrong place.'

Gerald nodded impatiently, glanced at himself in the wing mirror. 'You don't think the sun glasses might look a bit out of place in the dark? And the weather forecast said it might rain, as well.'

'Better than giving a full-frontal mug shot to a battery of CCTV cameras.' Dizzy closed the driver's door, rapped twice on the bonnet and stepped back. 'Don't jump any red lights, break the speed limit or stop for leggy hitch hikers in short skirts.'

The drive to Pendrake Close took longer than expected but it wasn't difficult to find, thanks to the noise; a barrage of fireworks, loud and aggressive, tossed into the front garden of a semi-detached, halfway down the cul-de-sac; mindless shrieks of adolescent rage, fuelled by a heady mix of cheap booze and swaggering bravado. And crashing, clattering glass, the unmistakeable sound of violence, unprovoked, indiscriminate and intimidating.

Gerald reversed carefully into the cul-de-sac and came to a stop within a few feet of the corner. He paused, took a couple of deep breaths and braced himself for the suffocating anguish of the woollen mask. With the window open, he decided, it might just be bearable and quickly slipped it over his head before he could think too much about it.

The madness at the other end of the road was played out in the wing mirror of the van; someone cavorting on the roof of a small red car; two boys with iron bars, laying into the vehicle with the savagery of primitive hunters at the kill. The firework thrower stopped to urinate over a crumbling brick wall; someone else pitched a brick into the darkness, punched the air with his fist, let out a shrill, manic scream. Three others gathered around him in a display of deference.

The rain swept in, as forecast, on a cold east wind but the frenzied attacks continued, unabated, while six men in black moved slowly, quietly, unnoticed, from the van, through the shadows towards the commotion.

And then the retribution; a virtuoso performance, choreographed with the grace and precision of a Sadlers Wells ballet and worthy of a standing ovation.

Rupert's team worked in pairs, focussing the full power of their punches on the stomach and the backs of the knees, simultaneously, in a coordinated assault. It was brief but brutal and, in a matter of moments, a gang of rampaging louts had been concertinaed into a crumpled heap.

And then a sudden quiet; Gerald's cue to back the van down the cul-de-sac. He pulled out to the centre of the road, slammed into reverse gear, and manoeuvred slowly and carefully along the narrow corridor of parked cars. But reversing had never been one of his strong points and backing an unwieldy van through such a confined space was the stuff of nightmares. He began to perspire.

The woollen mask, hot and clammy, clung to his face like a wet dishcloth; stifling, suffocating, unbearable. He tore the loathsome garment from his head and accelerated blindly to the opposite end of the road where the smell of spent fireworks hung heavy in the air and a few anxious faces peered out from the shadows of darkened rooms.

Somebody opened the rear doors of the van, shouted something to the others, and quickly jumped inside. A minor scuffle broke out as the first of four youths was bundled into one of the narrow compartments and secured with leather straps.

'You're not the old Bill,' he protested. 'You got no fucking right to touch us. We're just 'avin a larf.'

'Shut it.' Rupert's voice, uncharacteristically cold and aggressive, reverberated around the inside of the van. 'The laugh's over.'

'It's against the fuckin' law. They'll bang you lot up for this.'

'I said shut it.' Rupert recognised the ring leader, forced a rag into his mouth, sealed it with a strip of gaffer tape. 'I'm the only law in your pathetic little life tonight, so get used to it,' he said quietly.

Gerald wasn't altogether sure what was meant to happen next; they hadn't really talked about it. But things seemed to have gone off without a hitch and he guessed that it was probably time to leave. He stepped warily round to the back of the van, face half covered by his hand. 'Ready for the off?' he whispered.

Rupert quickly turned, stared at him in disbelief. 'Why don't you just print your name across your back? Perhaps your telephone number too.' He waved him away impatiently, gestured to him to close the doors.

Gerald decided this probably wasn't the ideal moment for explanations and apologies. He slammed the doors shut and climbed back into the driver's seat, watched by two young boys, barely teenagers, gaffer taped to a lamp post.

Muffled protests from four irate passengers in the back had died down by the time the white van turned off the Dorking road and headed up across the open fields towards the cluster of out buildings.

But relentless, torrential rain had turned the narrow track into a quagmire. The van slithered to a halt, wheels spinning in the mud, some fifty yards or so from The Shed, where Dizzy leaned casually against the open doors, arms folded, smoking a cigarette.

Gerald slipped down into first gear, accelerated hard, and sent another shower of sludge high into the air behind him while the van sank still deeper into the soft mud. After the third unsuccessful attempt, the van now dangerously skewed to one side, he signalled defeat with a few short blasts on the horn and waited, humiliated and embarrassed, for someone to do something.

Dizzy span his cigarette to the ground and disappeared into the darkness. He returned in a moment with a tractor and a length of heavy chain, dragged the van from the soggy mire and hustled four anxious youths into The Shed in the time it took Gerald to find his way back to the dying embers of the log fire and the dregs of a brandy glass.

Failure, Mr Cornfield had long since decided, was an unbecoming garment. It hung loosely about him like an old cardigan; ill-fitting and embarrassing, but always close at hand, waiting for him to slip it on and look stupid. He settled back in the chair and resigned himself to the inevitable ridicule and recrimination to follow.

But as the others took their places by the fire there were no lectures, no rebukes, no wails of condemnation, only Rupert's sincere thanks and warm congratulations on a job well done.

'Pity about the weather,' he said, rubbing his hair vigorously with a towel. 'Slightest drop of rain always seems to turn these fields into a bloody swamp.'

'It's certainly very muddy out there.' Gerald hesitated, glanced down at his trainers. 'Sorry, I should have cleaned myself up a bit before coming in.'

'Don't worry about it. Mud washes off.' Rupert rolled-back his left sleeve, carefully unwound an improvised bandage from his wrist. 'Blood, on the other hand, stains the furniture.' He tossed a red streaked handkerchief into the fire and hurried off to the bathroom.

Gerald glanced quickly at the others. 'How did it happen?'

'One of the little bastards had a knife,' Dizzy said eventually. 'Par for the course these days.'

'They *all* had knives,' Rupert shouted above the sound of running water. 'The tow rag with acne had a bloody air pistol as well.'

Dizzy shrugged. 'Most of them won't leave home without a knife these days, sometimes a machete. Next thing you know they'll tool themselves up with shotguns and pistols too.'

Gerald was painfully reminded of his own juvenile crime; a home-made catapult and the endless shame of breaking Mrs Hillman's bedroom window. He'd aimed at a red box kite which bobbed irresistibly above the trees in the field beyond so, to all intents and purposes, it was nothing more than a silly mistake. But nobody was interested in the mitigating circumstances and the sentence was handed down with no right of appeal; three Saturday mornings mowing Mrs Hillman's lawn, weeding the path, and emptying her cat's disgusting "clean" tray. The tray was rarely "clean" and the foul smell of ammonia lingered in his nostrils for weeks after. The awful sense of injustice flooded back and it crossed his mind that the boys from Pendrake Close might very well be feeling the same way.

'What will you do with them now?' Gerald asked, wondering if the somewhat brutal rounding-up and confinement in the shed might be considered punishment enough. 'I mean they sound as if they might be rather high-spirited to have around for too long.'

Dizzy shrugged, kicked a sighing log to the back of the fire, threw another on top. 'They're always a bit mouthy to begin with but a good slap before bedtime usually calms them down.'

'Slap? You mean a beating?'

'No, I mean a slap, as in leaving four red finger marks across the face.'

Gerald frowned. 'Sounds a bit childish. More like playground stuff. Slapping faces surely ranks alongside pulling hair, spitting, that sort of thing.'

'Got it in one,' said Dizzy. 'Treat 'em like naughty kids. Lowers their somewhat over-developed sense of self-importance.'

'Cleaning out cat trays has much the same effect,' Gerald said without further explanation. 'I suppose it all boils down to making the punishment fit the crime. Three Saturday mornings of hard labour for a broken window, a few nights in The Shed for a smashed-up car and a brick or two lobbed into someone's front garden.'

Dizzy fixed him with a quizzical stare. 'Whatever you say Gerry old lad. No worries.' He tossed his car keys high into the air for no good reason, caught them with cupped hands and made towards the door. 'I think it's probably time to get you home Gerry. Past midnight you know.'

'It's Gerald, if you wouldn't mind,' Mr Cornfield huffed. 'I think I mentioned it earlier.'

'And so you did,' Dizzy said at once. 'It's just that Gerald sounds a bit poncey, don't you think?'

Mr Cornfield got to bed a little after one o'clock but stayed awake until the early hours, wondering if Dizzy might have been right and his name might be just a bit poncey.

Chapter Nine

Winston's baritone bark echoed down Friday Street at exactly half past eight the following morning, while Mrs Black fumbled with the keys to Pycroft Cottage and, in a polite whisper which the dog always ignored, asked him to be quiet.

It was a waste of time, of course, a bit like asking bees if they'd mind leave out the buzzing bit. Winston's bark was an integral part of his being, like his slobbery black lips or the silly, stubby tail, but Mr Cornfield was beginning to warm to the great lolloping lump which barged through the front door each day with such single-minded enthusiasm.

Despite his obvious failings, Winston brought a touch of normality to Mr Cornfield's increasingly complicated life. Even the aging apple tree in the garden had so far survived Winston's twice daily visits; flourished even. It might have been a trick of the light but the leaves seemed altogether greener, healthier looking.

But dogs know when they've found a victim, someone they can manipulate, boss about, and Winston was no exception. He bounded into Mr Cornfield's bedroom, bounced across the bed and made two unsuccessful attempts to join him in the bath.

Mrs Black called out from the bottom of the stairs, told him to come down at once, said he was a naughty boy, but then quickly gave up and disappeared into the kitchen to make a cup of tea. Winston settled himself on the bathroom mat while Mr Cornfield dressed, then followed him downstairs and into the kitchen where Mrs Black sat, straight-backed and businesslike, at one end of the pine table.

'How did it go last night?' she asked, pouring herself a second cup of tea.

Gerald shrugged unconvincingly. 'How did *what* go?'

'Your appointment with Mr Clark-Hall.' She slid an open diary across the kitchen table. 'Eight thirty – Rupert – Tracksuit, it says. That sounds like jogging to me.'

'Something like that.'

Mrs Black wagged her finger importantly. 'Men of your age should be very careful. Too much physical activity can bring on a heart attack. Happens to joggers all the time.'

Gerald nodded, reached for a biscuit. 'We didn't go far. Couple of times around the block.'

'You'd be better off taking Winston for a little stroll every now and then. My husband always says...'

But Gerald wasn't listening and interrupted before he'd realised what he was doing. 'Mrs Black,' he said solemnly, and with a discernible hint of apology. 'Do you think my name's a bit poncey, Gerald I mean? Would Gerry be a bit more with it, less formal?'

'I don't hold with abbreviated names,' Mrs Black declared flatly. 'If your name's Gerald, your name's Gerald.' She paused, gave Winston a biscuit. 'Just as I'm Penelope and not Penny and Winston's most certainly not Winnie.'

'Not poncey then?' said Gerald.

Mrs Black took a little puff of her inhaler. 'A ponce is a man who lives off prostitutes so I don't think we need discuss that further.'

The phone on the kitchen wall rang out and brought the conversation to an abrupt close. Mrs Black reached up to answer it, sighed. 'It's Eddie Bates,' she said. 'Formerly known as Edward, no doubt.'

'I think it was Edwin actually,' Gerald said, sliding a chair nearer to the phone.

Eddie Bates had good news and slightly bad news. The good news was that the most beautiful woman in the world had agreed to have dinner with him that very evening. But, and this was the slightly bad news, she wanted to make it a foursome; asked him to bring along a partner for a girlfriend who was going through a bad patch.

'Naturally, I immediately thought of my good friend Gerald,' said Eddie. 'If anyone deserves a good night out, you do.'

'Me?' Gerald protested. 'Are you seriously expecting me to partner a complete stranger?'

'She's not a *complete* stranger. Her name's Valerie and she works at the hospital with Holly.'

'Holly? Who's Holly? You've never mentioned anyone called Holly before.'

'Actually I did but I wasn't holding out much hope for a date until today when, surprise, surprise, she said yes.'

'It's out of the question,' Gerald said emphatically. 'Blind dates simply aren't my style. And besides, I'm a bit shattered. Didn't get to bed until very late last night.'

'Sorry, I meant to ask. How did it go?'

Gerald lowered his voice. 'I don't think we should talk about it on the phone. Never know who may be listening.'

'Quite right,' Eddie whispered, suppressing an involuntary laugh. 'We'll meet up at the restaurant half an hour before the girls. Have a quiet chat over a glass of something cold and fizzy.'

'How many more times? I'm not coming.'

But Eddie ignored the protests. 'Casa Roma. Smart casual. Seven thirty. Don't be late,' he said, then quickly hung-up before Gerald could argue.

Gerald stared, exasperated, at the handset, dialled the first part of Eddie's number but then, somehow, allowed the moment to pass and poured himself a cup of lukewarm tea instead.

He wondered if Valerie might turn out to be a Val, and sounded out the possibilities in his head; Valerie and Gerald, or maybe Gerry and Val. He surprised himself by instantly warming to the less poncey option. And then a mental rummage through his wardrobe for smart casual; surely a contradiction in terms?

At seven o'clock, and after an unproductive day in which he'd found it unusually difficult to concentrate, Gerald examined himself in the hall mirror. Black blazer with silver buttons, grey flannels and a white shirt – no tie. Smart yet, at the same time, relatively casual and probably about right for the Casa Roma. He vaguely remembered going there once before, with Betsy. The bill was exorbitant, a rip-off. They never went again.

The short walk to the restaurant took considerably longer than he expected. In fact it wasn't a short walk at all and he'd obviously got the place muddled up with somewhere else, somewhere nearer, the Vecchia something or another. And then it started to rain.

A damp and bedraggled Gerald Cornfield arrived at the Casa Roma at quarter to eight and went straight to the gents to sort himself out. It was a full five minutes later when he joined his friend at the bar.

Eddie Bates swivelled around on the bar stool, glanced at his watch. 'I was beginning to think you weren't coming,' he said. 'Thought perhaps you'd chickened out, let me down.'

'But I told you I wasn't coming,' Gerald snapped back. 'So how could I possibly let you down?'

Eddie handed him a glass of Champagne. 'Stop grizzling and get that down you before the girls turn up. And, for the avoidance of doubt, this evening's on me.'

'That's very generous of you and much appreciated.' Gerald raised his glass, slowly sipped his drink. 'I just hope Valerie doesn't take an instant dislike to me.'

'Dislike you Gerald old son? What's to dislike?'

Gerald hunched forward, shook his head. 'Oh, I don't know. I suppose I'm a bit shy where women are concerned, and it shows.'

'But not so shy where the nation's scumbags are concerned eh? Showed your face to half a dozen of 'em last night I hear.'

'Who told you that?' Gerald asked indignantly.

'Does it matter? You took your mask off. Not a clever thing to do. End of.'

'It was dark, raining cats and dogs. Nobody got a good look at my face.'

'Hope you're right.'

'Of course I'm right.' Gerald insisted. He paused, let out a deep sigh. 'I suppose Rupert told you.'

Eddie nodded. 'Mentioned it this afternoon, down at The Shed.'

'The Shed? What on earth were *you* doing there?'

'Oh, just sorting out final arrangements for tomorrow night.'

'Why? What's happening?'

'Usual thing, probably,' said Eddie, cramming a handful of peanuts into his mouth. 'Drag a few tow rags off the street, lead them in the paths of righteousness. But there's talk of a brand new plan.'

Gerald felt suddenly left out, excluded, and he didn't like it. 'You're obviously privy to everything that goes on at The Shed,' he said with a spark of irritation. 'Probably driven the van a few times too.'

'Just the once.'

'Why didn't you mention it?'

'To be perfectly honest, I was waiting for you to have a go at it too, so we could sort of compare notes.' Eddie checked his watch, huffed. 'Why is it that women can never turn up on time?'

Gerald stared wistfully into his glass. '*Some* women turn up on time. Betsy was never late for anything. She always said punctuality costs nothing.'

'Hold it right there,' Eddie said, before Gerald could launch into one of his regular bouts of nostalgia. 'Can we agree not to talk about Betsy or Deirdre this evening. No mention of either of them. Deal?'

Gerald nodded but held back from actually saying yes; a small, silent protest on Betsy's behalf. He ran his hand down the sleeve of his jacket. Still a bit damp, even after two or three blasts of hot air under the hand drier. And the trousers were now uncomfortably clammy. 'Do you happen to know if this Valerie likes to be called Val or Valerie?' he asked suddenly.

Eddie turned slowly, looked him square in the face, frowned. 'How would I know? I've never met the bloody woman.'

'Of course not. Silly question. I just wondered.' Gerald hesitated for a moment before changing the subject back to more important matters. 'I suppose you'll be driving the VRU tomorrow evening then?'

'Nope. This time I'll be in the back with the others.'

It wasn't what Gerald expected to hear. Eddie's foolhardy plans to take a more active part in the evening raids might be seen as an example for him to follow, and that was out of the question. He took a handkerchief from his top pocket, dabbed the perspiration from his brow. 'Is that such a good idea? I mean, a man of your age, slugging it out with a gang of juvenile delinquents.'

But Eddie didn't answer. Instead, he nudged Gerald with his elbow; a short, sharp prod. 'Shtum,' he said in a tight-lipped, gravelly whisper. 'They're here.'

Gerald turned towards the door. Two women, talking together, arm in arm near the cash desk. One of them handed a wet umbrella to a passing waiter, whispered something to the other. They both giggled. A man in a red waistcoat checked the reservations book, pointed across to the bar.

Eddie gave a little wave, jumped to his feet and quickly arranged the bar stools in a half circle. 'I'll tell you what,' he muttered under his breath in the same rasping tone as before, 'Valerie's a little cracker.'

'I do hope you're not going to speak like that all evening,' said Gerald. 'You'll give yourself a sore throat.'

The two women marched towards them as one, arms firmly linked in a blatant declaration of unity, solidarity and mutual support; an intimate feminine alliance, seemingly inseparable, unstoppable, ready for combat.

There was something shamelessly aggressive about the look on their faces which reminded Eddie of the women who sometimes danced around their handbags at the social club, yelling "I Will Survive" whenever Gloria Gaynor's anthem for disgruntled divorcees shattered the calm of an otherwise pleasant evening. Holly Lockwood's foursome was beginning to look more like a girl's night out with him picking up the bill.

But Gerald had no such qualms. He saw only two pleasant middle-aged ladies enjoying a quiet meal with two equally pleasant, if slightly more mature, gentlemen, and nothing more; no need of Eddie's juvenile chat-up lines, no innuendos and expectations at the end of the evening, none of the inevitable embarrassment of rejection. And that, he'd already decided, was exactly as it should be.

It was Eddie, however, who made the first move, kissed the taller of the two women on both cheeks, took the other's hand. 'You must be Valerie,' he said.

'Vee will do,' she answered with finality, then smiled.

He smiled back; a faltering movement of the jaw which came and went like small ray of sunshine on a cloudy day. 'Right, now girls, I'd like to introduce you to my very good friend Gerald Cornfield.'

'Gerry, actually,' Gerald corrected without hesitation. 'And may I say how very pleased I am to meet you both.' He seemed unusually confident, gestured to them both to sit, nodded to the barman to pour the Champagne. 'I do hope you didn't get too wet,' he said with a look of genuine concern. 'It's a terrible evening.'

Holly Lockwood took a mirror from her shoulder bag, fiddled self-consciously with the neckline of a red cotton dress. 'Vee managed to find a place in the car park, thanks Gerry. Chocker block, as usual, so I suppose we were quite lucky.'

'Very lucky,' Eddie said, handing round the drinks. 'I finished-up at the other end of the road. Parked outside the old folks' home.' He laughed loudly, pounded Gerald on the back. 'You've already reserved a room there, haven't you mate?'

It was meant as a joke, of course, but it irritated and Gerald responded in kind. He turned to Holly. 'I hear we have you to thank for looking after poor Eddie's ankle,' he said. 'Do you specialise in geriatrics?'

Holly laughed, squeezed his knee. 'Don't be so wicked Gerry. He's not *that* old.'

Eddie looked mortified. 'No he bloody well isn't.' He reached for the Champagne bottle, handed it to Gerald. 'Here, do something useful while I check the table.'

'Only joking,' said Gerald. 'But take it slow now. Don't fall down.'

Vee sat perfectly still while Gerald filled her glass. He found himself staring at her hands, delicate hands, pale and smooth as alabaster; slender fingers, long, crimson nails neatly rounded-off at the end. There was a ring on her right hand; dark green, probably an emerald. It matched her eyes.

She ran her hands through long, auburn hair, pushed it back from her cheeks in a single, practiced movement. 'Have you known Eddie long?' she asked, edging closer as if she wanted to share a secret. 'You seem like good pals.'

Gerald's gaze switched to the full, generous mouth, the high gloss lips which shaped each wonderful word, and was at once mesmerised by one of her front teeth; an undeniably crooked upper tooth, slightly twisted to one side, yet altogether endearing and, in some explicable way, the most bewitching tooth he'd ever seen. 'I'm sorry,' he said, realising that he'd only been half listening. 'Bit noisy in here.'

'I asked how long you'd known Eddie,' she repeated, wondering if he might be slightly deaf.

Eddie was back before Gerald could answer. He looked pleased with himself, handed a single red rose to each of the women. 'An English rose for two English roses.'

'Actually I'm Welsh.' Holly smiled apologetically. 'Do I still qualify for an English rose?'

'Definitely. Besides, with the greatest respect, a long stem daffodil wouldn't have quite the same romantic appeal.'

'My wife Betsy was half Welsh,' Gerald whispered. 'On her father's side. Her mother was English, of course…'

'Perhaps we should order at the table,' said Eddie, bringing an abrupt close to Gerald's reminiscences about Betsy's fluent Welsh and how they'd often toyed with the idea of moving to Wales but never quite got around to it. 'We're over by the window,' he said jostling Gerald forward and pointing him towards a round, corner table.

But Eddie Bates wasn't the sort of pompous chap who keeps his dinner guests standing around while he struggles to make up his mind who should sit where. He'd already decided, placed name cards on the side plates, avoiding the whole embarrassing charade. And he'd played it safe with the usual boy, girl, boy girl arrangement too; Holly on his right, Vee to the left.

The waiter had presented everyone with leather-bound menus and snapped crisp, white napkins to life with a masterly flick of the wrist, when the Alvis drew up outside. A uniformed chauffeur stepped from the car, opened a huge, green umbrella and escorted his four passengers to the restaurant door. He gave a little salute before he drove off; nothing too ostentatious but sufficient to draw attention to the new arrivals.

'Flash bastard.' Eddie reached for a bread stick, snapped it in two.

Holly twisted round, looked across at the elderly gentleman now leading his entourage towards the bar. 'Do you know him?'

'I suppose you could say he's a business partner,' said Gerald. 'His name's Bevington. Major Edgar William Bevington.'

'And the redhead's called Katrina,' Eddie chimed in. 'She's his wife, in case you were wondering what the relationship might be.'

Vee dived into her handbag, found her glasses. 'Thought I recognised him,' she said, squinting through narrow, gold-rimmed lenses. 'The tall, fair-haired chap. Double-barrelled name.'

'Clark-Hall,' said Gerald.

Vee snapped her fingers. 'That's the one. Captain Clark-Hall.'

'Captain?' Gerald looked puzzled. 'Are you sure?'

'Positive. I saw his medical records only this morning.'

'Careful now.' Holly giggled raised a finger to her lips. 'Patient confidentiality and all that.'

Gerald nodded, patted her hand reassuringly. 'And quite right too,' he said, wondering how Rupert would have explained-away his knife wound at the hospital. He also wondered, more out of idle curiosity than genuine concern, who the tall, slender blonde hanging on Rupert's every word over at the bar might be.

But Eddie Bates had other things on his mind. He edged his chair closer to Holly Lockwood, opened a menu for them to share. 'What do you fancy?' he whispered. 'It all looks pretty good.'

She didn't hesitate. 'Insalata di Mari, with just a dash of Tabasco sauce, followed by Sogliola alla Griglia, off the bone, French beans and a mixed green salad. Garlic dressing, easy on the vinegar,' she said, without even glancing at the menu.

'You've been here before then?'

'A few times.'

Eddie felt slightly crestfallen but forced a weak smile. 'Recently?'

'Week or so ago.'

'I wish I'd known. We could have gone somewhere else.'

She grasped his hand. 'Don't be so silly. Anyway, I like it here.'

'I've been wondering,' Gerald announced suddenly. 'Do you think you should, perhaps, nip over and say hello to E.W.? Matter of courtesy, so to speak.'

Eddie's eyes widened. 'If you wouldn't mind, we're about to order.'

'It just seems a bit ill-mannered,' Gerald persisted. 'All of us together, in the same restaurant, without even a quick hello.'

The small vein on Eddie's forehead began to swell but nobody else seemed to notice. 'In that case they can come over to us' he said, speaking slowly and patiently. 'Will that do you?'

Gerald shrugged and settled back to read the menu.

'You're obviously friends as well of business partners,' said Vee. 'What sort of business are you in?'

Eddie spotted an opportunity to impress. 'Oh, a bit of this and a bit of that,' he replied casually, as if the details were too tedious to talk about. 'We've got shares in a couple of E.W.'s enterprises – cosmetics, fashion, that sort of thing.'

'Wowie,' said Vee, looking suitably impressed. 'I hadn't realised you were entrepreneurs.'

'We call ourselves Elderpreneurs,' Gerald corrected. 'Men of a certain age who still have the necessary energy and enthusiasm to dabble in commercial ventures.'

Holly looked surprised. 'I thought Eddie ran some sort of café.'

'More of a small restaurant,' Eddie said grandly. 'Part of a wider business portfolio.'

The conversation came to a temporary halt while a waiter recited a long list of specials, apologised for a seasonal shortage of fresh mussels and waited, pen poised, for their orders.

Vee was apparently watching her weight. A small, plastic calorie counter, produced from her handbag, ruled-out the garlic bread, warned against the pasta [especially the one with cream] and steered her towards the grilled fish, carefully avoiding the French fries on the way. Not that she needed to worry; Gerald guessed she was a size ten, maybe smaller, and obviously intended to stay that way.

Guessing Vee's age was more difficult. She looked no more than forty but little things she said suggested she might be older. She'd mentioned being eighteen when Maggie Thatcher first took office, so she'd probably be nearer fifty. But that was good news; it meant that Gerald wasn't old enough to be her father, even if he looked it.

A little way along from the Casa Roma, on the opposite side of the road, The Jolly Farmer had started to reverberate with a muffled beat; a steady, discordant thump which had more in common with the sound of jack hammers than musical instruments.

Gerald glanced at his watch, just gone nine. Soon the pub would be heaving; it was like that most nights. Then small groups of blustering youths would slowly spill out on to the street, fill the evening air with their profanities, occupy the corner like a conquering army. He'd seen it all before.

The sudden pang of fear which pierced the centre of his stomach at that moment was painfully familiar; a short sharp jab like a needle, reminding him of his inadequacy, confirming his vulnerability. If a handful of lager-fuelled louts were to single him out for their mindless violence, he'd show a clean pair of heels, make a run for it. That was the definitive plan, had been for a year or so. But it didn't make him a coward; not a bit of it. He'd told himself a thousand times. And if he ever found the time to go to martial arts classes, got to know a few tactical defence moves, it would be a different story altogether.

A roadside puddle burst suddenly across the pavement as a police car screamed past, lights flashing, sirens blazing. Gerald was wondering what villainy could possibly warrant such dangerously inconsiderate driving when Vee gently nudged his arm.

The waiter moved closer. 'When you're ready sir,' he said with an impatient smile that faded in a moment.

'So sorry,' Gerald said, thumbing quickly through the menu. 'I was miles away.'

Eddie stared at him with exasperation, slowly shook his head. 'If you could possibly make up your mind before the restaurant finally closes for the night, I'm sure we'll all be very grateful.'

'I'll have the wild smoked salmon,' Gerald snapped back immediately. 'Followed by grilled prawns.'

Vee unwrapped a bread stick, held it between two fingers like a cigarette, 'Fasten your seat belts,' she said, in a sultry Hollywood drawl. 'It's going to be a bumpy night.'

'Margot Channing,' Gerald said at once. 'And an excellent impression it was too.'

Eddie shrugged. 'Who's Margot Channing?'

'A character in a Bette Davis film,' said Gerald. 'All About Eve.'

'OK, who's this then?' Eddie borrowed Vee's bread stick for a cigar, raised an eyebrow, twisted his mouth into a jaunty half smile and, with an accent that owed more to the Wild West than the Deep South, delivered the classic movie put-down. 'Frankly my dear, I don't give a damn.'

'Boris Karloff,' said Vee, straight-faced. 'Bride of Frankenstein.'

Eddie shook his head, sighed. 'It was Jet Butler. Gone With The flaming Wind.'

'Rhett,' Gerald whispered. 'I think you'll find Clark Gable played Rhett Butler.'

'I'm sure it was Jet.' Eddie looked round the table for support. 'Jet,' he repeated. 'Like Jet Harris and The Shadows.'

'Wasn't it Cliff Richard and The Shadows?' said Holly.

'Yes, of course it was. I'm only saying Jet Harris was *in* The Shadows.' Eddie thought for a moment. 'And then there was Hank Marvin. He was in The Shadows too, played lead guitar.'

'His real name's Harry,' Gerald confided.

Eddie looked irritated. 'No it's not. It's Hank.'

'I meant Cliff Richard. He changed his name from Harry Webb.'

'When did he do that then?'

'I don't know exactly when he did it, but he definitely did it.'

Holly was beginning to regret ever mentioning Cliff Richard when Vee cut in quickly.

'Boris Karloff changed his name too,' she said with the beginnings of a smile. 'Better name than William Pratt, don't you think? Clark Gable was a William too, and Bette Davis's real name was Ruth,' she went on. 'Even the great Edward G. Robinson was born Emanuel Goldenberg.'

Gerald was impressed. 'Fancy you knowing that,' he said. 'I mean they were all a bit before your time.'

'So were Dickens, Shakespeare and Jesus Christ but I know a bit about them too.'

'Absolutely. It's just that many young people think you're from another planet if you happen to mention someone who was born before David Beckham.'

Eddie looked suddenly smug. 'Ever heard of Gerry & The Pacemakers?'

Vee thought about it, slowly shook her head. 'Sorry, no. Can't say I have.'

'Guessed as much,' he said.

The subject came to a timely close with the arrival of the first course when Vee neatly swung the conversation around to food and why a Mediterranean diet was healthier than most of the others. She seemed to excel on the subject, quoting the British Medical Journal on how it might protect against type 2 diabetes and heart attacks, and why olive oil apparently aided digestion and lowered cholesterol levels.

Gerald squeezed some lemon across his salmon. 'I'm not quite sure what a Mediterranean diet means,' he said. 'There must be a dozen or more countries bordering the Mediterranean Sea, not just Italy.'

'Does it matter?' Eddie stabbed at the whitebait with his fork. 'As long as it tastes OK, I don't care if it's from Sorrento or Southend.'

Vee looked at him in vague surprise. 'You can't really compare a lightly grilled sole and salad with deep fried skate and chips.'

Eddie was about to point out that the whitebait looked as if they might be deep fried too when he felt a hand on his shoulder. He looked down at the manicured fingers and Rupert Clark-Hall's signet ring.

'I do hope you're enjoying your meal,' Rupert said.

Eddie laid his fork at the edge of his plate, turned towards the voice. 'No complaints so far.'

Rupert hesitated for a moment, looked around at the others, smiled expectantly.

'My apologies,' said Gerald, jumping to his feet. 'May I present Miss Lockwood and...' He paused, turned to Vee. 'So sorry, I don't yet know your surname.'

'Actually Doctor Blythe and I have already met.' Rupert pushed back the cuff of his shirt, showed-off his bandage. 'She says I should be more careful with my kitchen knives.'

'Doctor Blythe?' Gerald repeated.

Vee shifted uneasily on her chair. 'Just a very ordinary hospital doctor.'

'A very *charming* hospital doctor, if I may say so.' Rupert smiled, nodded politely and turned to go but then hesitated. He took a card from his top pocket and placed it on the table, next to Eddie's glass. 'I'll be there for most of tomorrow,' he said quietly. 'Let me know what you decide.'

Eddie glanced at the card, slipped it into his wallet but said nothing.

'Decide about what?' Gerald whispered when Rupert had gone.

'Whether I want to invest in this place.'

Gerald looked astonished. 'You mean buy it?'

'Not exactly. More like buy a share in it.' Eddie Bates sipped his wine, glanced casually around looking altogether more important than before.

'I assume Rupert and E.W. will be shareholders too,' said Gerald with a hint of irritation in his voice.

Eddie nodded. 'That's the plan. Of course, I'll have to sell the eatery first but I don't see any major problems.'

Holly Lockwood fixed him with admiring eyes, parted her lips just a little. 'That is just *so* clever of you,' she breathed, edging closer. 'Buying my favourite restaurant. And you kept it all so quiet.'

Eddie shrugged. 'Early days. To be completely honest, I really hadn't planned to say anything at all at this stage of the game.'

But Gerald didn't believe that for a moment. He thought it far more likely that Eddie had staged-managed the whole thing to impress Holly Lockwood. It explained why he'd refused to go over to E.W.'s table earlier, where any talk of buying restaurants would have been beyond Holly's hearing.

'The deal could still fall through then?' Gerald asked casually.

'Nah.' Eddie dismissed the suggestion with a wave of his hand. 'If the balance sheet measures up to the food and service here, it's a done deal.'

'And if you can't sell the eatery?'

'But I will,' Eddie said flatly. 'There'll be new owners at the Casa Roma before you know it, and I'll be one of them.'

Holly Lockwood kissed him full on the lips; a long, lingering but utterly frivolous kiss which seemed to take him by surprise. She raised her glass triumphantly. 'To new owners at the Casa Roma.'

'New owners,' Vee repeated. 'And long may they prosper.'

Gerald felt obliged to add his good wishes. 'Best of luck,' he said, uncomfortably aware that he was sipping his fourth, rather large, glass of red wine. 'I hope it all works out for you.'

Plainly encouraged, if a little confused, by Holly's sudden show of affection, Eddie ordered a bottle of Champagne to wash down the crepe suzette. But then came the XO brandies; four doubles sent across to them with E.W.'s compliments.

Vee pushed hers to one side. 'I think I'd better call a halt before I start talking scribble,' she said, brushing some crumbs into a neat little pile with her napkin. 'And no more driving for me tonight either. I'll leave the car here, take a cab home.'

'Sounds like a good idea,' Eddie said, yawning loudly. 'It's just possible I might be a wee bit over the limit too.' He stared blankly at his mobile phone, prodded it to life with a plump finger, dialled a couple of wrong numbers. After the fourth attempt, when the battery went flat, he finally gave up and delegated the task of booking two mini cabs to a passing waiter.

The rain stopped soon after midnight and a pale, watery moon glimmered behind the clouds for a fleeting moment before fading into the darkness as two cars drew up outside the restaurant.

Eddie led the way outside, opened the door of the first car and waited until Vee had settled herself in the back, then grabbed Gerald's arm and pushed him forward. 'Perhaps you'll permit Gerry to escort you home,' he said. 'He's very well behaved.'

Gerald stood motionless while Eddie drove off with Holly Lockwood in the second car. 'I really must apologise for Eddie's disgraceful behaviour,' he said, peering cautiously inside. 'And you don't have to worry, I'm quite happy to walk home.'

Vee patted the seat beside her. 'Don't be so silly. We can't have you walking the streets at this time of night.'

Gerald glanced across to The Jolly Farmer, doors now open wide to a sleepy street, music screaming at the silence. And then the sound of breaking glass; a bottle tossed into the gutter. Somebody lit a cigarette, dropped the empty packet where he stood.

'Perhaps I *should* see you home,' Gerald said, easing himself into the back seat. 'Twenty-four hour drinking has a lot to answer for.'

Vee opened the window slightly, closed her eyes to a cool breeze. 'You and I have probably drunk more tonight than those mindless cretins but we won't smash up the neighbourhood, or try to kill each other.'

'I've no doubt they'll need an ambulance before long,' said Gerald, looking back at the crowd gathering outside the pub.

'Absolutely guaranteed. It won't have been a good night out unless someone ends-up in casualty.' She slowly shook her head, sighed. 'Patching-up violent, vomiting yobs is such an appalling misuse of over-stretched resources.'

'You're quite right, of course, but what's the alternative?'

Vee shrugged. 'Unfortunately I'm a doctor, not a politician.' She leaned forward, spoke to the driver. 'Just down on the left, wrought iron gates.'

The car swung into a gravel drive, past a *For Sale* sign, and up through a line of trees to a large but dismal house, a solitary porch lamp barely penetrating the gloom. Vee fumbled for her keys.

'Have you lived here long?' Gerald asked casually.

She looked at him with sad eyes. 'Just a few short months. Barely time to unpack really.'

'Sorry. I didn't mean to pry.'

'It's a long story.' Vee touched his hand, smiled wearily. 'Thanks for a lovely evening Gerry,' she said. 'I really enjoyed it.'

She'd reached the front door, key in the latch, before Gerald had mustered the courage to call after her. 'Perhaps we could do it again sometime?'

She turned, gave a little wave. 'Love to,' she said, and went inside.

Mr Cornfield shrank back into the car seat, flushed with embarrassment, but more than a little excited by the prospect of seeing Dr Blythe again.

Chapter Ten

But a fiver a week is loose change when you've paid a million or more for your house, so the residents of a private road, on the fringes of Pixley Green, had no reservations about signing-up with a new security company, specialising in property protection.

Katrina Bevington's sales pitch pressed all the right buttons with a subtle mix of flattery and financial logic, designed to calm the fears, anxieties and general sense of unease born of newspaper headlines about street violence and vandalism. Like-minded people with mutual interests and objectives, she called them; joint investors in a desirable neighbourhood; law-abiding citizens with the right to the quiet enjoyment of their prestigious homes.

And if cut-backs meant that over-stretched resources couldn't always be relied upon to maintain acceptable levels of peace and quiet in the vicinity, [Police were never mentioned by name] reliable private services were now available to protect discerning home owners and maintain the safety and security of the streets.

So all but two of the sixteen residents invited to Katrina's evening presentation were happy to hand-over their cheques for two hundred and fifty pounds – along with the responsibility for keeping undesirable elements out of Bartholomew Place.

But while one or two other up-market avenues and exclusive estates seemed happy to sign-up to the deal, the real interest came from the commercial sector; property companies with concerns about late night vandalism and the falling rental values for high street shops and offices which inevitably followed. A spate of smashed windows and spray can graffiti along the parade near the railway station had already closed-down two shops. And then came the break-ins and burglaries.

Safe Streets promised to change all that, reverse the fortunes of struggling traders in Station Approach, reclaim the area for local residents.

The first Gerald heard about it was when two official looking forms turned-up in the morning post. A couple of pencil crosses showed him where to sign as a director of the new limited company, and a scribbled note from E.W. assured him that this was merely a commercial interface with existing operations, so nothing to be concerned about.

Gerald didn't like the sound of it. His mouth dried as he dialled E.W.'s number, pulse racing more in anger than through any sense of fear and trepidation.

'Got your note,' he said as calmly as he could manage. 'Would you mind clarifying a few points?'

'Bit early in the day old chap,' E.W. grunted. 'Call you back after breakfast.'

But Gerald was insistent. 'It'll only take a moment. What exactly did you mean by a commercial interface with existing operations?'

'Precisely what I said. It's time we put things on to a more commercial footing, charge a fee, make a profit, that sort of thing.'

'You mean VRU operations?'

'Up to a point.'

'Charge a fee to break the law, in other words?'

'Absolutely not.'

'Then what *do* you mean?'

E.W. paused to sip his coffee. 'Look, I really don't think we should do this on the phone,' he said flatly. 'Drop round at eleven.'

It wasn't so much a social invitation as a military command. Gerald was exasperated but the next few hours passed slowly and his mood gradually gave way to quiet resignation. But by ten thirty, when he set out on the short walk to Lovelace Farm House, he felt only mildly depressed at the prospect of the inevitable bickering to follow.

E.W.'s idea of a reasonable discussion was to state and re-state his point of view in a progressively louder voice until everyone else agreed, or at least gave-up disagreeing. It was an arrogant, infantile attitude from a petulant, ill-mannered man; an aging Toad of Toad Hall, Gerald told himself, as the imposing residence came into view on the far side of the common.

'Got the time mate?'

Gerald instinctively checked his watch, turned to face a gaunt young man in a grey tracksuit, close behind him. 'It's nearly eleven.'

The other man quickly overtook him then stopped. 'Nice watch,' he said, rubbing his fingers through closely cropped hair as if he might be trying to remember something. 'Looks like the one I lost last week. Cheers for finding it.'

'I think you must be mistaken,' Gerald said importantly, trying to disguise his growing anxiety. 'I've had this watch for many years.'

The knife was unexpected. It appeared from nowhere like a conjurer's rabbit; a short, fat blade, no more than three or four inches long, gripped tight in a skinny hand, the letters H A T E tattooed across the fingers.

'Don't fuck with me granddad or I'll stick yer.' The youth stabbed menacingly at the empty space between them, his eyes cold and lifeless, his movements uncoordinated and erratic. 'The watch,' he screamed. 'Wallet, mobile, the fucking lot.'

So here it was, starring Gerald in the face, the violence he'd always dreaded, the decisive moment when he'd resolved to show a clean pair of heels, make a run for it. But he didn't. He stood perfectly still, rooted to the spot, vaguely aware of someone running towards him from the right; an accomplice probably, the man who'd snatch the watch from his wrist, ransack his pockets, pin back his arms while the knife was plunged deep into his chest.

Gerald Arthur Cornfield, loyal husband, widower, one-time sub-post master, and latter-day company director, braced himself, clenched his teeth, and closed his eyes to the inevitable agonies to follow. But there was nothing and, in a moment, he'd reopened them to a changed landscape; a jogger who'd passed close by, over to the left, and a would-be mugger running off in the opposite direction, towards the high rise flats.

His step quickened as he made for the relative safety of the road which sliced through the edge of the common, and cursed himself for surrendering to a scrawny, sub-species of humanity without so much as a whimper. It was degrading and humiliating and, worst of all, he felt like a collaborator in his own mugging.

But this unpalatable reality demanded a new perspective. Perhaps he was no more than an average trusting soul who'd been taken by surprise; unprepared, naive perhaps, but far from submissive? And hadn't he remained cool, composed, restrained even, in the face of danger? There were those who might well consider his response to be nothing short of courageous; standing his ground against violence, resisting the easy option to run away.

By eleven fifteen, when Mr Cornfield finally reached Lovelace Farm House, he'd assured himself that his response to the morning's fearful encounter had been exemplary.

E.W. was still having breakfast. 'With you in a minute,' he said, pointing his fork at the study door. 'Rupert will fill you in.'

Rupert, unusually casual in denims and a white T-shirt, was half sitting on a desk close to the window, one foot on the floor, the other resting on the rung of a chair. He stared out into the garden through a pair of binoculars. 'The little blighters are all over the bloody place,' he whispered. 'Scoffing everything in sight.'

'Slugs, caterpillars or rabbits?' Gerald asked, putting on a brave face after his ordeal on the common. 'I've got the lot in my garden, squirrels too.'

'Jumbo rabbits,' said Rupert. 'They've completely devoured E.W.'s delphiniums, chomped through a few clumps of his prize hostas and seem to be moving-in on the Floribunda roses. It's the young leaves they go for you see.'

Gerald looked up, surprised. 'You seem to know your plant life. I wouldn't have thought you were the gardening type.'

'Soldiers very often make excellent gardeners. Planting and nurturing, growing and tending – it's the direct antithesis of maiming and killing.'

'Does that mean you've done a lot of it – maiming and killing I mean?'

Rupert slowly slipped the binoculars into their case, threw back his head in silent contemplation. 'Enough to know I don't like it.'

'Surely nobody actually *likes* it?'

'Oh but they do,' Rupert insisted, as if a penchant for killing might, somehow, be perfectly reasonable. 'There are those who positively thrive on it.' He stood up, hooked his thumbs into the back pockets of his jeans. 'What's more, they usually make good soldiers.'

Gerald noticed the wrist bandage had disappeared, replaced by a small sticking plaster. 'How's the stab wound?' he asked. 'I see you've dispensed with the dressing.'

'Almost healed.' Rupert waved his hand around, made three or four fists in quick succession. 'See, good as new.'

'But supposing you'd been stabbed in the chest or neck? That would have been a very different story, wouldn't it?'

'That,' Rupert said with a deep sigh, 'would have been very unfortunate but extremely unlikely.'

'What makes you so sure? I mean, how do you defend yourself against a young thug when he's waving a knife under your nose?'

Rupert raised an eyebrow, nodded thoughtfully. 'That sounds more like a plea for professional advice than a random question. Would I be right?'

'Not exactly, no.' Gerald hesitated, took a deep breath. 'Well yes, sort of.'

'Someone's threatened you with a knife?'

Gerald nodded. 'On the common. Less than half an hour ago.'

'Were you hurt?'

'Only my pride.'

Rupert settled himself back on the edge of the desk, folded his arms. 'So let's see now, what would I have done? Well, after overcoming the initial disappointment that somebody had the temerity to threaten me, I'd apply my uppers to his lowers, or boot him in the balls, so to speak. Legs, you see Gerald, are so much longer than arms and always out-reach the hostile hand.'

'You make it sound so simple. But then you've probably done it loads of times.'

'My dear fellow, the kicking bit *is* simplicity itself. Anyone can do it.' Rupert span a cushion in front of him, kicked it across the room. 'Finding the courage to do it when the fear of retaliation grips your belly – that's the difficult bit.'

'What's the difficult bit?' E.W. stood, motionless, in the doorway, starring at the cushion in front of him.

'I was just saying that mustering the guts to strike an opponent is often more difficult than landing the blow itself,' said Rupert.

E.W. frowned. 'That's all very well but surely the prime objective is to land the *first* blow and make it count.' He crossed the room to his desk, slumped down heavily into a swivel chair. 'Two actors may slug it out for ten minutes in some daft Hollywood film but, in the real world, street fights last just a few seconds. The first blow nearly always decides the outcome because that's all it takes to put a man down for good.'

'Couldn't agree more,' Rupert said, jumping to his feet. 'But we really must be off or we'll be late.'

'Off?' Gerald repeated indignantly. 'I've only just arrived.'

E.W. seemed unconcerned. 'Quite so,' he said, rummaging through the desk drawer for an address book. 'I'd fully intended to update you, as promised, but something's come up so Rupert will tell you all about it on the way.'

'On the way? On the way where?'

But E.W. was already preoccupied with his book and waved away the question with a flick of his hand.

'We're going to school,' said Rupert. 'I think you might find it educational, especially after your ordeal on the common.'

* * *

Rupert's driving technique involved just two speeds; fast and stop. For the most part his right foot hammered at the accelerator pedal, grinding it into the floor like a discarded cigarette. But then, at red lights, road junctions and in deference to lollipop ladies who'd managed to reach the centre of the road without incident, he stamped hard on the brakes, sending a shudder through the car. Nevertheless, he remained totally relaxed throughout the journey, as if the transient world beyond the car windscreen was no more important than a figment of the imagination.

'What's your connection with the lovely Doctor Blythe then?' he asked casually. 'Personal or professional?'

'Well it's not professional so I suppose you'd call it personal.' Gerald tightened his seat belt, stiffened as the car swung into the roundabout. 'She seems a very nice person.'

'Known her long?'

'No, not really.'

Rupert nodded, smiled gently. 'I get the picture.'

'I'm not sure you do,' said Gerald, bracing himself for the traffic lights ahead. 'We had dinner together. That's it.'

'But you'll be seeing her again?'

'I really couldn't say. It's possible, I suppose.'

'That's the spirit Gerald.' Rupert gave the steering wheel a little slap with the flat of his hand. 'Sweep her off her feet.'

Gerald's face reddened. 'I'm not sure about sweeping anyone off their feet. Doctors are very busy people.'

'Don't be so daft. Doctors are looking for love, just like everyone else. Probably more so.'

'Like the blonde you were with at the Casa Roma, for example? She seemed quite smitten.'

'Lucy?' Rupert laughed suddenly, shook his head. 'She's a friend of Katrina. And, anyway, she's a blonde, not my type at all.'

'So what's *your* type then?'

'I generally go for redheads, thirty'ish, tall, slim, good sense of humour. And they must have a pert little bum. That's an absolute essential.'

'Katrina Bevington, for example?'

Rupert ignored the question. He braked hard, turned sharp left and accelerated up the narrow lane towards The Shed.

'I thought we were going to a school,' Gerald said, peering out across the open fields.

'And so we are… a class in Wado Ryu.'

'Woto what?'

'Wado Ryu. It's a style of karate which roughly translates as way of peace.'

'Isn't that a bit of a contradiction in terms? Surely karate's all about violence?'

'You've been watching too many Bond films,' Rupert sniggered. 'Karate simply means open hand, so no knives, no guns or any other weapons of violence, just the concentrated power of body and mind in a relatively placid form of self-defence.'

'Look, I do hope you won't take this the wrong way,' said Gerald, shifting uncomfortable in his seat, 'but could you get to the point. This martial arts stuff is all very interesting but what's it got to do with me?'

The car skidded to a halt behind the smallest of the three outbuildings where a dozen or more other vehicles were already parked in a neat line, three or four motorbikes close by. 'OK, I'll keep it brief,' Rupert sighed. 'As E.W.'s already told you, we're going commercial on cleaning-up the streets, which means we can turn a profit from keeping the peace.'

Gerald stared straight ahead, expressionless. 'How can you possibly talk about making legitimate profits if what we're doing is against the law?'

'But it's not. A legitimate security company, registered to receive fees for protecting client property, won't be breaking any laws at any time. It'll be totally above board.'

'So what will you do when violence breaks out? Call the police?'

Rupert's grin broadened. 'Come now Gerald, we both know that would be a complete and utter waste of time. Besides we'll have a uniformed officer on patrol, twenty-four-seven, in each of our client neighbourhoods.'

'One man? How could one solitary man be expected to tackle a gang of tearaways?' Gerald let the question fade into a whisper, having decided that he probably wouldn't like Rupert's answer anyway.

But Rupert was reassuring. 'Our chaps won't tackle anyone,' he said. 'Almost any form of retaliation by our representatives could be viewed as unlawful. And, as I've already said, we have no intention of breaking any laws.'

'How's this lone security officer going to keep the peace then?'

'Make a phone call. Delegate the problem to others.'

'Others?' Gerald snorted. 'Meaning a VRU team?'

Rupert shook his head. 'No, not exactly, but does it matter? Does anyone honestly give a damn who the local council employs to take away their wheelie bin rubbish, or what happens to it after? I don't think so. They just pay their rates and let others get on with it so why should our clients be any different? They don't care *who* clears the streets of unruly louts and the rest of our anti-social garbage, just so long as *somebody* does it.'

Gerald looked blank. 'I wonder,' he said quietly, as if he might be thinking aloud. 'Would they be quite so relaxed about it all if a gang of masked men turned-up suddenly and bundled their *problem* into the back of a white van.'

Rupert rolled his eyes, huffed a bit, but said nothing.

'Well, come on, it *would* look a bit odd, don't you think?' Gerald persisted. 'Some of those clients you say couldn't care less might ask a few awkward questions.'

'You have my firm assurance,' said Rupert, trying to look serious but not quite managing it. 'Nobody's going to see any masked men in white vans unless, perhaps, there's a jihadist Mr Whippy in the area.'

'Now that's the sort of thing that worries me about you. Why do you always have to reduce everything to a silly, schoolboy joke?'

Rupert pressed his finger to his lips. 'I'll let you into a little secret,' he whispered. 'Life's a series of very silly jokes, and most of them aren't very funny.' He pointed towards a small door to one side of the outbuilding, the words Keep Out daubed in white across the top. 'Behold a modest portal, Gerald, behind which we're attempting to blur the boundaries between positive and negative. Even as I speak, contradictory elements are being forged into a single, powerful force, uniting good with bad, right with wrong, friend with foe.'

'And that's another thing,' said Gerald. 'You try to make your more doubtful ideas sound as if they deserve a Nobel Peace Prize.' He paused, thought for a moment. 'These so-called contradictory elements... would they be your peace-loving karate kids by any chance?'

'Sort of,' Rupert replied with a note of obvious hesitation. 'But there's a bit more to it than that.' He stepped from the car, slammed the door shut. 'Come and see for yourself.'

A slow, rhythmic chant drifted across the car park, barely audible at first but then louder and more distinct as the two men made towards the outbuilding; male voices in unison; short, sharp, guttural roars; "ich" ... "ee" ... "ich" ..."ee". And then a yell; much louder, longer... "eeeeeee".

The door opened to a small reception area; a modest desk and a swivel chair to one side, bench seats around the walls and what looked like a shower room just beyond, forming an L-shape with the main building. To the left, double doors, half open to a gymnasium, where the distinctive smell of stale sweat lingered like the remains of an over-ripe camembert.

"ich" ... "ee" ... "ich" ... "ee" ...six men in crisp, white karate suits punched and kicked their way up and down the room with military precision, moving as one to the command of an older man who stood, expressionless and perfectly still, at the far end of the room, feet slightly apart, hands clenched into fists at his sides.

'Utaka Hayakawa,' Rupert whispered. 'Fifth Dan, three times All-Japan Universities karate champion when he was a young student.'

Gerald nodded politely but his attention had already strayed to the centre of the room and a young man with a familiar face. 'Isn't that one of those god awful kids we picked up in Pendrake Close a few weeks back? The one who knifed you?'

'Certainly is,' said Rupert quietly. 'But he's not such a kid... gone eighteen, old enough for National Service a while back.'

'And the rest of them?'

Rupert smiled. 'As you've probably already guessed, all former inmates of The shed.'

'Have I missed something here?' Gerald said, turning his head away. 'Wasn't the plan to give these kids a short, sharp shock and send them home, without identifying ourselves.'

'And that's exactly what we do with most of them. We pick 'em up, give 'em a slap, and send 'em home.' Rupert gestured towards the instructor. 'But Mr Hayakawa here has selected these particular lads for special training. There are others too.'

He'd barely finished the sentence when Hayakawa shrieked a string of new commands in rapid succession.

'Kiritsu.' Everyone stood to attention. 'Sensei Ni Rei.' A bow to their instructor. 'Otagai Ni Rei.' More bowing, this time to each other and the dojo, before filing out to the shower room. Hayakawa bowed and left through another door.

Gerald stepped back, away from the open door, and spoke in a discreet whisper. 'Where's the sense in teaching already violent kids how to be even more violent?'

'We're not,' Rupert said with finality. 'We're forging them into teams, *our* teams, winning teams.'

Gerald looked mystified. 'Teams?'

'OK, gangs, if you prefer.' Rupert's expression hardened, his voice instantly more serious. 'Make no mistake about this, my friend, we're talking about highly professional gangs, each more than a match for anything on the streets. But, and this is the important bit, they'll look just like all the other tykes routinely avoided by the police.'

Gerald had never wanted or expected to be associated with gangs of any description and certainly not Rupert's professional gangs. He slid trembling hands into his jacket pockets and paused to regain his composure. 'I think I'm beginning to understand,' he said quietly. 'The Shed's not so much about teaching tearaways a lesson as recruiting and training the more violent of them for commercial purposes.'

'It's a basic recipe borrowed from National Service training,' said Rupert. 'Take one stroppy little sod, beat and humiliate before slowly bringing to the boil. Leave to simmer for a few days, mix-in a liberal dollop of education and training, then sprinkle with self-respect and add a pinch of pride. Allow to cool before garnishing with professionalism and ability, and leave to mature.'

'I love the analogy but you make it sound as if these louts were hand-picked for the job.'

'Not far off. Let's face it, we've already rounded up some of the biggest trouble makers in the district, specifically for this project.'

'And if they decide to go it alone after you've garnished them with your professionalism and ability? What then?'

Rupert shrugged. 'Why would they do that? We'll pay them good money for Christ's sake, give their lives some semblance of order and direction. And, at the end of the day, it's a good career move for former no-hopers. Besides, nobody takes liberties with me without very soon regretting it.'

Gerald glanced round the empty room, now strangely silent after the shouting. 'I really don't understand why you need me in this,' he protested. 'You seem to have everything pretty well sewn-up.'

'Everything but a little matter of capital investment.'

Gerald chuckled nervously. 'Don't look at me. Every penny I can beg, steal or borrow is already tied-up in E.W.'s Elderpreneur companies.'

'I was coming to that.' Rupert took a small notebook from his pocket. 'Most of your money's invested in Full Bloom Cosmetics. Twenty of the original twenty-five thousand to be exact, which you'll get back when we sell the company.'

'And when's that likely to be?'

'Last week,' said Rupert, somewhat sheepishly. 'That is to say the deal's already done, bar a few signatures. But your investment shows you a healthy fifteen per cent profit and that, in a faltering economy, is a bit of a result.'

Gerald did a quick calculation, permitted himself a weak smile. 'So I get my twenty thousand back plus another three,' he said, cheered by the prospect of paying-off some of his mortgage.'

'And your twenty thousand reinvested will give you ten per cent of Safe Streets,' Rupert declared grandly. 'Plus dividends, of course, and free tuition in martial arts, if you fancy.'

'Actually I fancied shares in the Casa Roma but nobody offered them,' said Gerald, with a hint of pique. 'Besides, wouldn't you say I was a wee bit too old to take up martial arts?'

Rupert shook off the question. 'Don't concern yourself with a piddling spaghetti house when you're offered a stake in a company like SS,' he said.

'SS,' Gerald repeated. 'Some might say it's a fitting name for an organisation which employs thugs.'

'Watch my lips,' Rupert said slowly and deliberately. 'Only accredited, uniformed officers on the pay roll at any time. The gangs are purely incidental.'

'They'll just happen along at the opportune moment.'

'Precisely.'

'Deal with any unpleasantness and go.'

'Got it in one.' Rupert checked his watch and made towards the door.

'But that's not the whole story, is it?' Gerald called after him.

Rupert turned, fixed him with a determined stare. 'Of course not Gerald,' he said in a half whisper. 'It's just the beginning. If we can harness the power of the wind and waves, why not the natural aggression of young men?'

Chapter Eleven

They'd promised a quiet, informal affair; just a few early evening drinks at the Casa Roma, a little get-together with friends. But that, as it turned out, was a bit like inviting someone to a breakfast without mentioning the wedding.

If anyone had bothered to inform Gerald that the Mayor of Pixley Green was to be guest of honour at a Champagne party to launch the new venture, he'd have almost certainly worn his navy suit instead of the brown tweed jacket with the leather elbow patches. And then there were all the other dignitaries; the local MP, full of promises and self-importance, at least three town councillors, the lady who ran the repertory theatre, a bevy of shop keepers, and the manager of the Honda dealership near the roundabout, who hinted at recession-busting discounts for corporate buyers, having sold no cars in weeks.

Gerald blamed E.W. for the embarrassment. It was, after all, his idea to celebrate in such extravagant style, without a word of warning. And the post of managing director [or Chief Executive Officer as up-to-the-minute companies like Safe Streets apparently now called it] hadn't once been mentioned. He'd never been offered the job so he couldn't possibly have accepted it. But there it was, in raised print on beige visiting cards, Gerald A. Cornfield, CEO.

He scanned the restaurant, smiled at the sea of faces, tried to appear confident and assured while E.W. expounded on the company philosophy, explained how Gerald Cornfield's unique vision for neighbourhood security was about to become a reality and, finally, called upon "the man himself" to tell them all about it. The unexpected announcement sent a wave of panic through Gerald's stomach, like a final flight call for someone who can't find their boarding pass.

Eddie Bates stood on a chair and led the applause, punctuated by his coarse, intermittent, football terrace whistle. It was one of

Gerald's pet aversions; that and the mindless whooping which inevitably followed.

Gerald was incensed but quietly determined to keep his emotions in check. He buttoned his jacket, ran the flat of his hand across his hair and politely cleared his throat for a brief response; no more than a few reluctant words of thanks, to be delivered without the slightest trace of sincerity or conviction.

But that's not how it happened. A fleeting glance across the restaurant, at the decisive moment Dr Valerie Blythe stepped through the door, changed everything in an instant. Their eyes met, cosmic forces realigned, and by a strange and unexplained process of symmetry, a self-confident man of conviction slipped quietly and unnoticed into the placid and receptive body of Gerald Arthur Cornfield.

'I have a very simple question for each of you,' he began with the acquired ease of an experienced raconteur. 'Did anyone happen to see a uniformed police officer on their way here this evening?'

The question was greeted by complete silence until a matronly woman raised her hand. 'Do police *cars* count?' she asked. 'Only I noticed one parked outside the kebab house, just up the road.'

A newly-assertive Gerald Cornfield smiled broadly. 'Parked police cars most certainly count,' he said. 'But only if the police officers are inside them and not elsewhere, maybe ordering fast food.'

'Didn't see anyone,' she shrugged. 'Not in the car, anyway.'

'Unfortunately the only police officers you are likely to see these days will probably be in cars rather than on foot,' said Gerald. 'And most of them will be on their way somewhere else.'

Clarity and conviction surged through him like a rush of adrenalin, clearing his conscience for what he now felt obliged to say. 'It's been long time since Bobbies patrolled our streets but that's progress, we're assured. Patrol cars are more efficient, they tell us. Politicians would have us believe that police work is completely different today than in the past... more scientific. Patrolling the streets is neither practical nor effective anymore, they say. And then the ultimate excuse, there's a shortage of officers. Well I say piffle.'

Gerald paused, eyes narrowed, thrust his hands into his jacket pockets. 'Our police force is altogether too tied-up with politically correct red tape and form-filling,' he declared. 'But even a 999 call is unlikely to bring our *PC* PCs running to your home unless, of course, you use what's known as "excessive force" to prevent your neighbourhood burglar from making-off with your worldly possessions, apprehend the mindless vandal who's just lobbed a brick through your front window, or strike back when a street mugger demands your watch and wallet. In a topsy-turvy world such behaviour will guarantee a speedy response from our constabulary, with a string of charges against you, the victim, ranging from assault and GBH to false imprisonment or kidnap. The real villains of the peace, however, will probably claim compensation for trauma, violation of their human rights and loss of self-esteem.'

It seemed to strike a chord with the audience and brought a wave of spontaneous applause. Some rapped on tables, others cheered while, alone at the far end of the room, E.W. Bennington nodded his own quiet endorsement with a satisfied smile.

'But that's not all,' Gerald said solemnly. 'What we have here is growing criminality, often compounded by the police force itself. Over four hundred police officers were convicted of serious crimes in the past three years, yet more than forty per cent of them are still in their jobs? Don't take my word for it. The facts are readily available, thanks to the Freedom of Information Act.'

Rupert Clark-Hall leant back against the bar and ran a finger across his throat, like a knife to the jugular. Gerald took the hint. Time to cut to the chase, explain the fundamentals of the company before his audience lost interest.

'Bringing a degree of safety to our streets is not an exact science,' he began, with a slightly theatrical note of humility. 'But we've tried very hard to create our own unique formula for at least partial success. It's a mixture of reliability, integrity, professionalism and, above all, realism.'

A camera flashed in front of him, three or four times in rapid succession. The crouching photographer slipped quickly back among the guests, like a sniper into the shadows.

Gerald was blinded for a moment, in a haze of white light. 'We're not attempting to compete with an apparently overstretched police force,' he said, blinking his eyes, trying hard to refocus. 'But, make no mistake, we'll guarantee a visible presence of security officers, day and night – a constant reminder that anti-social behaviour of any description will not be tolerated in neighbourhoods where we operate.'

It was at this pivotal moment in Gerald's presentation that E.W. gave the signal for two people to appear from behind an improvised curtain which discreetly screened the door to the toilets. A tall, well-built man and a woman who looked as if she'd stepped straight out of a glossy magazine, rather than the ladies loo, were dressed entirely in black; chunky, woollen tracksuits, the pants tucked into calf length leather boots, tops zipped-up over polo-neck sweaters, and black berets with a gold SS badge pinned to the front.

E.W. shook a Champagne bottle, fired its cork at the ceiling. 'You see before you a reliable, practical and, above all, credible alternative to the Old Bill,' he yelled. 'Will you please join in me in raising your glasses in a toast to the Black Berets?'

Gerald felt a flush of pride as he shook hands with the quietly confident couple at his side and posed for the photographer, now rather more demanding than before.

'Put your arms round 'em both,' he shouted. 'Tighter, closer together. Big smiles. Straight into the camera.'

The whole performance began again with a second photographer who wanted them sitting round a table, then standing together, arms linked. 'Like the three musketeers,' he said. 'One for all, and all that stuff.' Finally he wanted the same sort of picture out in the street with a policeman, if they could find one. But they couldn't, so the idea was abandoned for a close-up shot of Gerald, fingers steepled like a pontificating priest during a sermon.

And then came the questions. Two reporters, notebooks at the ready, pens poised, took it in turns to probe the company's operations. How many officers would be on the streets at any given time? What percentage were women? How were they recruited? Were they specially trained? Was the job well paid? And the questions got steadily trickier. How would they deal with trouble makers? Would they use force? Did they have powers of arrest? Were there back-up teams? And, most importantly, did they plan to liaise with the police?

Gerald had always been irritated by politicians who side-stepped awkward questions. Some had turned the avoidance of truth into an exact science, waffling on about strategies and philosophies and how they'd "deliver" this or that to the electorate, as if they might be talking about the morning post.

But skirting round the important issues, blurring reality just a little, telling the odd white lie when necessary, suddenly seemed like a good idea. Gerald talked vaguely about an Englishman's home being his castle, upholding the traditional values of law and order, cementing relationships within the community, maintaining a benign vigilance on our streets. At the end of it all he'd said nothing of importance but two reporters seemed happy to write it down.

'I believe our very presence will prove to be an effective deterrent to potential law breakers while providing auxiliary eyes and ears to support our constabulary in their struggle against crime,' Gerald declared flippantly, bringing the questioning to an abrupt close.

Rupert handed him a glass of Champagne. 'Excellent,' he whispered. 'A born diplomat if ever I saw one.'

E.W. nodded approvingly from across the restaurant, his eyebrows uncharacteristically fixed in the surprised position. He mouthed the words "good man", or it might have been "god damn". It really didn't matter.

The applause rang in Gerald's ears, testimony to a hidden talent, the ability to inspire, motivate and impress which had burst forth from somewhere deep inside him like the first gush of an oil well. And, the best part, Vee was there to see it all, his moment of glory.

He spotted her, standing alone, a little way back from the main group, green eyes sparkling, stunning in a simple black dress, tight as a skin, auburn hair sleeked back from her face. She smiled gently, touched her lips, but then turned away as if she might be looking for someone else.

Gerald hesitated, made a couple of small circles with the base of his glass on the table beside him and, after a moment's deliberation, decided it probably wouldn't be too presumptuous to join her. He straightened-up, tweaked the cuffs of the tweed jacket and had already started across the room towards her when Rupert emerged from a little cluster of people, arms outstretched, a glass of Champagne in each hand, and kissed her fondly on the cheek.

Eddie Bates coughed twice, deliberate attention-grabbing barks, directed at Gerald's left ear. 'There were no tongues down any throats,' he whispered. 'Just a quick peck. Nothing to get upset about.'

But Gerald wasn't upset, he was inspired and had already decided this was the moment for resolute action. He reached out, gently plucked the Champagne glasses from Rupert's hands and, in a single, sweeping gesture, presented one to Vee before leading her off towards a tray of canapés. The smug smile confirmed it was an act of piracy.

'Sorry to whisk you away like this,' he said, taking her arm. 'But would you mind answering a couple of questions for me?'

She stared at him quizzically, shook her head. 'My goodness Gerry, it all sounds very important.'

'Actually it's *extremely* important.' He hunched forward, looking into her eyes. 'The answers you give this evening could possibly alter the course of our lives.'

'Heavens, that's serious stuff,' she grinned. 'You'd best get started before I lose my nerve and make a run for…'

'OK, first question,' he said, before she'd quite finished the sentence. 'What's your favourite sort of music?'

She shrugged. 'I like most music but, if I had to choose, it would be classical.'

'And would you say you were a town or country type of person?'

Vee took a handful of peanuts, thought for a moment. 'I think I'm happiest in the country. Towns tend to stifle me, too many people.'

Gerald seemed pleased with her answers. 'The last time we were here you ordered fish,' he said, gesturing towards the window table. 'Do you prefer fish to meat?'

'I suppose I do, yes.' She finished her drink and placed it on the table behind her. 'Now would you mind telling me where all this is leading?'

'Could I ask just one more question? Very last one, promise, then I'll stop.' He searched the ceiling for the right words but then gave up, took a deep breath, and simply blurted it out. 'Do you believe in fairies?'

Vee laughed suddenly, eyes wide with surprise. 'Is that a trick question or is it meant to be serious?'

'Absolutely serious.'

'You're quite mad,' she said as her laughter faded. 'Totally bonkers.'

'So, would that be a yes or a no then?'

She hesitated, sighed, looked him square in the face. 'What you really want to know is do I believe in magic?'

Gerald nodded. 'But only if you want to tell me.'

'I think I did, once upon a time. Not so sure now.'

'In that case would you permit me one *absolutely* final question?'

She stared at him, expressionless, waiting for him to continue.

'Will you marry me?'

'You're barmy,' she said, and quickly finished her drink.

'No, seriously, think about it. We both like classical music, country living, and grilled fish. That's a pretty good start, isn't it?'

'I've never thought of Mozart and monkfish as particularly good reasons to get married.' She sighed, wondered how this could possibly be the endearingly bashful gentleman she'd met just weeks earlier.

'I'll take that as a yes then.'

She took his hand, squeezed gently. 'I'd prefer you took it as a no, Gerry. At least for the moment.'

'I'm so sorry,' he said at once. 'That was incredibly insensitive of me. Downright impertinent too. Would you please accept my sincere apologies?'

'Apologies accepted but only if you get me another glass of Champagne,' she said trying to lift the mood. The emerald eyes flashed and she drew closer, her hands clasped demurely in front of her. 'Then it's my turn to ask the questions, like whether you're really that quiet, unassuming chap I met here for dinner a few weeks back or the inspired orator who just wowed his audience.'

Gerald leant back against the wall, nodded thoughtfully. 'That's a very good question,' he said. 'Unfortunately I'm not sure I know the answer.'

Dr Blythe's lips found Mr Cornfield's cheek and settled there for an exquisite moment. 'I think you know exactly who you are, Gerry Cornfield,' she whispered. 'And it's not that quiet chap from Pixley Green post office, is it?'

Chapter Twelve

The month of January hadn't long been torn from the calendar on the kitchen wall but spring was in the air. And for Gerald Cornfield, aged sixty-one and a quarter, the word sexagenarian was, quite suddenly, more to do with the *sex* bit than the *agen* or the *arian*.

He remembered feeling like this only once before, half a century ago, when Yvette West and her flame red hair first stole his schoolboy heart in the queue for Saturday morning pictures, outside the Rialto cinema. But theirs was a tragically short romance which ended when the Eleven Plus exam elevated her to a grammar school on the other side of town while he was despatched to the local secondary modern. And that, sadly, was that. They went their separate ways.

The heady euphoria of this first innocent passion was never quite recaptured and, by the time dear, sweet Betsy stepped into his life, by way of the village hall where she sometimes helped-out with the teas, the feeling had long-since faded into the mists of childhood memory. Until now.

Now it was back with an overwhelming intensity which far exceeded his pre-teen infatuation with the irresistible Yvette; a world away from the comfortable, undemanding affection that had bound him to darling Betsy for so many years. This was fiery, dangerous, an all-consuming madness of the mind.

Gerald's daily routine, the unshakeable foundation for so many years of quiet contentment, was thrown into chaos. He woke each day at six, a full ninety minutes before the radio alarm crackled to life, and occupied much of his newly-acquired time laid out on the bathroom floor, hands clasped behind his head, struggling towards something resembling an upright position. Stomach crunches, they called them, designed to sculpture six-pack abdominals from the fleshy folds of an unambitious belly.

And a jog around the common after work, according to informed sources, not only improved the respiratory system, strengthened the heart, and toned the calf and thigh muscles, it also helped to wean former TV addicts from the sedentary comfort of their reclining chairs. Gerald hadn't reached for the remote in weeks.

But the most welcome change in his life was the sudden and unexpected absence of dread. Dread no longer stalked him like a masked assassin. It slipped quietly away, without fuss, taking with it the haunting fear of the future; incurable disease, physical attack, unexpected bills, baldness, toothache, flat car batteries and, of course, the ultimate dread of death. Dread had seemingly been banished by the gentle hand of Dr Valerie Blythe.

And with Gerald's new found confidence came the clothes. Bold, striped suits and loud ties, hushed by the classic restraint of crisp white shirts and pocket handkerchiefs, announced that he was a man of style with a sense of humour which extended to his two-tone, black and white brogues. It was a uniform borrowed from another era when the tragedy of a world war finally gave way to the exuberance of the 1920s. Gerald had never before understood such careless flippancy but, with encouragement from Vee, a new mantra began to make sense; fear nothing, have fun, and let tomorrow take care of itself.

While Gerald wasn't altogether comfortable with the concept of a totally unplanned tomorrow, he was constantly reassured by Eddie Bates' laid-back attitude to life. Eddie not only lived for the moment, he somehow managed to put the future on hold whenever and wherever he fancied. Silly things, like not choosing a holiday destination until he arrived, case in hand, at the airport. OK, he might, perhaps, have packed for the sun rather than the slopes, but that was the extent of his forward planning and the final selection was always left until the very last minute, and the biggest discounts. Eddie worked hard at being unpredictable. 'Keep life guessing and it won't pin you down,' he'd say, as if erratic behaviour guaranteed a unique freedom of opportunity.

Gerald got the point. Maybe order and routine were just a sedative which gently closed the eyes to life's more adventurous options, numbing the spirit into blind, passive contentment while the rest of the world hurried-on by.

But Gerald's eyes were now opened wide, the world sharply in focus, and he liked what he saw. His one regret was that it had taken the best part of a lifetime to wake up to a gamut of possibilities.

Mrs Black listened to him with growing astonishment, but without interruption, while he explained how the Chief Executive Officer of a substantial company like Safe Streets couldn't possibly operate from the dining room of Pycroft Cottage. The address lacked credibility and, besides, Major Bevington had already signed the lease on a self-contained office suite close to the high street.

He omitted the bit about winding-up the business of Older & Wiser and, with it, her five per cent stake; no point in confusing her with the finer details of diminished share values and limited trading prospects in the face of an economic downturn.

Instead he focused on the upside and being part of a team in a growing company, with a salary increase to match her new status as PA to the CEO. Then there was the extended holiday entitlement, private health benefits, and a designated area for Winston.

'What do you think?' Gerald asked her at last.

Mrs Black clicked the top of her ballpoint pen, took deep breaths through her nose, lips sealed tight in a conspiracy of silence.

Gerald smiled. 'That's settled then,' he declared, rubbing his hands together enthusiastically. 'New job, new challenge. I just know you're going to love it.'

'Settled, is it?' she snapped. 'So I don't get a choice in the matter?'

'But of course you do. You can seize this wonderful opportunity or move on to pastures new, with my blessing. The choice is entirely yours.'

'You've changed,' she said. 'Not the same person at all.'

'Changed?' Gerald asked drily. 'In what way changed?'

'You used to take things more slowly, think about what you were doing. Now it's all smart suits and snap decisions. Doesn't become you.'

She was right of course, Gerald knew it, but he didn't have an explanation to offer; not a simple, logical explanation that she'd be likely to understand anyway. He shrugged. 'It's probably just a phase. Some kind of hormonal imbalance.'

'I blame that Eddie Bates. Bad influence he is.' Mrs Black shook her head, sighed. 'You're too gullible, easily lead. That's your trouble.'

'I surrender,' he whispered, waving the white handkerchief from his top pocket about his head. 'But dear, dear Mrs Black, will you or will you not be coming with me to Safe Streets' new offices?'

'I'm not at all sure,' she said, after a brief pause for contemplation. 'I'll have to give it a bit more thought.'

And it was a full two days later when, after due consideration but still with lingering doubts and the usual concerns about Winston's toilet arrangements, she found herself in the foyer of the smoked glass office building in the centre of the town.

The lift button marked *Penthouse* whooshed her directly to a small but sumptuous suite on the fourth floor, overlooking the high street and a random huddle of drab, cheerless shops below. But the lofty elegance of black leather and gleaming chrome, set in a sea of plushy, white axminster, seemed a world away from the mundane reality outside and in total harmony with Mrs Black's personal aspirations and expectations. She loved it, every little bit of it, even the small area of scrubby wasteland at the back of the building, next to the supermarket car park, ear-marked for Winston's personal requirements, at least until someone built on it.

Shortly before nine the following Monday morning, a substantially up-dated Gerald Arthur Cornfield settled himself behind a wide mahogany desk and resolved to become the acceptable, client-friendly face of Safe Streets [Security] Limited while, just a few miles away at The Shed, well beyond public scrutiny, Rupert Clark-Hall took the natural-born hostility of a growing number of young men and painstakingly forged it into an unofficial support force for the company's security officers.

It was a tough regime, based on military principles, where hand-picked hot-heads learned the fundamental lesson that aggression without control is a run-away horse; a mass of unbridled muscle and mindless energy galloping towards inevitable disaster and self-destruction.

A few learned it the hard way, from the neck up, where broken noses, blackened eyes, and swollen, blooded lips quickly identified the smart arses among the newer recruits. But, with or without the pain, a small but highly-disciplined unit started to take shape.

Except it wasn't one unit, it was two. And while the first confined its covert activities to neighbourhood security, the second was harder to pin down. An auxiliary unit, Rupert called it. A back-up team with a slightly broader brief, he said, and left it at that.

Gerald screwed up his face, closed his mind to the potential reality of Rupert's devious plans, and told himself it was none of his business.

He checked Mrs Black's handwritten instructions for the fourth time before pressing the small red button which brought his computer flickering to life, then waited, with mounting unease, while an avalanche of dubious e-mails cascaded down the screen; an embarrassing catalogue of pills, creams and potions which not only guaranteed a larger penis but also promised long-lasting firmness whenever required. And amid the farcical, if slightly offensive offers, lurked a surfeit of subterfuge and skulduggery; urgent, badly-spelled, demands for confirmation of his account details from bogus operators masquerading as well-known banks and building societies; messages from deposed African kings and princes, anxious to deposit their multi-million pound fortunes in Gerald's bank account for safe keeping, if he'd kindly hand over his sort code, account number, and any other access details. Phishing, they called it in informed circles; internet bait to hook the gullible and steal their savings.

Gerald couldn't help wondering if the E in e-mail stood for Exploitation.

But blatant con tricks weren't the only perils prowling the internet's super highway. There were infections; malicious viruses, worms, Trojans and a host of other invasive yet invisible cyber creatures which crawled into computers and skulked around, doing their worst, until flushed out with the internet equivalent of antibiotics. E for Evil.

Gerald hankered after the chic simplicity of the fountain pen, personalised communications on quality notepaper, the practised flow of a unique signature in rich, royal blue ink. The computer, on the other hand, lacked both style and common sense; an illogical, electronic mind which closed down only when you clicked the button marked "Start". E for Exasperating.

And E for E.W. with his short, sharp, impolite e-mails. 'Need to see you asap,' he declared a few weeks later, without explanation, in a late afternoon communiqué marked urgent.

'Look forward to it,' Gerald replied. 'We'll put the kettle on.'

A moment later Mrs Black peered round the door. 'Major Bevington just rang to say your meeting will be at Lovelace Farmhouse in twenty minutes, and not to be late.'

'Cheeky bastard.' Gerald slammed his desk drawer shut, reached for his jacket.

'Will you be back?' Mrs Black checked her watch, gave him a superior look as he made towards the door. 'If anyone calls, I mean.'

Gerald shrugged. 'Doubt it. Probably one of E.W.'s lengthy sermons about corporate procedures and reducing operating costs.'

But it wasn't.

E.W. greeted him with the congratulatory smile of a headmaster at prize giving, his chest puffed-up with pride, hands clasped behind his back. 'Well done dear boy,' he began before Gerald had quite settled himself in a leather armchair. 'First class job... company launch and all that.'

Gerald nodded, unbuttoned his jacket. 'No problems so far.'

'And none anticipated, I'm sure.'

'Absolutely not.'

'Excellent.'

The brief but unusually polite exchange terminated abruptly and the room fell silent.

Gerald shifted uneasily in his chair and waited, for E.W. to get to the point.

'Are you interested in politics?' E.W. asked eventually.

'I've always voted, if that's what you mean.'

E.W. stared down at his feet, cleared his throat. 'And always for the same party, I wouldn't mind betting.'

'Pretty much.'

'Regardless of their policies?'

'Because of their policies. The two main parties haven't fundamentally changed too much over the years, apart from claiming old, socialist Labour is actually New.'

'You're happy with the traditional left right contest then?' E.W. grunted. 'In the red corner, Government intervention and state control and, in the blue, commercial enterprise and personal freedom?'

'Hadn't really thought about it.'

E.W. turned towards the window. 'Perhaps it's time you did. You seem the sort of chap who might very well flourish in the world of politics.'

Gerald hunched forward, elbows on his knees, chin cupped in his hands. 'Anything's possible. Somebody once told me that Winston Churchill became prime minister for the second time when he was seventy something.'

'A mere child. Gladstone was eighty three when he formed his last government.'

'But that was another world, another time,' said Gerald. 'Politics is a young man's game these days, not for the likes of old fogies like me.'

E.W. turned to face him, smiled. 'But isn't that precisely why our political system is in absolute chaos? Bursting with career politicians, straight out of university, who couldn't run a works canteen, never mind a country. And most of them making disastrous decisions on a daily basis.'

'And you honestly think I'd be any better?'

'You could hardly be any worse. Let's face it, they're nothing more than a bunch of self-important chancers with ambitions to make the world a better place… for themselves.' Gerald paused, looked about him. It was a room he hadn't seen before, E.W.'s inner sanctum; bookshelves from floor to ceiling, regiments of leather spines, the silent army of a well-read man. His eyes were drawn to the top shelf and a fat, faded book, set apart from the others, laying flat on its side.

'*Mein Kampf*,' E.W. said at once. 'The thoughts and philosophies of the gentleman who gave us World War Two. An interesting, if depressing read. Borrow it if you like.'

'I'm not at all sure I'd be very interested in what Adolf Hitler had to say.'

'Perhaps you'd find Karl Marx more to your taste? *The Communist Manifesto*, over there, ironically, on the far right.'

'Not really,' Gerald muttered. 'One extreme to the other.'

'Nothing wrong with ideological extremes. They're what's shaped today's mainstream politics.'

'Maybe. But I think we've swung rather too far to the left, too many liberal souls with good intentions but appalling judgement.' Gerald reached for a book, flipped open the first few pages. 'Churchill obviously spent a life-time in politics. It says here he was elected member for Oldham in 1900, at the tender age of twenty-five, so I've probably left it a bit late to get started on a new career, wouldn't you say?'

'Too late for a lifetime in politics, perhaps, but still plenty of time to make a difference, have a go at changing things for the better.'

The grandfather clock in the hall struck six. Gerald glanced at his watch. 'It's certainly an interesting thought,' he said with a half-hearted chuckle which seemed to dismiss the whole idea. 'But I'm sure that's not why you wanted to see me.'

'On the contrary.' E.W. sat down in the chair opposite and stared hard, hands clasped, prayer-like, in front of him. 'How would you feel about running for parliament, as an independent candidate.'

Gerald hesitated for a moment, slowly shook his head, searching for the words to reject E.W.'s suggestion without appearing rude or ungrateful. 'Don't get me wrong, I'm flattered, really I am. But I don't see how I'd find the time to run Safe Streets and also run for parliament.'

'Don't be daft,' E.W. snapped back. 'The Commons is full of part-time politicians with second jobs. The Lords too, only they aren't quite so secretive about it. And, besides, it would be a logical extension of your commercial activity.'

Gerald looked confused but forced a narrow smile. 'Not quite sure what you mean.'

'Think about it,' said E.W. 'It's only a small step from keeping crime off our streets to keeping criminals out of our country. Protecting this royal throne of kings, this sceptered isle... this precious stone set in a silver sea... a moat defensive against the envy of less happier lands... isn't that how it goes?'

'This blessed plot, this earth, this realm, this England,' Gerald continued without hesitation. 'Shakespeare, Richard II, act 2. A sixteenth century masterpiece but they'd probably book you for incitement to racial hatred if you repeated it, out loud in a public place, in this day and age.'

'And that's the problem.' E.W. settled back, stretched out his legs, slid his thumbs into his waistcoat pockets in a Churchillian pose. 'We have a government passing laws to which the indigenous population is forbidden to object yet we continue to call ourselves a democracy. The whole thing's bizarre, straight out of the totalitarian mind-set of madmen like Stalin.

'Perhaps legislation is sometimes necessary to influence public attitudes?'

'Poppycock. Public attitudes are meant to influence legislation, not the other way around. Anything else is dictatorship.'

Gerald thought about it, conceded a hesitant nod, but wondered why someone with such emphatic political views hadn't talked about his own parliamentary ambitions. 'May I assume you have plans to stand for election too?' he asked.

'Absolutely not.' E.W. stiffened, looked away. 'I simply forge the weaponry of political warfare, make the bullets for others to fire.'

'So what would that make me?'

'You, Gerald, are already a champion in the struggle against crime and injustice – head of an effective crime prevention company and prospective parliamentarian in the defence of this sceptered isle.'

Gerald lowered his gaze, forced a wry smile. 'And what political bullets would you hand me to fire?'

'The staggering seventy million pounds it will cost us this year to house and feed *failed* asylum seekers who should, in law, have already been deported, will do for starters?' E.W. spoke in the angry, rasping tones he always used when he reeled-off important statistics. 'That's a massive jump on the four million pounds we spent just a few years ago,' he went on, barely pausing for breath. 'And thousands more potential immigrants line up on the coast of France each and every day, intent on entering Britain illegally, hidden away in the backs of lorries. But the most depressing fact of all is that, deliberately or through sheer incompetence, this government's total failure to protect our borders threatens our very way of life.'

'They'll integrate in time, accept our culture and traditions,' said Gerald. 'Isn't that why they come here?'

E.W. laughed suddenly but the indignant look and the clenched fist told another story. 'Don't kid yourself its warm beer and changing the bloody guard that attract immigrants here,' he snapped. 'The bastards swarm across Europe like ravenous locusts, bypassing Italy, Germany, France and dozens of other countries closer to home, to feast on *our* succulent benefits system, devour *our* juicy unemployment hand outs, gobble-up free housing, free health care, and free education for their kids. And that's why acres of green fields and open spaces are transformed into new estates to house the invaders. Then there's all the additional pressure on the NHS and an already failing education system, which routinely turns out kids who can't read, write, or add-up because they're taught in classes where half of them don't even speak English; sufficient to say that a once thriving economy is being flushed down the toilet, taking our way of life with it.'

Gerald shrank back into his chair. 'Are things really that bad? I mean, just how difficult can it be to protect our borders?'

'It should be the easiest thing in the world. We're a bloody island, for Christ's sake, which is why this government's continued failure looks increasingly like a deliberate act of vandalism.'

'But where's the logic in that?'

'Absolutely bloody nowhere.' E.W.'s frown hardened as he spat out the words. 'Logic is the result of rational thought. Vandalism, on the other hand, is merely mindless sabotage, frequently inspired by envy.'

'Sorry, you've lost me,' Gerald cut in. 'Sabotage?'

E.W. rose slowly to his feet. 'I'm not alone in believing its part of a long-term plan to change our social landscape forever, decimate middle England, the part of it they hate the most. And flooding the country with immigrants, who will inevitably show their gratitude at elections, is one way to achieve it.'

Gerald scratched his head thoughtfully. 'I don't honestly see how one independent MP is going to make very much difference.'

'A dissenting voice in the Commons would, of course, be the more diplomatic of two quite different, but complimentary, approaches to the problem.'

'The second being?'

'A less diplomatic approach. Let's call it positive communications at the source of the problem or, more precisely, presenting a persuasive argument at the port of Calais.'

'But so many different languages? Surely a communications nightmare?'

E.W. brushed aside Gerald's concerns. 'Violence is the Esperanto of persuasion. It's a beautiful language which cannot be misinterpreted, misunderstood or, most importantly, ignored.'

'And no doubt spoken fluently by everyone in Rupert's so-called auxiliary unit,' Gerald jibed. 'A back-up team with a slightly broader brief – isn't that how he describes it?'

The door opened suddenly and Katrina burst into the room waving a mobile phone, at arm's length in front of her like a live grenade. She handed it to E.W., flashed Gerald a fleeting smile as she passed, and left without a word.

E.W. snapped to attention as he pressed the phone to his ear. 'Report', he barked then listened, silent and expressionless for about a minute. 'Well done, that man,' he said finally, before slipping the phone into his pocket.

Gerald began to feel uncomfortable. 'Perhaps I should be off now,' he said, buttoning his jacket. 'I can see you're busy.'

E.W. shook his head, thought for a moment. 'Stay awhile. I'd like you to be fully briefed on today's action in Calais.'

Gerald raised an eyebrow but asked no questions, hoping his silence might somehow disassociate himself from whatever had taken place that afternoon in France.

'The attack went well,' E.W. announced flatly. 'And a timely intervention it was too.'

Gerald looked away, let loose a few dissenting sighs while E.W., undeterred and brimming with self-importance, continued with his news.

'Apparently breaking into Britain is no longer enough for illegal immigrants. Now they're mugging British tourists at knife point on the roads leading to the port.'

'But surely the French police...'

'Will turn a blind eye,' E.W. interrupted before Gerald could finish. 'They blame us and our ridiculous benefits system for creating the problem in the first place, so we can't expect much sympathy or cooperation from that quarter.'

Katrina returned with a bottle of Perrier Jouet under her arm, four Champagne glasses hanging, bottoms up, between her fingers. 'I didn't hear any screams of rage so I assume we're celebrating,' she whispered, as she placed them on a small round table beside E.W.'s chair. She looked up with an expectant smile. 'We are, aren't we? Celebrating, I mean.'

E.W. nodded. 'Rupert will be here shortly with the details.'

Katrina slid a pouffe across the floor and sat down, hugging her knees like a small child waiting for a bedtime story. 'There was nothing about it on the six o'clock news.'

'It'll take a while for them to work out what happened,' E.W. grunted.

Gerald swallowed hard. 'What, exactly, *did* happen?'

Katrina threw back her head, arched her neck, and spoke softly to the ceiling. 'We told a gang of foreign freeloaders to bugger off.'

'And will they?' Gerald asked.

She shrugged, span around to face him. 'You'll have to ask Rupert. But he sounded quite perky on the mobile.'

E.W. opened the Champagne. 'We've struck a blow for cash-strapped pensioners who get less consideration from this government than illegal immigrants,' he said, filling each of the glasses in turn. 'They're even talking about bribing the bastards to go home when what they deserve is a boot up the arse.'

'And they got it today, didn't they?' Katrina giggled mischievously. 'A dozen or so boots, if I'm not mistaken.'

'More,' E.W. corrected. 'Twenty men, ten motorbikes, one day trip to Calais.'

'And zero casualties.' Rupert Clark-Hall leaned against the open door in a leisurely pose, casual in an extravagantly white velour tracksuit, hands thrust deep into the trouser pockets. 'Can't vouch for the other team though.'

Gerald stared hard at Rupert as he sauntered into the room. 'You didn't go dressed like that, did you?'

'I didn't go at all,' he yawned. 'But it's been a tough day all the same and a bit of bubbly will go down very well right now.'

Katrina handed round the glasses, raised hers in a toast. 'To severely kicked arses,' she shouted. 'And many more of them.'

'Kicked arses,' Rupert echoed, glancing quickly at Gerald for his reaction.

Gerald forced a weak smile, sipped his drink. 'As always, you make it sound like a sixth form game Rupert. Thrashed 'em at ruggers, kicked their arses at cricket. Surely this was a bit more serious?'

'Much more serious.' Rupert perched on the arm of Gerald's chair. 'They're a vicious load of bastards by all accounts.'

'From the beginning,' E.W. demanded. 'Including all the cock-ups.'

Rupert frowned. 'My chaps don't do cock-ups, particularly when they're outnumbered ten to one.'

'Two hundred of them?' Gerald interrupted. 'That's an army.'

'Probably more, nobody was sure. Dizzy reckons most of them were slumming it at a makeshift camp in nearby woods they call The Swamp, while the others made no secret of hanging around the lorry parks. Another bunch, which including some women and children, were squatting in empty houses just beyond the port itself.'

Katrina knelt in front of him, topped up his glass. 'You went straight for the camp I hope.'

Rupert shook his head. 'Not right away. First we sent three men into the lorry park to hand out leaflets. Simple message, four languages, unambiguous. *"Go home if you value your life."* Seemed to hit the spot.'

'That's the stuff,' E.W. snorted. 'Clear cut options'.

'Wasn't it a bit foolhardy?' said Gerald, 'I mean, three men handing out multi-lingual death threats to a mob.'

Katrina pursed crimson lips. 'Bait,' she whispered. 'Something to lure the quarry into the trap.'

'Took longer than we expected to get 'em riled,' Rupert continued. 'Perhaps some of them couldn't read or maybe our translations weren't so hot. Anyway, they eventually got the message and all hell broke loose. A crowd of them chased our three to a small clearing on the fringes of The Swamp where the rest of the team were waiting.' Rupert paused, held out his glass for a refill. 'We jumped them, gave 'em a good slap, torched the camp, and legged it, post haste, to the bikes. I don't have too much in the way of detail from that point on in the proceedings.'

E.W. nodded thoughtfully. 'But no casualties or arrests?'

'All present and correct, as far as I know.'

'And no unexpected problems on the way?'

'Maybe one,' Rupert sighed. 'Dizzy thinks the fire may have taken hold, spread across the woodland towards the town.'

E.W. seemed unconcerned. 'If you hoard inflammable rubbish, you must expect fires.'

'Isn't that a bit unfair?' said Gerald. 'Surely the French don't want asylum seekers in Calais?'

'Of course not,' E.W. snapped. 'They want them in Dover.'

Rupert rose slowly to his feet. 'Calais will be crawling with police after our little raid so nobody will be crossing the Channel without a passport – which will be a first.' He emptied his glass, placed it on the tray, kissed Katrina gently on the cheek. 'Just what the doctor ordered,' he said. 'But I've got to be on my way. The lads will be at The Shed for a debriefing in an hour. There's to be a repeat performance in three days.'

Gerald watched him leave the room, Katrina's arm around his waist, and waited until the door closed behind them. 'Well that'll certainly set the cat among the pigeons,' he said. 'But I don't see how violence in France can be complimentary to the work of an independent MP in the Commons.'

'What happened in Calais today would have the tacit approval of most people in Britain,' said E.W. 'Our task is to make it acceptable for them to admit it.'

'One man, alone, with no party support and no prospects of ever being in government? No chance.'

E.W. leaned forward and spoke quietly. 'I'd wager that thirteen million disgruntled pensioners would rally to a party which promised to give them a voice.'

Gerald sank back into his chair. 'I get it,' he sighed. 'We've put up with New Labour, why not Old Codgers?'

'Not quite, but you're on the right lines.'

'Are you serious?'

'Completely,' E.W. answered at once. 'The issues are obvious. Healthcare, pensions, law and order, dignity, respect. The manifesto almost writes itself.'

'But you've jumped from sponsoring one independent MP to creating a new political party in the space of thirty minutes.'

'Let's just call it a *movement* for now.' E.W. stood up, reached into his inside pocket for a small, black notebook and flipped it open. 'You might like to know that only two of the government's six key policy decisions this month were announced from the green hide benches of the Commons. The rest were slipped into the public domain from various floral couches in TV studios.'

'Meaning what?'

'That Parliament has become irrelevant. Public opinion is shaped through the media in a tally of press conferences, interviews and chat shows. With an army of oldies behind us we can influence decision making no matter who's in government.'

Gerald cringed. 'I don't like the word oldies. Sounds like a pile of worn out records from the fifties.'

'Does a bit, doesn't it?' E.W. conceded with a faint smile. 'But at least it's honest, straight to the point. None of that senior citizen nonsense.'

Gerald stood up, stretched. 'If we *have* to be categorised by our age, I think I'd prefer to be an elder than an oldie,' he said, making towards the door. 'Seems to have a more positive ring to it.'

'Yes, I suppose it does. Certainly demands respect rather than sympathy. More dependable, trustworthy, that sort of thing. Which brings me to another matter...' E.W. placed a comforting arm around Gerald's shoulder and drew him closer. 'How would you feel about getting married?'

'Married?' said Gerald, slightly taken aback. 'Why do you ask?'

E.W. beckoned, led him into the hallway where he paused to straighten a framed photograph of himself on the wall. 'Great men must have a woman in their lives,' he declared emphatically. 'It's the way of things. People don't trust bachelors. Unreliable, you see.'

'How about widowers? Can they be trusted?'

E.W. dismissed the question with a wave of the hand. 'We must all live in the present, old chap, not the past. It's high time you were remarried.'

'I'll give it some thought,' said Gerald, buttoning his jacket to leave. 'Always assuming I can find a willing accomplice.'

Chapter Thirteen

They'd kicked him to death outside his own house, booted his head like a rugby ball. A pensioner, brutally murdered for asking a gang of kids to keep the noise down, according to the reports.

The local TV news said it was the mindless killing of an innocent man who'd dared to confront local rowdies. Teenage thugs without a conscience, they called them. Heartless monsters.

But the attack was largely ignored by the national networks who filled their evening news bulletins with tales of terrorism, political shenanigans, rising unemployment and a falling pound. The premature demise of former taxi driver, Stanley Skinner, wasn't sufficiently newsworthy.

Mr Cornfield stared at Mr Skinner's picture in the local paper; a snapshot taken on holiday with his wife a year earlier. Now he was dead, and for no good reason.

Almost at once, the police announced that two local youths were helping them with their enquiries, that they were confident of finding the attackers, but nobody had been arrested or charged.

There was one particular line in the story that caught Gerald's eye; a quote from a social worker who thought irresponsible supermarkets were to blame. It was their cheap liqueur that fuelled the wave of street violence. Supermarkets, she said, had a lot to answer for. Mr Cornfield thought about it. By the same logic, supermarkets could be blamed for many more of society's ills; high fat foods which caused obesity, instant dinners in a bag which destroyed home cooking and family meals, supermarket packaging which contributed to environmental problems. And surely the very existence of the supermarket itself had killed off many of Britain's high street shops? Yes it was all the fault of supermarkets, everything from microwaved food to murder most foul, and a bit more besides, but only in a crazy world where people no longer accepted responsibility for their own actions.

Mrs Black dabbed her eye with a tissue. She'd known the Skinners well, Stan and Maureen. Lovely couple, lived only minutes away. Quiet bloke, he was, genuine sort, easy to get on with. Had a smile for everyone. Always there to lend a helping hand. Shouldn't have happened, not like that. No respect, she said, not these days, not anymore.

A daughter and some neighbours had said much the same thing on the TV news. Gerald imagined they'd probably be saying something similar in Somalia, Romania or maybe Iraq if they ever heard about the attack at Calais. Whether violence was right or wrong seemed to depend entirely on your perspective at the time.

But, one thing was certain, if Safe Streets had been patrolling Stan Skinner's neck of the woods on the night he was attacked, he'd probably still be alive. The thought loitered in Gerald's mind for the rest of the day, nagged at him like a persistent toothache. Safe Streets offered well-off residents the BUPA equivalent of home security while the less fortunate put their trust in an overstretched, under-funded, NHS-style police force, bound-up in red tape and bogged-down by bad management.

Way of the world, Gerald told himself. Nothing's for nothing; you get what you pay for. And that might have been an end to it if he hadn't met up for a drink with Eddie Bates that same evening.

A quick sharpener at The Crow, Eddie's antidote to the toil of the day, raised an important question.

Eddie just threw it into the conversation without prior warning. 'Who do you suppose stumped-up the readies to invade Calais's multi-cultural YMCA then?' He stood perfectly still, eyes fixed on his friend, his glass of whisky held in suspended animation close to his lips. 'Someone must have funded that particular little day trip, eh?'

Gerald shrugged. 'I hadn't really thought about it.'

'Didn't come out of your Safe Streets budget, did it?'

'I don't think so,' Gerald answered slightly hesitantly. 'No, definitely not, I'd have known about it.'

Eddie emptied his glass in a single swig, burped loudly. 'You see what I'm saying mate?' He reached for his wallet, took out a slip of paper. 'Ever heard of something called Stopwatch?'

Gerald shook his head.

'Mainly funded by private business, unofficially backed by at least one trade union, operating well below the radar. Dedicated to keeping immigrants out of Britain in general and England in particular.'

'You mean keeping illegal immigrants out of Britain?'

'I mean *any* immigrants at *any* time, my friend. All of 'em.'

Gerald stared at his glass, ran his finger slowly around the rim. 'Stopwatch, you say. That's a new one on me,' he muttered without looking up. 'How come you know so much about it?'

'E.W.'s wined and dined them a few times at the Casa Roma. Being a good restaurateur, I make it my business to know a bit about the clientele.'

'And you know for sure they funded the raid on the immigrant camp?' Gerald asked, his tone now more impatient.

'Certain. But that's not the point I'm trying to make.'

'What exactly *is* your point then? Do you even have one?'

Eddie laughed suddenly. 'Hold your horses mate. This is The Crow not the Old bleeding Bailey. I just thought you should be aware that the lads from The Shed are being hired-out for private parties, so to speak.'

'Like Calais?'

'Calais's a good example,' said Eddie. 'But they've apparently turned-up at a few gigs closer to home.'

Gerald looked surprised. 'Hang on a minute,' he said, settling himself on a bar stool. 'There aren't enough of them to just *turn-up* here, there and everywhere.'

'Sure about that?' Eddie raised an eyebrow. 'How many do you reckon there are then?'

Gerald shrugged. 'Can't be certain, but I know twenty went to Calais so I'd guess there are maybe twenty-five or so, top whack.'

'Guess again and multiply by four,' said Eddie

'A hundred?'

'Near as damn it.'

'How do you know?'

'Elementary my dear Cornfield. Rupert was joking around the other evening, said something about Dizzy being his first "centurion". So I put two and two together and made a hundred.'

Gerald thought about it for a moment. 'Sorry, no pun intended, but it doesn't add up. I mean, how could he have trained that many kids so fast? And why would he need them in the first place? I think you *must* have got it wrong.'

Eddie eyed his friend's blue and white striped suit and two-tone brogues, blinked a few times, smiled smugly, but said nothing.

'You've definitely got the wrong end of the stick,' Gerald insisted.

Eddie slowly shook his head. 'Sorry my little pin-striped person, but I haven't,' he said dismissively, the words slightly slurred. 'It's been confirmed, well sort of anyway.'

'Confirmed?'

'By Holly.'

Gerald tried to stifle his irritation. 'And what in hell's name has Holly got to do with all this?'

'Very little, as it happens. It's Vee.' Eddie turned away, signalled to the barman for more drinks. 'Holly says she's been doing a Florence Nightingale at... and this'll interest you... some farm buildings near Dorking. Ring any bells with you?'

'Holly told you that?'

Eddie nodded. 'Apparently Vee's asked if she'd help out from time to time.'

'Ridiculous,' Gerald huffed. 'This is Surrey not the Somme.'

Eddie slid a ten pound note across the bar, handed Gerald his drink. 'A toast to our brave young ladies on the Western Front,' he spluttered, unable to control his laughter.

Gerald wasn't amused. 'How many of those have you had this evening?'

Eddie peered into his glass as if the answer might be engraved on the bottom. 'This tiny, weeny little Scotchy poo is only my second,' he declared solemnly, raising two fingers in the air by way of confirmation. 'Then again, one or two large ones from lunchtime may have caught-up with me when I wasn't looking.'

Gerald forced a timid smile, acutely aware that his affable, giggling friend was about to transmute into a charmless, argumentative oaf. All the warning signals were there; the sudden bout of nit-picking, the carelessly loosened tie, the wagging finger close to your face, the raised voice. It was time to go. 'Gotta be off,' said Gerald as chirpily as he could manage. 'Busy day tomorrow. Early start.'

But Eddie Bates wasn't listening. What began as a few critical remarks about the barman's diamond ear stud, quickly developed into a noisy rant about young men who looked more like girls these days and how some of the older ones, who should know better, had taken to wearing poncey suits.

Gerald turned his back on the jibe and stepped out into the chill evening air. He took a deep breath to clear his head; smoking had long since been banned in The Crow but the sour smell of tobacco still lingered like an obstinate stain.

His mobile phone warbled suddenly to life, vibrating somewhere in his jacket, but then fell silent and still as he fumbled through his pockets and flipped it open; "Missed Call", it announced accusingly, as if he'd been somehow negligent in answering. And then, as he pressed command buttons designed for an alien civilisation with ballpoint fingertips, the message finally disappeared from the screen.

The clock above the library at the other end of the road chimed eight, reminding Gerald that he hadn't eaten since breakfast. He told himself the call to Vee was nothing more than a courtesy to see if she'd been trying to contact him. And it would only be polite to invite her for dinner, always assuming she was free.

A taped message said Dr Blythe was unavailable and to leave a message but then Vee's voice cut-in suddenly. 'Hello, hello… sorry… thought I'd turned the damn thing off.'

'Have you eaten?' Gerald asked with a silly little laugh that always seemed to slip out when he was nervous and unsure of himself.

'David?'

'It's Gerry actually, Gerald Cornfield. Um, I was just wondering if you might be free for dinner.'

'So sorry. You sounded like somebody else.' She paused for a moment. 'Dinner, tonight you mean?'

'Well, yes, if you're not too busy. Just a quick bite somewhere, nothing special.'

'Right,' she whispered hesitantly, then paused again. 'Actually it's been a bugger of a day, one way and another. Not sure I'd be very good company.'

'Sounds like a slice of pizza and a glass of wine might cheer you up a bit.'

'Pizza, yes,' she said, still sounding uncertain. 'I could get some delivered I suppose. Not really in the mood for going out, if it's all the same with you.'

'No problem. Leave it to me. I'll pick-up a couple on my way over. What do you fancy?'

'Oh, whatever. You choose. But would you be a dear and give me half an hour to sort myself out? I've just this minute got in and the place is a mess.'

'Quite understand, really,' Gerald spluttered, feeling suddenly awkward and intrusive. 'I'll be there at nine o'clock.'

'You're a darling. Sorry to be a bore.'

Gerald stood, motionless, staring at his mobile phone, half wishing he'd never made the call and wondering why he'd suggested pizza, his least favourite food; cardboard with cheese on, as Eddie Bates called it.

But that's how things happened with Vee. Even a simple invitation to dinner seemed to find him listing the reasons why she should accept, as if her very presence was a prize to be won. And then she'd somehow manage to modify his plans to fit-in with hers, like tonight. They'd seen each other just three or four times and always, somehow, on her terms, but this was the first invitation to her home. And so, at precisely nine o'clock, he stood at Vee's front door, two pizza boxes and a bottle of Merlot in a plastic bag by his side.

She looked different; the long, auburn hair bunched back into an untidy muddle by a couple of tortoiseshell slides, her face pale, devoid of make-up, the smile strained and grudging.

'My goodness Gerry,' she said, thrusting her hands into her jeans pockets as she stepped forward to kiss him on the cheek. 'You *do* look snazzy.'

'Pizza delivery outfit. We dress to impress.' Gerald took the pizza boxes from the bag and followed her into a room with wooden picture rails and faded floral wallpaper, dominated by a tiled fireplace with an iron grate nestling in the mouldering ash of another time. 'Awful, isn't it,' said Vee. 'Straight out of World War Two, untouched by the passing years.'

'It does all seem very original,' Gerald replied tactfully. 'Probably worth a few bob to a collector of forties memorabilia.'

Vee shrugged. 'Who knows. I just want out of here asap.' She gestured for him to sit.

He eased himself into one of a pair of elegant, white sofas. 'These obviously didn't come with the house,' he said, plumping up a fat cushion beside him. 'What was your previous place like?'

'It was a flat, brand new, overlooking the river, near Wandsworth.' She placed a side table at either end of the sofa, set a wine glass and paper napkin on each. 'All very swish but much too perfect, more like a show flat than a home.'

Gerald glanced down at the worn linoleum, faded brown and red diamond patterns which reminded him of his parent's North London semi. He turned to speak but she'd left the room.

'I suppose moving here must have been a bit of a culture shock,' he called out.

'Not really,' she shouted from the kitchen. 'It's a fine house with great potential, but you have to look past the current mess and visualise it finished.' She returned with knives and forks, handed him a cork screw. 'Unfortunately we never got around to even starting and now it's too late.'

Gerald nodded sympathetically, sighed as he opened the wine.

'What's that line? Life's what happens when you're busy making other plans.'

'John Lennon,' she said with a sudden look of sadness. 'He summed it up so well, don't you think. An absolute genius with words.'

Gerald drew closer to fill her glass. 'Didn't John Lennon also say something about love being all you need?'

The microwave pinged and Vee turned quickly away. 'Sounds like dinner is served.' She disappeared back into the kitchen, returned a few moments later with two plates of sliced pizza on a tray.

Gerald waited until she'd settled herself at the opposite end of the sofa. 'Pizzas all look the same to me so I went for vegetarian, thought they'd be the safest bet.'

'They're fine,' she replied dismissively.

Gerald peered at her across the rim of his glass. 'Look, I really should apologise for barging in on you like this. I've probably messed-up your entire evening.'

She shook her head. 'Nothing to mess-up. I was all set to nod-off in front of the TV.'

'I find that difficult to believe. Surely you're more of the gallivanting-about-town, enjoying yourself type.'

'I'm afraid gallivanting isn't high on my agenda after a ten hour shift.'

'No, I suppose not. Must be totally exhausting.'

'You get used to it.'

'Don't suppose you get much spare time.'

'No. Not much.'

Gerald placed his glass carefully on the side table, dabbed his mouth with a paper napkin. 'It's good of you to find time for the lads down at The Shed,' he said. 'I'm sure it's greatly appreciated.'

'Ah yes, The Shed.' She turned slowly to face him, fixed him with emerald eyes. 'I wondered when you'd get around to that.'

Gerald shrugged. 'Just curious. None of my business really.'

'Nonsense. You're the boss. Of course it's your business.'

'I meant your involvement as a doctor. That's entirely your affair, nothing to do with me.'

She settled back with her drink, sighed gently. 'So it's OK for me to patch up your employees but you'd rather be spared the gory details?'

'That's not what I meant.'

'Then what, exactly, *did* you mean?'

Gerald hesitated, brushed imaginary specs from his jacket front. 'To be completely honest, I'm a bit concerned about the way things seem to be developing. I don't want you mixed-up in it.'

'How about what I want?'

'Look, I just want to be sure you understand what you're getting yourself into.'

'And I appreciate your concern, Gerry. Honestly. But I think I know what I'm doing.'

'Well I'm glad one of us does, because I'm damned if I do.'

Vee's frown softened into a tired smile. 'Now you're beginning to sound like that quiet chap who used to run Pixley Green post office. What became of the other man, the one with a mission who wowed us at the Casa Roma press reception?'

'Oh he's pretty much the same. It's the mission that's changed.'

Vee slipped off her shoes, swung her legs on to the sofa, tucked her feet under a cushion. 'Changed?' she repeated, as if no such word existed in the English language.

'Completely changed,' said Gerald, his face flushed with indignation. 'The plan was to train a small group of kids to deal with street yobs and bring a bit of order to local neighbourhoods. And, may I say, I don't have a problem with that concept. But the small group seems to have become an army, raided an immigrant camp on the other side of the Channel, among other things, and opened its own casualty ward, with you as resident doctor. So I'd say the mission's changed, wouldn't you?'

Vee shook her head. 'I'd say it's progressed.'

'Then you've obviously been privy to a lot more information than me because I knew nothing about any plans to create a full scale private army.'

'Well, you may not have noticed, Gerry, but the world's a bit short on super heroes at the moment. And when Superman's unavailable and Batman's busy, you have to make do with a small army instead – same job description, more people involved.'

Gerald closed his eyes, shook his head in disbelief. 'I just love your analogy,' he whispered. 'Really I do. It's straight out of Marvel comics. Supergang saves the world.'

'I'm afraid the world may have to wait.' Vee stood up suddenly, crossed the room to the window, peeked out as if she might be expecting someone. 'Everyone knows Westminster's corrupt enough to be twinned with Gotham City and there's more violent crime on our streets than Metropolis on a bad day.' She turned to face him. 'I'd say we've got quite enough to be getting on with right here.'

Gerald grunted, leaned forward, elbows resting on his knees. 'How long have you been involved in all this?'

'Not sure. I suppose it was shortly after I patched-up Rupert's wrist. He's very persuasive.'

'Did you know E.W. wants me to become a politician?'

She smiled. 'Actually it was my suggestion. I think you'd be magnificent. You're loyal, industrious, honest, conscientious – everything most politicians aren't.'

'You made no mention of charisma and diplomacy, the two qualities that seem to define a successful politician in this day and age.'

'Mere cosmetics. Permatan and politeness are no substitute for the real thing.'

Gerald stared at the grey, cheerless hearth with a growing sense of unease. 'They're not telling me everything, are they?' he whispered. 'I'm being kept in the dark for some reason. Why would they do that Vee?'

She poured herself another glass of wine, sat down beside him. 'I called Rupert immediately after you called me, asked him to come over. He'll explain everything.'

'So it took a telephone call from you before he deigned to tell me what's going on? Is that it?'

'Ask him yourself,' she said as a car's headlights flickered across the latticed windows. 'I'm sure he'll tell you everything.'

A car door slammed, the sound of footsteps on gravel, and then silence.

Vee mumbled something about another wine glass, glanced at herself in the mirror as she passed, and quickly disappeared into the kitchen.

Gerald stood for a moment uncertainly. 'Shall I get the front door?' he called out.

'Not necessary, old chap.' Rupert sauntered into the room wearing blue corduroy and waving a bunch of keys above his head like a championship trophy. He threw off his jacket and flopped down on the sofa opposite. 'That looks like a reasonable brew,' he said, with a casual glance at the wine label.

'French Merlot,' said Gerald.

Rupert stroked his chin thoughtfully. 'To be perfectly honest I prefer Chilean wines these days... seem to have a bit more body than the French stuff... not so buggered about... younger soil, you see.'

'Well you can thank Gerry for this rather nice *French* stuff,' Vee cut in. She thrust a glass into his hand.

Rupert watched her pour the last of the wine, gave her a cheeky grin as their eyes met. 'Tell you what, darling,' he cooed with obvious relish, 'perhaps I'll open a bottle of that Shiraz we bought a week or so back?'

It was the word *darling* that drew blood, pierced Gerald's pride with rapier precision, left him wounded, crestfallen. 'Please don't bother with more wine on my account,' he said at once, pointing to his watch. 'I've got to be off.'

Rupert shrugged, quickly drained his glass. 'Up to you old chap but I understood you were feeling a bit neglected, left in the dark on one or two issues.'

'It seems to me I've been left in the dark on rather too many issues.'

'And so you have, Gerald, so you have. I admit it. The question is are you prepared for enlightenment?'

'Well, I wasn't actually expecting the angel of the Lord to descend in a fiery chariot, if that's what you mean,' Gerald replied. 'But I'll probably understand most of what you've got to say if you speak very slowly and don't use too many long words.'

'Then I hope you'll not only understand but also support and applaud what I'm about to tell you.'

Gerald tapped his fingers impatiently on the side table. 'I'll do my best,' he sighed. 'Always assuming this isn't going to take all evening.'

'Have you ever heard of *keeni meeni* ?'

'I've heard of *eany meany,* but, as I recall, there was a *miney mo* tagged on the end somewhere.'

'*Keeni meeni,*' Rupert continued, undeterred by Gerald's sarcasm, 'is Swahili and means deadly snake in the long grass.'

Gerald reached for his empty glass. 'Perhaps we should have a drop of that Chilean stuff you mentioned? Sounds like this is going to be a very long story.'

'I'll get the wine,' Vee said at once. 'You two carry on.'

Rupert stood up and waited until she'd left the room, then sauntered over to the window, his back towards the other man. '*Keeni meeni* was a codename adopted for covert operations by special forces. They were an under-cover elite – dedicated, efficient, highly professional and, above all, deadly.' He hesitated for a moment, then turned around. 'I want you to understand, Gerald, that our gallant little band is every bit as efficient and effective as *keeni meeni* at its best. They have the training, the ability and the mind-set to become a very special force for progress.'

'Then again, some might call them adolescent thugs,' Gerald interjected. 'Bullyboys, even.'

Rupert tut-tutted, shook his head. 'Come come Gerald, it's all about perception. A thug with a responsible leader is a soldier. A bully in a worthy cause can be a hero. Even Her Majesty's armed forces would be little more than nationalised hooligans without a chain of command and a bit of discipline.'

'Call them what you like,' Gerald snapped. 'The fact remains that your gallant little band is getting out of hand.'

Vee came into the room quietly, placed a bottle of wine on the side table, and left again without speaking.

Rupert called after her. 'Shall I pour you a glass?'

'Perhaps later,' she replied. 'Got a few things to do.'

The door snapped shut behind her and, for a brief moment, the two men stared at each other in silence.

Gerald spoke first. 'Are you two living together?'

Rupert pinged his glass with a fingernail. 'Seconds out. Round one.' He laughed suddenly, flopped down on the couch.

'Well, are you?' Gerald persisted.

'Certainly not. I drop in from time to time, strictly business. That's it.'

'*Darling* doesn't sound much like business.'

'I call lots of women *darling.* Doesn't mean I'm screwing them.'

'So why would you *drop in* from time to time?'

Rupert stabbed the corkscrew into the wine bottle with purpose, twisted hard and yanked it out. 'None of your damn business,' he said, smelling the cork before filling each of their glasses. 'But if it'll bring your little inquisition to a close, I can tell you that Vee lets me use the place for business meetings when she's not here.'

'Why would you have meetings here, when we've got a prestigious penthouse suite in the centre of town?'

Rupert threw back his head and spoke quietly to the ceiling. 'Best not to muddle things,' he said. 'The office is strictly Safe Streets territory. This house, on the other hand, is neutral territory. What's more, it's on the market and will soon have no connections with any of us, which makes it an ideal venue for some of my more confidential meetings.'

Gerald clasped his hands calmly in front of him and waited, silent and expressionless, for Rupert to continue.

'You have the distinctly patronising look of a judge who's reached a verdict before he's even heard the charge,' Rupert said. 'Perhaps you should wait to hear all the evidence.'

'I wasn't aware anyone was on trial.'

'You seem to put everyone on trial, demand they prove their innocence in the Court of Gerald Cornfield.' Rupert's expression slowly softened into a smile. 'Look mate, just give people a chance. Don't assume we're all cheats and liars...at least not *all* of the time.'

Gerald stared wearily at the floor. 'Do you think we could get to the point of your *keeni meeni* story now? I mean, that is why you came here this evening, isn't it?'

'Not entirely, no,' said Rupert. 'Ours is a tiny militia but it supports a very big philosophy which, with any luck, will change the political landscape of Britain.'

'What exactly are you planning to do?' Gerald asked, helping himself to some more wine. 'Blow up the Houses of Parliament?'

Rupert shrugged. 'No point. Parliament is little more than a monument to a democracy which no longer exists. Sure, the great unwashed still vote political parties into power, based on manifesto promises, but then governments do as they bloody well please for the next four or five years, shadowed by an impotent and incompetent opposition, before the whole sorry performance is repeated and another load of lying bastards eventually take office.'

'Forgive me,' Gerald mumbled through a stifled yawn. 'But I think I've already heard all this from E.W. Lots of ideological stuff about why parliament has become irrelevant and how I could magically transform myself into some kind of political champion for the older generation, but nothing specific.'

Rupert nodded impassively. 'E.W. got the distinct impression you approved of his concept.'

'Can't think why. It's not so much a concept as a few random thoughts. Like I said, nothing specific to either like or dislike.'

'Then let me get specific,' said Rupert, suddenly more serious. He stared at Gerald with steel blue eyes, cold and penetrating, the usual schoolboy humour gone from his face. 'We're talking about a shadow government, a ghost power-base which will put Britain first and bring about the changes the whole country talks about but which no government has ever had the balls to deliver.'

Gerald sat perfectly still. 'Like what?' he asked, without looking up.

'Like enforcing a new *Magna Carta* of shadow laws. We'll make governments accountable, protect our borders, punish criminal behaviour, reward the industrious, penalise the freeloaders and spongers, enforce immigrant integration, deport immigrant law breakers, restrict the health service to British citizens, reinstate the authority of teachers over pupils, deliver dignity to our pensioners, and give parent power back to our families. Will that do for starters?'

'I'm not sure how you'd hope to achieve all that,' said Gerald after a moment of contemplation. 'But it sounds very right wing.'

'What you mean is it sounds very *right*, full stop,' Rupert retorted. 'Right's not a position on the political spectrum, it's fair, reasonable and, above all, for the benefit of the nation. It's plain, bloody logic.'

'But it's not politically correct, which is why our political masters won't go for it – not in my lifetime, anyway. We've travelled too far down the PC path to Brussels.'

'Well, they're going to get it whether they go for it or not,' Rupert said, rising to his feet and rubbing the small of his back with clenched fists. 'This is about enforcement not electioneering.'

Gerald looked up at the other man, slowly shook his head. 'How could your *tiny* militia – your description – ever hope to take on a national police force?'

'We wouldn't even try,' Rupert said with finality. 'Instead we'll be the deadly snakes in the long grass, unseen but lethal, *keeni meeni*. And we'll put the fear of god into this government, the armies of liars and cheats, the criminals, the gangs, the people who would exploit England and turn it into a third world state.' He stopped abruptly, stretched his arms high above his head, sighed.

'What's this got to do with me then?' said Gerald.

Rupert smiled. 'I should have thought that was obvious. For starters, you're already on the fringes of all this through your work with Safe Streets. But there's another, more important issue. You may not know it, old chap, but you have a face that people trust. And that's not a personal opinion, it's a scientific fact.'

'Scientific fact? I very much doubt that.'

'Oh but it is,' Rupert continued. 'You see ideal facial proportions are universal, regardless of race, sex and age and are based on a specific ratio. If the width of the face from cheek to cheek is 10 inches, for example, then the length of the face from the top of the head to the bottom of the chin should be exactly 16.18 inches.'

Gerald listened, bemused, while Rupert explained, in more detail, how worldwide scientific studies proved that men with narrow faces were seen as more trustworthy than those with more rounded, fuller faces. And the good news was that Gerald's facial proportions were, mathematically at least, as near to ideal as you get.

OK he was no Brad Pitt or even Eddie Bates' screen hero *Jet Butler,* but then sexuality and physical attractiveness were often viewed with a degree of suspicion by the general public; Rupert made several references to detailed research from three different universities which proved the point. But then, after a full five minutes of tenuous comparisons with the great and the good, concluded that Gerald Cornfield was blessed with a countenance that the entire world would trust.

'When did you measure my face?' Gerald asked quietly when Rupert had finished. 'More importantly, how could you have measured it without me knowing?'

'Photographs,' said Rupert. 'It can be done from photographs.'

Gerald's eyes narrowed. 'What photographs? When?'

'Our photographer took a couple of mug shots at the Casa Roma, I think, during the Safe Streets launch party. Anyway, what difference does it make?'

Vee stood for a moment in the doorway. She'd changed into a silky blue kimono, fixed her hair, put on a bit of make-up. And there was a faint aroma of perfume. 'I'll have that glass of wine now, if I may,' she said, 'always assuming you two have finished your little chat.'

'Near as damn it,' Rupert answered. 'I was just telling Gerry here how we'd very much like him to become the ambassador for our cause, the public persona of our private pressure group.'

Vee crossed the room to the window, drew the curtains shut. 'And what was Gerry's answer?'

'I think Gerry will need a day or so to think about it,' said Rupert.

Gerald emptied his glass, placed it on the table beside him and turned slowly towards Vee's smile, bewitched by that endearing front tooth; upper right six, he'd checked. And, for the second time in his life, he sensed cosmic forces at work; the same process of symmetry which had implanted a self-confident man of conviction into the placid body of Gerald Arthur Cornfield just a few weeks earlier.

'It's exactly the sort of challenge I'm looking for,' he heard himself say. 'When do we start?'

Vee kissed him gently on the cheek. 'Soon, Gerry,' she whispered. 'Very soon.'

Chapter Fourteen

It was a great deal of money, the best part of one hundred thousand pounds, but E.W. was insistent; advertising would produce first hand evidence, detailed case histories, a tally of valid complaints to get their new campaign underway. Full page advertisements duly appeared in three different national newspapers the following Monday morning.

By Thursday it seemed clear they'd underestimated both the power of advertising and the mood of the nation. The first flood of replies swamped the reception area then spilled over into the boardroom; testimony to the failure of essential services, detailed accounts of incompetence, negligence, and broken promises, with the blame laid, more often than not, at the door of number 10 Downing Street.

But the torrent of mail was exactly what they wanted – needed. While government departments spewed forth bogus statistics to support their claims of delivering on promises and expectations, evidence of abject failure now lay in neat little bundles on the plushy, white carpets of Safe Street's penthouse offices.

To Gerald's way of thinking, government talk of "delivering" health care, education, law and order, and all the rest of it, conjured up a vision of white vans from Whitehall, speeding across the nation's highways to drop things off, to order, at everyone's front door. And, anyway, the word they were looking for wasn't "delivering" but "providing", only "providing" wasn't always what they actually did and the posturing of devious politicians couldn't change that shameful fact.

Mrs Black's blood pressure tested her Ramipril tablets to the limit over the following weeks as she opened a steady stream of letters, each envelope another sachet of despair from a disillusioned nation. She read them all, often out loud, like criminal indictments in a court of law. A national disgrace, she called them with a solemn, judgemental nod of the head; outrageous, inhuman, beyond belief.

E.W. spent an entire day selecting the most outrageous and inhuman stories for a press conference where their authors took centre stage to paint a picture of government incompetence on a grand scale; tales of hospital beds in corridors, geriatric patients in cupboards, immigrant invasions of inner cities, violence in suburban streets, entire neighbourhoods in fear, and a police force in denial. But then, beyond belief, first-hand accounts of anarchy in the classroom, school leavers incapable of reading, an education system in disarray.

Gerald Cornfield gripped the sides of the lectern, leaned very slightly back, eyes focused on the banner draped across the far wall of the room. *England Expects*, it said in big black letters on a background of blue and white squares, with red and yellow lines and crosses. And then, underneath in smaller letters *The Elders*.

He cleared his throat, scowled, and ran through the damning evidence of government deficiencies. It was a totally new experience; so many cameras and lights, rows of seated reporters, notebooks and pens at the ready, nothing like the local press party which had launched Safe Streets. But then this was about national government and the way it had let us all down, not some minor, local initiative to tackle neighbourhood crime.

The first question came from a tall, lean woman with spikey, blonde hair and an impatient smile. She stabbed at the air with a pen, pointing towards the banner on the wall behind her. 'What's it mean?' she asked.

'It's the numeric flag code,' said Gerald. 'Nelson's signal from HMS *Victory*. England expects that every man will do his duty.'

'Bit cryptic, isn't it?' she said.

Gerald smiled politely. 'It was certainly clear enough two hundred years ago at the battle of Trafalgar.'

'And The Elders?' she shrugged. 'Who are they?'

'Page four,' Gerald waved a copy of the press statement in front of him. 'Last paragraph. A few like-minded people who believe our government has let us down.'

She glanced quickly at the statement on her lap. 'Another pressure group then. But what do you expect to achieve, in strictly practical terms?'

'We hope to see more positive government action to remedy the many failings we've highlighted for you today.'

'Amen to that,' she said, flipping through her notes. 'But hope isn't going to change government policy, is it?'

Gerald paused, glanced across the room to where Rupert stood by the open door, mobile phone clasped to his ear. The superior grin and the quick thumbs-up confirmed everything had gone to plan.

'Perhaps we can influence government policy in some small way,' Gerald continued with renewed confidence. 'Time will tell.' He needed no prompting, knew it by heart, but unfolded the sheet of notes from his inside pocket and laid it out on the lectern in front of him anyway. 'I can confirm that the planning laws, which have been so deliberately biased in favour of travellers by our Communities Secretary, have today inspired a group of travelling families to settle on some vacant land in the Wiltshire village of Merston Common. It's a Green Belt site, previously turned-down for residential housing, but that won't be an issue for travellers who must, in the words of the Communities Secretary, be treated differently. He may, therefore, be pleased to know that the field in question is just a few yards from the boundary of his own home so he'll be able to drop in for a cup of tea.'

'How come you know about it?' asked a reporter from a local TV station.

Gerald felt a flush of pleasure surge through his body but managed to hold back the smile that now struggled for freedom with the muscles of his face.

'We were pleased to act as matchmakers between our travelling friends and the field in question.'

A reporter called out from somewhere towards the back of the room. 'Does the Secretary of State know about it?'

Gerald shrugged. 'I've no idea. But I feel sure he'll welcome his new neighbours with open arms. He is, after all, the champion of travellers rights, the man who insists they should be treated differently from the rest of us.'

'Where did these travellers come from?' someone asked.

Gerald referred to his notes. 'Apparently they were relocated from private land to the north of the county where the locals are not entirely happy with the current legislation.'

'Legally evicted then?' A radio reporter in jeans and a T-shirt, emblazoned with the station's waveband, approached the lectern. He held his microphone at arm's length, close to Gerald's face.

'Relocated, by mutual consent,' Gerald repeated.

'No legal proceedings for repossession then?'

Gerald stared at the yellow, latex microphone head and reminded himself that his words were being recorded. 'Absolutely none,' he said emphatically. 'No need. It was all done in a spirit of mutual cooperation.'

But it was time to move on, the moment they'd scheduled to produce the list; two pages, filled with times and dates, one man's log of telephone calls to the police, each call totally ignored. A chronicle of wasted time, Gerald called it, a diary of despair, testimony to police indifference.

Copies of the list were quickly handed out while a white haired gentleman was helped to the lectern where he stood, uncertainly, waiting for Gerald to introduce him.

William "Sparky" Flint, a frail old man of seventy-eight with sad, sunken eyes, stared blankly at a confusing world. He touched his forehead with trembling fingers, searching through painful memories he'd tried so hard to forget. His voice quavered and faltered as he relived the terrors that dominated his nightmare world.

He'd been threatened, intimidated, and attacked by neighbourhood vandals for more than a year. They'd thrown bricks through his windows, set light to his dustbin, daubed paint on his front door and posted excreta through his letter box. Sometimes they urinated on his doorstep, smashed bottles on his front path or ripped planks from his tiny picket fence to throw at passing cars. But the police had visited him only once, when his cat was injured by an airgun pellet. A smashed windscreen and slashed tyres on his Vauxhall Viva warranted no more attention than a *Police Aware* sticker and a warning that the vehicle was a potential hazard, a danger to the general public.

"Sparky" hesitated, took a freshly-ironed handkerchief from the top pocket of his jacket and wiped his eye. 'Sometimes there were three of them, other times just the two,' he said quietly. 'But they just wouldn't leave me alone. The same thing, day after day, shouting and screaming, throwing anything they could get their hands on. It never stopped. Dead man walking, they called me, shouted it out at the top of their voices late at night, they did. I haven't had a proper night's sleep for a long time, one of the reasons I've got the trouble with my heart.'

The room fell silent while a distressed old man was helped to a chair, strategically place to the right of the lectern.

Gerald stared at him for a moment before he spoke, remembering the night he'd driven the VRU to Pendrake Close and witnessed, first hand, the savagery of a few mindless teenagers. 'It's an all too familiar story,' he said. 'A vulnerable man, failed by the police, abandoned by his neighbours, all of them seemingly too frightened to intervene. They all abdicated responsibility, turned a blind eye, while an innocent man suffered this torture for months on end.'

The yellow microphone quickly lunged forward. 'Have you reported these incidents to the police?'

'You've heard how Mr Flint phoned the police each and every time this sort of thing happened but they simply failed to respond. Do you seriously believe they'd show any interest in the retrospective details?'

'So you haven't actually done anything?'

'I didn't say that.' Gerald stiffened, gripped the sides of the lectern still tighter. 'There have been no attacks on Mr Flint for more than a week and we don't anticipate any reoccurrence of the previous behaviour,' he said flatly.

'How can you be so sure?'

Gerald stared straight ahead and, for a fleeting moment, felt an uncontrollable urge to describe, in graphic detail, how three young thugs had each changed their perspective after being wired-up to a twelve volt car battery in a shed near Dorking. But he managed to resist the temptation; too much information and contrary to the planned media strategy. Instead, he announced that the perpetrators had seen the error of their ways and promised to make amends for their behaviour towards Mr Flint.

A striped-suited newspaper reporter in the front row shook his head in disbelief. 'Make amends?' he repeated. 'How?'

'Picking up litter, cleaning windows, painting fences, mowing lawns, that sort of thing,' said Gerald. 'Manual tasks to help repair the damage they've caused.'

The reporter tugged at the cuffs of his jacket, frowned. 'And you seriously think they'll do all that?'

'They've already started.' Gerald's face creased into a smug smile. 'It came as a bit of a shock to everyone,' he said with delicious irony.

He waved away calls to explain what he meant by the cryptic comment and launched into a diversionary attack on the Home Secretary; a man he blamed for the collapse of law and order, who'd made an absolute mockery of Britain's justice system.

'The Minister lives in a cocoon of high security where crime exists only as a set of remote statistics, diluted for human consumption,' he yelled, hoping he'd successfully changed the subject. 'Perhaps he'd have more consideration for people like "Sparky" if his own home had ever been vandalised.'

It was a question that resonated with the media during the next few days when news of a paint bomb attack on the minister's constituency home dominated the headlines. Red, white and blue emulsion trickled down the front of the house in a unique display of patriotic vandalism, emblazoned across the front pages.

Close neighbours reported hearing motorbikes in the early hours of Sunday morning while an eyewitness talked about a barrage of paint-filled missiles bombarding the house. Rumours that a series of volleys from paint guns were aimed directly at security officers were still unconfirmed the day the police invited Mr Cornfield to help them with their enquiries at Pixley Green police station.

'Who's going to win the Derby then?' Detective Sergeant Anderson asked him.

Gerald looked puzzled. 'I've absolutely no idea. Why?'

'I'll ask the questions if it's all the same with you.' The detective sergeant sipped his tea as he slowly turned the pages of his notebook. 'Perhaps horse racing's not your subject. I can understand that, sport of kings etcetera, so I'll ask you who's going to win the FA cup?'

Gerald's eyes narrowed. 'Is this some kind of a joke?'

'I'll take that as another no then, shall I?' D.S. Anderson slapped his notebook shut and folded his arms. 'Would I be right in saying you don't have any special powers to predict the future.'

'None that I know of,' Gerald answered, sensing what was coming next.

'Not a clairvoyant then?'

'I've never said I was.'

D.S. Anderson had the self-satisfied look of a chess player about to call checkmate. 'Then how did you know the Home Secretary's house was going to be daubed with paint?'

'I didn't,' said Gerald. 'I simply said that he might have more consideration for other victims if his own home had ever been vandalised.'

'And as if by magic, bugger me, that's exactly what happened. Now wasn't that a coincidence?'

'I suppose so.' Gerald forced a weak smile. 'What can I say?'

'You can say, for the benefit of the tape, that you organised the paint ball attack on the minister's constituency home.'

Gerald shrugged his shoulders, sighed. 'But that would be a lie. I didn't.'

It was at this pivotal moment in his questioning that D.S. Anderson's whole demeanour suddenly changed and became more brusque, his words clipped and spoken through tight lips. He wasn't a happy man, and said so half a dozen times during the next hour. There were less than subtle hints that the assailants had been captured on CCTV and vague talk about witnesses being able to identify at least one of them. He took obvious pride in emphasising that *anyone* involved in a wanton act of vandalism against the property of a government minister would be pursued and brought to justice.

'I've been wondering,' Gerald said quietly, after he'd finished. 'Would ordinary people have been moved to such desperate measures if the police had shown the same concern for the property of an elderly pensioner?'

'It was a reprisal then?'

'I couldn't possibly comment, but it seems like poetic justice.'

The D.S. nodded. 'You think so, do you? Well I can tell you that the law calls it criminal damage, and that gets you a custodial sentence.'

'Do you intend to charge me?' Gerald asked him, with a quick glance at his watch. 'It's just that I have a business to run and I've been here for just over two hours.'

Detective Sergeant Anderson rose slowly to his feet. 'You're free to go,' he said. 'But don't go too far. I'll probably want to see you again.'

The afternoon sun dazzled and danced on the pond as Mr Cornfield crossed the common towards Lovelace Farm House and the hastily convened debriefing meeting with E.W. He paused for a moment, close to where a small boy crouched in the reeds, examining the contents of a fishing net. A couple of Aylesbury ducks thrashed across the surface of the water towards the safety of the willows on the opposite bank as he approached.

'Catch anything?' said Gerald.

The boy looked up, solemnly shook his head. 'There used to be newts but they've gone.'

'Wrong time of year, perhaps.'

'Most likely they're all dead,' the boy said bluntly. 'Things eat them.'

'Surely some of them survive, don't they?'

The boy thought about it, rubbed his eye with wet fingers. 'No, I think they all die... and then new ones get born instead.'

Gerald nodded. 'Perhaps you're right. You can never tell with newts, wouldn't you say?'

But the boy now chasing butterflies in the long grass beyond the pond was too busy to hear.

Natural childhood curiosity, Gerald wondered, or maybe a glimpse of something altogether more sinister. He wasn't at all sure. Could a child's pursuit of the small and defenceless be a precursor to the teenage abuse of the old and defenceless? The thought dawdled across his mind and remained there for the rest of the day.

The mood at Lovelace Farm House was buoyant; E.W. noticeably smug and triumphant, Rupert Clark-Hall's innate arrogance shining through a very thin veneer of false modesty, Katrina Bevington in a state of mild euphoria about ministers getting their *"cumeuppance"*, and Eddie Bates, uncharacteristically quiet, reading the morning papers near the open French doors.

'No charges then?' E.W. snorted.

'No bloody evidence.' Rupert wrapped his arm around Gerald's shoulder, squeezed. 'This is an innocent man if ever I saw one.'

'Not entirely,' Gerald sighed. 'I think you'll find I'm what they call an accessory after the fact. Or maybe it's *before* the fact? I'm not altogether sure.'

'You're neither.' Katrina handed him a glass of lemon tea in a silver holder, gestured toward a plate of assorted cakes and biscuits. 'Drawing attention to ministerial shortcomings isn't a crime. And you can't be blamed for the subsequent actions of others.'

'Incitement to violence.' Eddie Bates looked up from his newspaper, nodded solemnly. 'They can do you for incitement to almost anything these days. You don't have to actually *do* anything illegal, you just have to *talk* about it.'

Gerald sipped his tea and cast his mind back to the police interview. 'Detective Sergeant Anderson said it was criminal damage.'

'Criminal damage?' said Rupert. 'Paint Bombs?' The words exploded from him like blasts from a double barrel shotgun. 'Nothing more than a bit of harmless fun. And directing homeless travellers to a vacant field? That's surely a social obligation, enshrined in some daft-arsed human rights legislation.'

'The police said they've got CCTV footage, even made some positive identifications,' said Gerald.

Katrina flopped down into one of the fireside chairs. 'That's total bollocks,' she said. 'Everyone wore pig masks so the only positive IDs will be for Pinky & Perky.'

Gerald smiled wryly, sat himself down in the chair opposite. 'Too much information,' he whispered. 'Probably best all round if I don't know all the gory details.'

'That's bollocks too.' She hunched forward, looked him straight in the eye. 'OK, so you're the good guy in the white suit, wearing the innocent smile, making all the public announcements, while Rupert's lot do the dirty deeds. But we're all in this together.'

Gerald reached for a digestive biscuit, dunked it in his tea and settled back in the chair. 'But we mustn't let the facts blur the facade. If I'm to be the acceptable face of passive criticism and concern, it's important that I'm not suspected of complicity in any subsequent violence.'

'Wrong,' she said flatly. 'It's important for them to suspect your involvement providing they can never prove it. That's the route to respect.'

E.W. hovered behind Katrina's chair, placed his right hand affectionately on her shoulder like a guardian angel. 'Why do you suppose Sinn Fein and the IRA were such a successful double act?' Katrina covered his hand with hers. 'You see the point I'm trying to make Gerald,' she said. 'Tacit complicity, that's the key to it all.'

'A bit like that international investment guru chap,' Eddie chimed in from across the room. 'Foreign sounding name... always predicting the imminent collapse of some country or another's currency... then seems to make a fortune when it does. All the financial whizz kids listen to him because they secretly believe he's to blame.'

Katrina screwed-up her face. 'I think I prefer the Sinn Fein simile,' she said. 'The Elders should be seen as the political wing of a covert army, nothing to do with financial gain.'

'Steady on woman,' said Rupert, sounding suddenly anxious. 'Don't let's lose sight of the economic realities. We need money, and that means financial support from elsewhere.'

Eddie Bates folded his newspaper, slapped it down on the table. 'Way of the world,' he said. 'Big business backs the Tories, trade unions bankroll the Labour party, and some well-wisher who should get out more, bungs a few quid to the Lib Dems from time to time. Fact is political parties are *all* sponsored by vested interests.'

'People with compatible philosophical perspectives,' E.W. corrected. 'The support we want comes from individuals and organisations who share our aims and objectives but who don't try to dictate the agenda.'

Gerald nodded impatiently. 'I hear what you're saying,' he snapped. 'But can we get back to the original point? Look, I don't have a problem standing-up in public, pointing the finger at government disasters, and exposing their long list of cock-ups, U-turns, and downright bloody lies. I'll be pleased to state the case for change from now until doomsday, and when Rupert's lot kicks-off somewhere, lobbing paint bombs or moving travellers into someone else's front garden, I'll flatly deny any involvement whatsoever. My problem is how can I possibly tell the police I know nothing about it... but I know a man who does?'

'Alibis,' E.W. grunted. He took a long sip of his lemon tea and stared out across the garden. 'The barrier between suspicion and proof.'

Rupert spelled it out. 'They'll all make the link between what *you* say publicly and what *we* do covertly but, with cast iron alibis, the police can't prove a thing.'

'And here's the nub of it guys.' Katrina wagged her finger importantly and waited until she had everyone's attention. 'As Gerald will be the only point of contact between the police and an aggressive but elusive enemy, putting him behind bars would be counterproductive.'

A sudden shiver trembled though Gerald's body as the words tripped lightly from her lips. 'Am I supposed to be reassured by that?' he said.

Katrina stared back with indifference. 'Certainly not. Chances are you could be detained under anti-terrorism legislation, imprisoned for an indefinite term, without trial, and never heard of again.'

'She's joking,' Rupert cut in quickly. 'Don't let her wind you up.'

Katrina's expression softened into one of her alluring smiles. 'Of course I'm joking,' she cooed. 'Didn't I just say it? Putting Gerald behind bars would be counterproductive?'

Gerald tried to return the smile but his face refused to cooperate.

Chapter Fifteen

Maybe it hadn't been conducted with quite the precision and credibility of Messrs Gallup or MORI but E.W.'s survey of the over sixty-fives was complete. And the results were conclusive.

One hundred thousand men and women ticked the *"Yes"* box next to the first question; *Do you think Britain's pensioners deserve a better deal?*

But in an inspired polling adaptation designed, he said, to accelerate and enhance the democratic process, E.W. and his team had limited their research to just two thousand people. This number was then "reconciled and elevated on a predictive basis" by the results of question two, which asked; *How many of your friends and relatives beyond retirement age would be likely to agree with you?* Nearly everyone had ticked the *"Up to 50"* box in preference to the other two options... *"Up to 100"* and *"More than 100"*.

So, allowing for a three per cent margin of error and following seasonal adjustment, [mature adults being less cooperative during inclement weather] it was clear that there would be close to unanimous support for a pensioners' declaration from "The Elders".

The official document, which was printed on expensive-looking, hand torn paper, enshrined five democratic innovations. The first underpinned the accepted social philosophy that the worth of the servant is equal to that of the master. And since members of parliament continually reminded us that they were the servants of the public, it followed that the public should enjoy the same level of state pension as their constituency MP.

Two further edicts dealt with the introduction of zero tax levels for workers of pensionable age and the creation of a mobile medical service, dispatching dedicated GPs to the doorstep, eliminating long waits in crowded surgeries, and reducing the spread of infection.

There were the usual demands for tighter immigration control, but the icing on the cake was E.W.'s "Elderpreneur Lottery", a national draw with big cash prizes, staged in conjunction with the

Post Office. And the good news was that it would cost nothing to run; not a penny.

E.W. produced a £5 postal order from his wallet and leaned it up against the bottle of Perrier water on Mr Cornfield's boardroom table. 'I want you to pay careful attention to the miracle about to take place before your very eyes,' he announced in his most commanding voice. 'You will bear witness to the transformation of this common or garden postal order into a lottery ticket with its own, unique, twenty digit serial number.' He waved a blue felt-tip pen around it two or three times, stood back, and waited for reactions from his audience of two.

Mrs Black reached for her glasses, shuffled her chair closer to the table, deftly avoiding Winston's stubby tail. 'Nothing's changed,' she said. 'Still looks like a postal order to me.'

'And so it is,' E.W. declared flatly. 'Not a damn thing has changed. And that's the beauty of it.'

Gerald looked mystified. 'Sorry, but what's the beauty of it?'

'A lottery ticket which costs us nothing to produce but which will be instantly available, over the counter, at post offices throughout the country. Printed and distributed by HMG.'

'But it's still a postal order,' said Gerald.

'Not when people send one to us, it isn't,' E.W. snapped back with more than a hint of irritation. 'Then it's a lottery ticket. We'll simply announce the winning ticket in our weekly draw, people will check the twenty digit reference number on their post office receipt and, voila, someone, somewhere, will be a lottery winner.'

Mrs Black shook her head disapprovingly. 'Sounds illegal to me.'

'I'm indebted to you for your legal advice,' E.W. answered with more than a hint of sarcasm, 'but it might be best if you concentrated on taking the minutes of the meeting.'

'*Is* it legal?' Gerald asked. 'I mean, have you checked?'

But E.W. was in no mood for a debate. Hadn't he already polled the views of pensioners, drafted a declaration for a better deal, and invented a zero cost, fund-raising lottery to finance his plans all in the space of a few days? Dammit, this was a time for action, not nit-picking and arguing about legalities.

There was a brief period of total silence before Mrs Black rose suddenly from her chair, grabbed Winston by the collar and ushered him from the room, in the way a protective mother leads a child from impending danger. She closed the door behind her with some mumbled protests about vice rings and gambling syndicates, and how she had better things to do with her time.

E.W. took a handkerchief from his pocket and stood, awkwardly, brushing dog hairs from his trouser leg. 'I really don't know why you put up with that woman or that ridiculous animal.'

'Because I like them, I like them a lot. They put the world into perspective,' Gerald answered with a conviction that surprised even him. 'Mrs Black is a past master at puncturing over-inflated egos while Winston refuses to allow people to take themselves too seriously in the first place.'

A faint, acid smile flicked across E.W.'s face. 'If you say so,' he said, raising his eyebrows in an unspoken question. 'Your personal relationships with sheepdogs and secretaries are no concern of mine.'

'Then we should move on,' Gerald said with a polite nod. 'I assume you have plans for your declaration.'

'Of course.' E.W. blinked solemnly, checked the phantom holster. 'Declarations must be declared or they remain just a load of meaningless words on paper.'

Gerald turned to face him, chin slightly raised. 'And I'm to do the honours, I assume?'

'Who else? You're our spokesman.'

'When and where?'

'Can't give you a *when* just yet but Downing Street's definitely the *where*.'

Gerald stared at him, bemused. 'Downing Street? That's a bit over the top, isn't it?'

'Why? The declaration's intended for the prime minister and the prime minister lives in Downing Street.' E.W. paused for a moment, turned towards the door. 'That animal... Winston. English sheepdog isn't it?'

'*Old* English sheepdog.'

'An *old* English sheepdog called Winston.' E.W. pondered the thought. 'Could be an ideal mascot for a visit to number ten.'

Gerald smiled. 'I'm afraid Mrs Black looks after Winston's diary. Perhaps you should have a word with her before you leave.'

E.W. leaned back in his chair and shook his head. 'Think I'll leave it to you, old chap,' he said, tapping a little military beat on the table with the tip of his pencil. 'England expects. England expects.'

Gerald watched from the fourth floor window as E.W. stepped into the waiting Alvis convertible and was driven swiftly away.

'Apparently it *would* be legal.' The pronouncement came from Mrs Black as she cleared the boardroom table. 'I checked with the post office people. Nothing to stop anyone using a postal order to fund a bet, they said.'

'What about running a lottery? I wouldn't mind betting you need some kind of a licence for that.'

Mrs Black shrugged, fed a left-over chocolate biscuit to Winston.

'He's going to look like an old English *pig* dog if you keep feeding him like that,' Gerald said. Then, after a brief pause and seemingly as nothing more than an afterthought; 'I wonder if I might borrow him for an hour or two one day soon?'

'Borrow him?' Mrs Black sounded only mildly surprised. 'Why on earth would you want to do that?'

'E.W. thinks Winston would make a perfect mascot when we deliver the declaration to Downing Street.'

Mrs Black searched Gerald's face for signs of guilt but, having satisfied herself that there were none, agreed to Winston's secondment to Downing Street, with one important proviso; she would accompany him.

And the Downing Street issue wasn't raised again until the final briefing, three weeks later, when E.W. announced that whether or not Mrs Black came along was irrelevant as he expected more than two hundred people to accompany Winston on his historic march to number ten... which would be after the rally in Trafalgar Square.

Gerald instinctively disliked the idea of *marches* and *rallies*. The tired format of mindless protest, he called it. No more than an organised day out for people with too much time on their hands and too few thoughts in their heads. Besides, two hundred people marching down Whitehall would be insignificant, compared with the hundred thousand E.W. claimed in his survey, so no point.

But, in a democratic show of hands, Gerald was out-voted and a wet and windy afternoon, the following Sunday, found him unceremoniously, and somewhat precariously, standing on an upturned plastic crate addressing a small group of supporters. You couldn't really call it a crowd, probably less than the two hundred E.W. had promised, but they gathered in an orderly fashion and with obvious enthusiasm on the south side of the square, in the shadow of Nelson's Column, facing down Whitehall.

"Sparky" Flint, pride of place near the front, sat perfectly still in a wheelchair, a sheet of white card on his lap, the words *Fair Play for Pensioners* printed in black. Behind him, a sea of black and white placards, carried aloft by a disparate band of elderly men and women with umbrellas, most of them looking far too cheerful for a serious demonstration. Close by, megaphone at the ready, Major Edgar William Bevington wore a suitably solemn expression as he chatted with press reporters, while his wife pressed leaflets into the hands of passers-by.

Gerald read aloud the important bits from the leather-bound declaration while Katrina orchestrated a gamut of cheering and applause, and then they were off, in the direction of Parliament Square, led by Winston, [accompanied by Mrs Black], on the short but very vocal march to the gates of Downing Street.

'What do we want? Fair play. When do we want it? Now.'

The clichéd chant was something Gerald had hoped to avoid. Apart from sounding like the demands of a petulant child, it had always struck him as totally selfish and lacking any semblance of compromise. But still it came, resounding across Whitehall's Portland stone facades, assaulting the silent dignity of the Cenotaph, steadfastly ignored by a pair of mounted guards from the household cavalry, unmoved and unimpressed by the passing rabble.

This was it, the foundation of the civilised world, democracy in action, public opinion on the march, escorted by a handful of tolerant but patently disinterested police officers.

'What do we want? Fair play. When do with want it? Now.'

The chanting had become more jaded, less heartfelt, by the time they reached Downing Street but the focus was now on Winston who barked excitedly as press photographers moved in for a series of close ups. Mrs Black was politely moved to one side and Winston took centre stage, carefully positioned for pictures between Gerald and "Sparky" Flint's wheelchair.

'Arms round the dog'… 'heads closer together'… 'big smiles…'

The photographers shouted their instructions to a background of tooting horns and bellowed witticisms from passing motorists.

'That the new member for Barking then?'... *'Godda bone to pick with the PM mate?'...* *'Country's going to the bleedin' dogs.'*

There was a security check by armed policemen at the gates to Downing Street before Gerald and Winston [accompanied by Mrs Black] were escorted to the door of number ten where someone accepted the declaration and went quickly back inside without a word. It was all a bit of an anticlimax.

They returned to the group as the last of the photographers disappeared into the crowds of tourists and a sudden and unnatural quiet descended. The chanting gave way to bursts of embarrassed giggling and self-conscious chatter as the previous sense of purpose seemed to drift away with the rain clouds on the afternoon breeze.

The group gradually dispersed, made towards underground stations and parked cars, promised each other they'd stay in touch and spread the word to relatives and friends.

Winston settled down in the back of E.W.'s Alvis, sandwiched between Gerald and Mrs Black, lolling from one to the other as the car accelerated around Parliament Square, down towards Millbank and on to Chelsea Bridge, Katrina at the wheel, E.W. a catnapping passenger beside her.

'Was it worth it?' Gerald asked nobody in particular. 'I mean, did today make one iota of difference to anyone?'

Katrina glanced back at him through the rear view mirror. 'But of course it did,' she said with a resolute slap of the steering wheel. 'For goodness sake, didn't we present the prime minister with the detailed demands of one hundred thousand over sixty-fives?'

'Oh please,' Gerald groaned. 'E.W. asked two thousand pensioners if they wanted a better deal and made-up the rest over a cup of coffee.'

She shrugged her shoulders. 'Same difference. It's exactly what pensioners need... what they deserve. And it's time the government did something about it.'

'I'll tell you what they'll do about it,' Gerald said. 'Sod all. They'll totally ignore us,'

Katrina nodded. 'I'm afraid that *does* seem to be the most likely outcome.'

'So what was the *point* of today's little charade?'

'First the word, then the deed,' she said enigmatically.

Gerald sighed. 'Which, in plain English, means what?'

E.W. half turned his head towards the back seat and spoke in a hushed voice. 'If they ignore our polite request, we'll demonstrate that actions sometimes speak louder than words.'

'And what could you possibly do?' Gerald sniggered. 'Paintball number ten? Set up a travellers' camp in the gardens at Chequers?'

E.W. looked at his watch, smiled, but said nothing.

'I'd also like to know the answer to that, if you wouldn't mind,' Mrs Black cut in.

'All things being equal,' Katrina said, sliding a Debussy CD into the player, 'we've probably already done it.'

Gerald gripped the back of her seat, drew himself forward. 'Done what?'

'Borrowed someone of importance.'

'How do you mean, *borrowed*?'

Katrina opened the car window, took a deep breath. 'Borrowed as in kidnapped,' she said.

Their eyes met in the rear view mirror. 'A top member of the cabinet no doubt?' Gerald asked, confident that she was probably joking.

She shook her head. 'Not possible. Security's too tight.'

'Look, I'm sure you already know this,' Gerald said with a hint of irritation, 'but the British government has a long-standing policy on this sort of thing. It is, quite simply, that they *never* negotiate or yield to the demands of kidnappers – not *ever*? And there are no exceptions to the rule.'

Katrina nodded. 'That's because kidnapped victims aren't usually members of their own family. But I wonder if they'd be more inclined to negotiate if the prime minister's father had been taken.'

Mrs Black wrapped a protective arm around Winston's shoulder and drew him closer.

'Are you serious?' Gerald sank back into the deep leather seat, hands covering his face. 'Kidnap the prime minister's dad? He's probably a frail old man. What if he dies?'

E.W.'s head jerked back. 'Not so very old, actually. Early seventies perhaps and fighting fit.'

A wave of panic surged through Gerald's body like an electric shock. 'The trauma alone could kill him,' he said, struggling to loosen his shirt collar, tugging at his tie. 'He might have angina, blood pressure... all sorts of terrible things... diabetes, maybe, and god knows what else. Suppose he's got glaucoma, arthritis... I don't know... haemorrhoids... all that sort of stuff? He'd need medication.'

E.W. dismissed Gerald's concerns with a nonchalant flick of the wrist. 'All taken care of, old chap.'

'Asthma can be fatal too.' Mrs Black clasped her inhaler to her mouth, took two puffs in quick succession. 'Even for people who don't usually have it.'

Katrina rolled her eyes. 'He suffers from nothing more serious than a hiatus hernia... that and a weak bladder, neither of which are life threatening.'

A knot which had formed in the centre of Gerald's stomach began to tighten. 'How can you be so bloody sure?'

'Medical records.'

'You've checked his records?'

'Dr Blythe checked his records.' Katrina turned, stared at him across her shoulder. 'What difference does it make?'

Mrs Black clasped her hand to her throat. 'If you don't keep your eyes on the road, we'll have an accident,' she said through clenched teeth.

Katrina tightened her grip on the steering wheel, accelerated up to the car in front, braked suddenly, lurching her passengers forward.

'That was a bit bloody stupid,' Gerald snapped. 'Haven't we got enough problems without you crashing the car?'

She took her hands from the wheel, ran them slowly through her hair. 'Back seat drivers irritate me... always have done.'

'And childish idiots have much the same effect on me, so grow-up or stop the car and I'll get out.'

'That goes for me too,' Mrs Black said. 'You're behaving like a fifteen year old schoolgirl.'

'Enough.' E.W. slapped his hand on the dashboard. 'If you could all stop the barracking for a moment, we've got work to do.'

Gerald stiffened. 'I've just done my bit. And it didn't involve kidnapping anyone.'

'You did your bit very well, if I may say so... magnificent, an example to us all.' E.W. paused, as if to let this rare compliment linger a while between them. 'But may I now crave your indulgence and cooperation for the next bit... the tricky bit.'

'Keeping our cool while the police go ballistic,' Katrina chimed-in. 'The plod will try to cover their arses by making early arrests. And that inevitably means you Gerald.'

'Me? But a couple of hundred witnesses and half a dozen press photographers can prove I was in Downing Street all afternoon.'

'Which is a very credible alibi,' said E.W. 'So while they may assume you're involved, they'll have great difficulty proving it.'

'Because he bloody well *wasn't* involved,' Mrs Black yelled back, unable to control her anger. 'And I'll stand up and say so if I have to.'

Gerald gently squeezed her hand. 'Much appreciated,' he whispered. 'But I'm sure it won't come to that.'

E.W. interrupted with a loud harrumph. 'Our problem, or should I call it our opportunity, is that our ransom demands have a marked similarity to today's declaration.'

'I think you should definitely call it our *problem*,' Gerald retorted. 'No doubt they're identical.'

E.W. nodded, settled back in his seat and closed his eyes.

Katrina giggled. 'He could sleep pushing a supermarket trolley.'

'But then, unlike me, *he* won't be facing kidnap charges,' said Gerald.

'Just remember what I told you before,' said Katrina earnestly. 'It's important for them to suspect your involvement but essential they can't prove it. That's the route to respect.'

They dropped off Mrs Black soon after four and waited while Winston charged ahead of her up the garden path towards the open front door. She gave a little wave without looking back.

Gerald pictured squad cars blocking the road as they turned the corner into Friday Street a few minutes later, but there were none. Everything wonderfully normal for a Sunday afternoon; the new people at the chalet bungalow mowing their front lawn, someone washing their car, two women in deep conversation, on their way to the park with a small dog.

'I suppose it'll be on the news,' Gerald said as he stepped out of the Alvis. 'The kidnapping, I mean.'

Katrina shrugged. 'Depends if or when they announce it.'
Gerald turned, nodded thoughtfully. 'I suppose so, yes.'

'Well done that man.' E.W. leaned across the front seat, arm resting on Katrina's shoulder. 'First class effort. Carry on.'

'And don't forget,' Katrina said with one of her saucy winks, 'you know nothing about any kidnapping, nothing at all.'

Gerald stood, hands in pockets, at the kerbside as they drove off, feeling suddenly alone and vulnerable. He smiled ruefully, shook his head, and wondered what Betsy would have made of it all.

Chapter Sixteen

Pins and needles in his left arm woke Mr Cornfield at six fifteen the following morning, but as the reality of the previous day flooded back into his consciousness, a sudden pang of fear and trepidation trembled through the very core of his being.

He lay perfectly still watching the early morning light creep silently across the ceiling and prayed for the wisdom and courage to deal with whatever this day might bring.

The radio alarm scattered his thoughts at exactly six thirty with a brief summary of the news; no mention of the prime minister or his father, nothing about kidnappings, not even a reference to pensioners in Downing Street.

Gerald swung his legs to the floor and stared at his reflection in the wardrobe mirror. He certainly didn't look like a criminal but, somewhere deep inside, he felt like one. Wouldn't an innocent, honest man call the police, tell them everything he knew? He rejected the notion in a moment. This was nothing to do with crime and kidnapping, it was about positive negotiation on behalf of the nation's pensioners. And, besides, nobody would be harmed in any way so there'd be no crime to answer... would there?

The banner headline in the morning newspaper was something to do with rising oil prices and, to the right of the main story, the picture of a blonde. Mr Cornfield fancied he recognised the face; an actress perhaps, or was she that singer? He quickly flipped through the rest of the paper but stopped, abruptly, on page eight and the picture of Winston, "Sparky" Flint on one side, he on the other. The caption said pensioners had marched to Downing Street. It mentioned Gerald by name, but didn't really go into too much detail about the declaration.

Winston seemed to be smiling. He wasn't, of course; his mouth just went like that when he was panting. "Sparky", on the other hand, was definitely smiling, in marked contrast to Gerald's own sombre expression.

Po-faced, that's what Eddie Bates would call it. 'Cheer up mate, it might never happen,' he'd say. But it *had* happened. Even if it wasn't yet on the news or in the papers, it *had* happened.

Or had it? Maybe they'd bungled it, been arrested. Perhaps they were still being questioned. Possibly they'd called it all off at the very last moment.

The phone call to Rupert Clark-Hall was brief, the conversation guarded.

Gerald spoke tight-lipped and quietly. 'Everything OK?'

'Fine thanks.'

'No cause for concern then?'

'No.'

'I'm in the Daily Express this morning.'

'You're also in the Mail, Times, Telegraph and Sun.'

'My goodness. Excellent. [pause] So no problems?'

'None I can think of. Must dash. Bye.'

The telephone clicked and went dead but rang out again the moment Gerald replaced the receiver. The voice was unfamiliar, a man. He sounded elderly.

'Would I be talking to Mr Gerald Cornfield?'

'Yes. Who's that?'

'Oh, nobody of importance. We've just read about your campaign in today's Sun.' He hesitated, cleared his throat. 'I do hope this isn't an inconvenient moment? Only I can always call you back some other time.'

'What can I do for you?' Gerald said, stifling his impatience.

'We just wanted to say well done, so to speak. Fair play for pensioners and so on... you can rely on our full support... my wife and I, that is.'

'Very kind. Thank you.'

'Not at all... it's *us* who should thank *you* for trying to do something about it... wonderful.'

'I'm only a tiny part of a fast-expanding movement,' Gerald said at once, almost without thinking. 'Pensioners deserve a fair deal and we'll do whatever it takes to get it for them.'

The words rang in his ears as he put the phone down. *"Whatever it takes."* ... so wonderfully unambiguous, unwavering. It was a total commitment to success, single mindedness personified, no half measures, a guarantee to get there at all costs, fair means or foul. And if the prime minister's dad had to be slightly inconvenienced in the process, then foul means before fair.

There were two more calls, in quick succession, both complimenting him on the Downing Street declaration, each pledging their support for the cause. It was all very flattering, of course, a welcome boost for a flagging ego, but after two or three more calls, it was clear that he'd have to give some serious thought to going ex-directory.

At eight o'clock he set off for the office, buoyed by the messages of support and with a definite spring in his step, pausing only to acknowledge a few pats on the back from some of the regulars at the newsagent's shop where he'd picked-up a selection of morning newspapers.

The telephone was already ringing when he finally found the right key to open the office door. He immediately dropped the bag of newspapers and the keys on the reception desk, quickly stretched across and reached for the hands-free button.

'Safe Streets,' he gasped. 'Can I help you?'

'I called you at home but you weren't there.' Mrs Black sounded agitated, her voice uncharacteristically subdued.

'That's right, I came in early.'

'I think it might be best if I stayed at home today,' she announced flatly. 'Feeling a bit queasy... been up most of the night... probably something I ate.'

Gerald sympathised. 'Best to stay at home, take it easy.'

'I expect I'll be OK tomorrow,' she said, 'all things being equal.'

'Right. Fine. Hope to see you tomorrow then.'

He sat on the edge of the desk wondering if Mrs Black was genuinely sick or simply distancing herself from a potentially high-profile kidnapping. Perhaps a bit of both, he decided.

The fax machine juddered to life on the other side of the room, discharged a single sheet of paper, instantly recognisable as yet another blurb about discount car hire rates. They turned-up every day, first thing, and went straight into the waste bin with the rest of the junk mail from the morning post, but Crazy Cars, or whatever they called themselves, persisted, as if repetition and the passage of time might somehow make their special deals more appealing.

Gerald had settled himself at his desk, grumbling aloud about wasted paper and the cost of fax ribbons, when it occurred to him that somewhere in one of Downing Street's back offices, an overworked underling probably felt exactly the same way about his so-called declaration, and a mountain of other petitions, demands, and pleadings from a dissatisfied nation.

He pinned five press cuttings to the cork board on the wall behind him and refocused one of the spotlights above for maximum impact. *Pooch Power for Pensioners* screamed the largest of the headlines. *Dogged Determination of the Oldies*, said another. *Dog Leads Whitehall Walkies*, the most laboured, contrasting with The Daily Telegraph's straightforward *Over Sixties Deputation to Downing Street*.

Gerald's watch said it was only nine thirty but it felt as if it should be much later. He dialled the speaking clock. *"Nine, thirty-one, and forty seconds."*

But how many more seconds would tick by before someone somewhere finally said something, interrupted radio and TV programmes to announce the kidnapping, showed pictures of the prime minister's father before his capture, speculated on the captor's motives, talked about police suspects?

Internet search engines were still unfamiliar territory for Gerald Cornfield so when he Googled the word *Kidnapping*, half expecting a cascade of news bulletins, he was disappointed to find little more than a page or two about how to survive the ordeal. *"The common hostage responses of fear, denial, and withdrawal are all experienced in varying degrees. You may be blindfolded, drugged, handled roughly, or even stuffed in the trunk of a car. If conscious,"* it advised, *"follow your captor's instructions."*

Some of the internet material linked kidnapping with terrorism, talked about solitary confinement, ransom payments and the execution of hostages. But, worst of all, it seemed to imply that kidnapping was akin to murder.

"Nine, forty-two, and ten seconds."

Time for some answers. Gerald grabbed the telephone and rose, purposefully, to his feet, the veins in his left hand swelling as his grip tightened while he punched out E.W.'s number with a rigid index finger. A pompously annoying voice answered.

"Sorry. The person you have called is unavailable. Please call again later."

He slammed down the phone in a childish but entirely satisfying gesture, and sank back into his seat.

Googling the word *News* produced better results. It took him to the BBC's on line news service and a summary of the main stories of the day; a scandal in the French government, spy swaps between the US and Russia, fears over the future of the Euro, another high profile celebrity divorce. But no mention of a kidnapping.

A little after ten thirty the telephones started to ring; five or six business enquiries, some VAT information from the accountant, a sales pitch from a stationery supplier and a wrong number, followed by a call from Katrina Bevington.

'Sorry we weren't in when you rang,' she said. 'E.W.'s at a meeting with some of his cronies and I've only just got back from the hairdressers.'

'I just wondered what was happening,' Gerald said in a hushed voice.

'Well now then, let's see,' she chuckled. 'You and that shaggy dog are all over the morning papers, that's for sure.'

'Yes I saw the coverage,' Gerald said, trying to sound upbeat about it all. 'Really rather good, wasn't it? But I was thinking about another issue, the one we talked about yesterday.'

'Well you just stop thinking about other issues. You've quite enough to occupy your mind already.'

Gerald gripped the handset tighter, felt his anger rising. 'Listen to me Katrina. This is important. I want to know exactly what happened yesterday,' he demanded, the voice now louder than before. 'And I want to know now.'

'Goodness me, will you just listen to yourself,' she trilled, the Irish accent more marked than usual. 'Shouting the odds and behaving like a trackside bookie on Derby day. Calm yourself down, try to think beautiful thoughts, and join me for a little bite of lunch.'

'Lunch?'

'Twelve thirty, Casa Roma,' she said, then hung up.

He slumped back in his chair, trying to remember the code which would divert the office phones to the answering service. Star, twenty-one, then the number, followed by the hash key? It sounded right but he still couldn't remember the number.

A cursory glance through Mrs Black's card index system found it under P for Phones, just before P for Prime Minister which listed two Downing Street telephone numbers. There was another card, P for Police, with Detective Sergeant Anderson's contact details, including his mobile phone number.

Gerald thought about it on the way to the Casa Roma. Maybe the police had contacted the office the day they'd picked him up for questioning. Perhaps they'd left their details with Mrs Black.

In all the best crime thrillers, the Detective Sergeant hands the suspect his card with explicit instructions to call if he remembers anything important. But D.S. Anderson obviously didn't know that. He simply said; 'Don't go too far. I'll probably want to see you again.'

No doubt Mrs Black would be able to clear up the mystery. He'd make a note to talk to her about it when she was better.

Katrina Bevington swung round on her bar stool as Gerald entered the restaurant, a Champagne glass suspended, upside down, between her first and second fingers.

'Perfect timing,' she said, picking at the neckline of a scarlet summer dress. 'How is it you're always so incredibly punctual?'

'Good manners.' Gerald kissed her lightly on the cheek, rested his elbow on the bar. 'I've always thought it rather rude to keep people waiting.'

'Did you hear that barman? A glass of Champagne for my guest and the tiniest refill for me.'

Gerald cleared his throat and got straight to the point. 'Tell me exactly what happened yesterday afternoon,' he said quietly but firmly.

'Let me see now.' She fixed him with laughing eyes that said she wasn't going to be rushed. 'At approximately three forty-five, we borrowed the prime minister's daddy and took him for a drive.'

'And he's OK, no problems?'

'As far as I know.'

'But why nothing in the press?' He drew closer, spoke in a hushed voice. 'And no arrests?'

She gave him a playful shrug. 'Well now, I can't be sure but it might have something to do with the fact that we gave the prime minister's daddy back soon after midnight.'

Gerald stared at her wondering if this was a joke. 'How do you mean, gave him back?'

'I mean Rupert returned him ahead of schedule, sooner than we'd originally planned.' She signalled to the barman. 'Can we have that Champagne when you're ready?'

'Sorry, I don't understand.' Gerald stopped abruptly, waiting until the barman had poured the drinks. 'What was the point of that?'

She sipped her Champagne, ran the tip of her tongue around her lips. 'We proved we could do it, showed them we mean business, and delivered an ultimatum, all in the space of eight hours. That's impressive, don't you think?'

'But it can't have been that simple. How did you do it?'

'A couple of fellas, looking very much like police officers and driving something that looked very much like a squad car, apprehended him on his way home from the golf club and escorted him to The Shed.'

Gerald's face changed from anxious to angry in a split second. He took a deep breath and prepared to speak, but said nothing.

Katrina emptied her glass and glanced at the chalk board menu on the opposite wall. 'Afterwards, we dropped him off at West End Central police station, slap bang in the middle of Savile Row,' she said.

'In a squad car?'

She shook her head in disbelief. 'Now that would be just plain silly for goodness sake.'

Gerald's expression slipped from angry to exasperated.

'We used a motorbike,' she said in her softly reassuring voice. 'But it was long gone and lost in the London traffic before the prime minister's daddy had even reached the custody desk.'

'Nobody got the registration number?'

She shrugged. 'Wouldn't have made any difference. We borrowed the bike too.'

A waiter handed Gerald the menu, said something about the asparagus being fresh and waited, pen poised, to take their orders.

'I'm not very hungry,' Gerald said.

Katrina's long red finger nails tapped impatiently on the bar. 'I'll have grilled monkfish and a side salad.'

The waiter turned back to Gerald. 'Perhaps a little smoked salmon, sprinkled with some black pepper and lemon? Very light, very appetising.'

'He hates smoked salmon.' Eddie Bates leaned casually against a mock Roman pillar at the other end of the bar, a tea towel slung carelessly over his shoulder, a broad grin on his face, hands thrust into the pockets of a blue and white striped apron. 'That's right, isn't it mate? Too greasy, too fishy, too salty... too bleedin' everything.'

'Too expensive,' Gerald said. 'I eat only wild salmon, not the stuff they fill with antibiotics, so the price is usually a bit steep, that's all.'

The waiter interjected. 'We serve only Scottish wild salmon. Nothing farmed at the Casa Roma.'

'I know,' said Gerald. 'I've had smoked salmon here before.'

Katrina handed back the menus. 'Bring my guest a plate of Scottish wild smoked salmon and some thinly sliced brown bread,' she said, waving the waiter away.

'Lunch is on the house,' Eddie said as the waiter passed him. 'Mr Cornfield here is something of a celebrity.' He took a press cutting from his apron pocket, unfolded it, read aloud; *"It's high time Britain showed more respect for its elders, recognised the contribution they have already made to our society, and rewarded them with a fair and reasonable basic pension."* Great stuff, Gerald,' he said. 'Can't say I go much on the picture though. You look as if the dog has just farted.'

Katrina smiled a small, fierce smile which told Eddie Bates he wasn't wanted. 'I think we'll go to the table,' she said, rearranging the folds on the front of her dress. 'Gerald and I have things to discuss.'

'No playing footsie under the table,' Eddie quipped on his way back to the kitchen. 'E.W. will have my scallops for starters.'

Gerald laughed, genuinely amused. 'Let's have a beer at The Crow,' he called out. 'Make it soon.'

Eddie turned, made a phone with his finger and thumb. 'Give us a call.'

'I've never quite worked out what you two have in common,' Katrina said. 'You're a caring, sensitive man... he's the type who doesn't give a shit.'

'Takes all sort, don't they say?'

Katrina smiled. 'Spare me the clichés, please.'

'OK, put it this way,' Gerald said, avoiding eye contact. 'When your world comes crashing down around you, it's people like Eddie Bates who help you to build it back up again.'

Katrina's smile faltered. 'Shall we talk about something else?'

'That *is* why we're here, isn't it, to talk about *something else*?'

'OK. We sent the PM's daddy back some very clear demands,' she said, cuddling her bare arms as if there'd been a sudden fall in temperature. 'Immigration, street crime, health, pensions... it was all there, just like the declaration.'

Gerald took a bread stick, nodded. 'You said as much yesterday.'

'But I didn't mention the ultimatum.'

'Surely kidnapping the prime minister's father was a clear ultimatum? Do as we ask or you won't get him back.'

'No, that was a warning, proof that we could do it.'

'And the ultimatum? What was that?'

'We've demanded they demonstrate positive action towards meeting our agenda within the next four weeks.'

'Or what?' He stared at her, unmoving, waiting for the punchline. 'It all sounds very fine but what can you actually do?'

'We'll snatch members of the government,' she said, as if the idea had just occurred to her.

Gerald laughed out loud. 'No you won't. You won't get anywhere near them. They're protected twenty-four seven.'

She shook her head. 'Trust me, they're not.'

'Don't be so silly, they must be. You hear about it all the time.'

Katrina gently touched the sides of her mouth with a corner of her serviette. 'Listen to me,' she said, striking a more regal pose. 'I'm not talking about cabinet ministers. There are over three hundred *other* MPs on the government benches in the Commons, and a further two hundred lords and ladies in the upper house. Do you seriously think all five hundred or more have been assigned a security guard to monitor their every movement?'

'To be perfectly honest, I hadn't thought about it at all,' Gerald said, trying to conceal his mounting concern. 'But I bet Her Majesty's Government will now give it some very serious thought.'

The food arrived with a bottle of chilled Chablis but the mood at the table remained a few degrees colder – icy, in fact.

Chapter Seventeen

There were questions in the House.

The Leader of the Opposition shuffled some papers and leaned across the dispatch box. He felt sure the rest of the House would join him in asking the prime minister to convey his sincere good wishes to his father, following press reports of his recent ordeal.

And then came the question, his first question of the day.

Could the prime minister inform the House what measures were being taken by the police and security agencies to ensure that this sort of thing didn't happen again?

The prime minister thanked his honourable friend, and other members of the House, for their kind wishes and assured them that a full review of security arrangements, both inside and outside the Commons, was already underway. He would, of course, update the House on progress but was sure they'd understand that, in the best interests of parliamentary security, he would be unable to disclose sensitive information either now or in the future.

And that was that. Lobby correspondents probed for further details but were referred to the statement given to the House during prime minister's questions. Downing Street remained tight-lipped over the whole affair, prompting media speculation that the incident might have been a bungled attempt at hostage-taking by Islamic fundamentalists.

An official police statement confirmed they were treating the incident as a kidnapping and had ruled out terrorism. Their investigation was now focused on an undisclosed list of demands made by the alleged kidnappers but they were also pursuing other lines of enquiry. There was the usual stuff about making satisfactory progress and early arrests but nothing about anyone helping the police with their enquiries.

Gerald Cornfield was, if nothing else, a realist and was resigned to the probability that any "early arrests" would include his own.

You didn't need to be Hercule Poirot to spot the link between his well-publicised Downing Street declaration and demands made by kidnappers the very next day, yet the police seemed to have ignored it.

Rupert Clark-Hall's signet ring resonated on the rim of a half-full whisky glass, bringing the meeting to order. Members of the *Shadowy* Cabinet he called them as they settled in their chairs either side of a long, oak table; the type that might have graced a Mediaeval banquet in an altogether different time. But, for this evening at least, it was central to the baronial elegance of one of the neighbouring buildings to The Shed.

He stood, prince-like and perfectly still, at one end of the table while Dizzy passed around the evening's agenda; Vee Blythe, hands clasped modestly in her lap, to his right, Katrina Bevington, scribbling last minute notes, on his left. E.W. presided at the opposite end of the table, Gerald to one side of him, Eddie Bates to the other, with six of Rupert's key men seated in the middle each, it seemed, with half-filled glasses of whisky. Gerald recognised them at once from the raid on Pendrake Close. There was something about their pristine appearance; the crisp white shirts, navy blazers with gold, embossed buttons, sensible black, lace-up brogues, and the neatly parted hair. It gave them a look of schoolboy innocence at the start of a new term.

Rupert raised his glass. 'To Bookie.'

The others followed. 'Bookie,' they chorused. 'Best of the best.'

Eddie looked bemused.

'Colonel James Bookman,' Gerald whispered. 'Killed, apparently, in a parachute accident.'

Eddie turned to E.W., shrugged. 'How come we weren't offered a drink?'

'Because you weren't in the regiment.' E.W.'s instant response sounded more like a reprimand than an explanation.

'*The* regiment?' Eddie scowled. 'What regiment's that then?'

'If you don't know, you don't *need* to know.'

'Bit like the Masons then?'

Rupert's whisky glass rang out for the second time before the argument could continue. He glanced quickly at the agenda, looked up, his expression more serious than before. 'I'm afraid Downing Street isn't taking us seriously,' he said. 'There's been no response to Gerald's declaration and no attempt to contact me following the snatch of the PM's father.'

Gerald pondered the announcement for a moment, wondering if it was good news or bad. 'I have to admit I'd expected some kind of standard letter of acknowledgement from number ten. On the other hand I don't quite understand how they are supposed to contact an anonymous kidnapper.'

'E-mail,' said Katrina. 'We gave them a throw-away hotmail address, kidnappers@hotmail.co.uk would you believe.'

'Hotmail,' Gerald echoed. 'Surely they'll be able to trace you?'

Katrina shook her head. 'The registration details are all false but we can log onto *kidnappers* anytime, anywhere, to pick up responses from Downing Street or the police.'

'But there have been none.' Rupert forced a weak smile but his voice betrayed his anger at being ignored. 'We'd quite expected Gerald to be hauled in for questioning by now but they haven't even bothered to pay him a visit.'

'Oh I expect they'll get around to it soon enough,' Gerald murmured forlornly. 'They're probably just playing cat and mouse for a while.'

Katrina sighed as if she was bored. 'Which is why we intend to borrow a prominent back bencher for an indefinite period,' she said flatly. 'That should help to focus their little minds.'

'And if it doesn't?' Vee asked her. 'What then?'

'We'll just have to wait and see, won't we?' Katrina looked away, searching through her briefcase. She took out a beige folder, placed a newspaper cutting on the table in front of Rupert.

He stared at it for a moment, reread the first few paragraphs before holding it out at arm's length as if it had an unpleasant smell. 'This young gentleman's unsavoury activities have been the subject of extensive press coverage in recent weeks,' he said, pointing to the picture of a hooded youth kicking an elderly lady in the back. 'You've probably read that he delights in kicking or punching old people for reasons which remain unclear and seem somewhat lacking in logic.'

Katrina looked up from her notes. 'He's seventeen, unemployed, and out of control. And, from what we can see, the police are not particularly interested. Petty crime, they call it.'

Rupert nodded. 'I've singled out this particular yob for special mention because the enormous press coverage devoted to his behaviour has given national importance to a local lout. And that's exactly what we needed.'

'He's here with us this evening,' Katrina said with a happy smile. 'Next door, in The Shed.'

'And so I have a question for you,' Rupert continued. 'What would be a suitably high-profile deterrent for this celebrity thug? The sort of thing that will keep him in the media headlines.'

Gerald glanced around the table at the others. 'I think we probably need a bit more notice,' he said. 'It could take all evening to come up with a worthwhile idea.'

Eddie Bates shrugged. 'Seems to me we should make him look a complete prat. Dress him up in something daft, tie him to a lamp post somewhere and give the nod to the press.'

'What about a tutu?' Katrina giggled. 'Always looks pretty daft on a man.'

Dizzy gave her a puzzled grin. 'Tutu?' he repeated.

'Ballet skirt.' Katrina entwined her arms above her head in a pseudo ballet pose. 'And white tights too, of course.'

'Chained to the railings at Buckingham Palace,' Eddie chimed in. 'Loads of tourists, lots of cameras, good get-away route down The Mall.'

Rupert seemed unimpressed. 'OK, Buck Pal in a tutu. Any other suggestions?'

'The fourth plinth in Trafalgar Square,' said Gerald. 'The empty one. We could put him on top.'

'Brilliant.' Katrina clapped her hands with delight. 'In tutu and tights.'

'I was thinking of painting him white,' Gerald continued. 'Like a statue.' He paused briefly, permitted himself a smug grin. 'Like the statue of David, in fact. Stark naked.'

'Logistics.' One of Rupert's men, with the build and arrogance of a matador, fixed him with a penetrating gaze. 'How do we ensure he stays on the plinth?'

'It's pretty high,' said Gerald. 'He couldn't possibly get on or off without a ladder or something.'

'But he could fall off,' the other man countered. 'Break his legs or his bloody neck. So not a good idea.'

Vee quietly eased her chair back from the table, turned slightly to face the others. 'They relied on some highly effective punishments for anti-social behaviour a few centuries back,' she said. 'Why don't we follow their lead and set up a pillory?'

Katrina dismissed the idea in an instant. 'Wouldn't work,' she declared emphatically. 'Pillories have to be firmly fixed in the ground and there'd never be time for all that sort of palaver.'

'OK, a portable pillory.' Vee slid a hurried sketch across the table to Rupert. It showed a horizontal piece of wood with holes for the head and hands, fixed to a vertical post, and set on a heavy wooden base. 'You could take them all over the place… the ultimate humiliation.'

Rupert finished his drink, slammed the glass down on the table. 'Sounds good,' he said, 'always assuming we can make it work.' He turned to Dizzy. 'What do you think?'

'Absolute doddle.' Dizzy rocked back on his chair, made a pistol shape with his hand. 'Just tell me when and where,' he said, firing an imaginary bullet at the ceiling.

'Marble Arch, soon as you like.'

Dizzy nodded in agreement but looked confused.

'Once the site of the notorious Tyburn gallows,' Rupert explained with obvious relish. 'Rather fitting, don't you think?'

Vee could see that Gerald had reservations about the idea. He'd started to fiddle with his tie, the way he always did when he was unsure about something. 'Something worrying you Gerry?' she asked, leaning forward so he could see her face. 'You look a bit doubtful.'

'Oh, I was just thinking,' he said. 'Pillories involved throwing rotten eggs, mouldy vegetables and things, didn't they? Don't you think someone could get hurt, blinded even.'

E.W. made a little snorting sound. 'I don't think you'll find too many rotten eggs or mouldy vegetables laying around on the pavement at Marble Arch.'

'What about empty lager cans?' Gerald said. 'Or bottles even. They're all over the place.'

Dizzy rolled his eyes. 'He's right. Some half pissed arsehole's bound to lob a bottle or something.'

'It's a possibility,' Vee conceded. 'But unlikely. And anyway, I'd bet there'd be no more than a quarter of an hour between us setting up the pillory and the police hauling it away again.'

'OK, settled,' Rupert cut in impatiently. 'A pillory it is, but we must be absolutely sure the press have time to get a good picture. I'll send a couple of the lads to mingle with the crowd in case they start throwing bricks.'

Vee chewed her pencil thoughtfully. 'It really is *the* most fantastic concept, isn't it?' she enthused. 'A classic, instantly recognisable as a device for community punishment, and such perfect imagery for press photographers too. Perhaps we should seriously think about adopting the pillory as a sort of trademark. Maybe we could set one up outside the Old Bailey or in front of the Law Courts in The Strand. It would help to reinforce the criminal justice aspect.'

Gerald was a little surprised by Vee's cold, calculating attitude; doctors were meant to care for people not subject them to public humiliation. While he had to admit the pillory was a highly original idea and a well-deserved touch of poetic justice for the oafish lout in question, he was concerned that Vee showed no more emotion than if she'd just prescribed ointment for a skin rash.

On the other side of the table Eddie Bates stared into his lap and fiddled with his mobile phone; probably texting somebody or picking up messages from his answering service. He looked up from time to time, gave the occasional nod and offered intermittent grunts of approval in a futile pretence at paying attention. But he wasn't listening to any of it. Gerald could tell. Eddie Bates' mind was elsewhere.

Katrina Bevington presented her hit-list of backbench candidates suitable for future "borrowing", along with her personal selections, based on their potential news value. There was the chap from the Midlands who'd been a surprise defector from the Lib Dems to Labour, and the member for somewhere in east London who'd claimed his girlfriend's beauty treatments on parliamentary expenses. Both seemed likely to attract media interest but, on Katrina's recommendation, the honourable member for Coventry South was duly elected.

Gerald admired her bluntness and the child-like logic with which she magically argued absurd ideas into absolute sense in a matter of moments. Her finely-tuned powers of persuasion had slipped neatly into overdrive and the meeting seemed to defer to her every whim in the matter of the honourable member's forthcoming abduction. He'd be snatched in London, possibly from his flat near Chelsea Bridge. They'd transfer him to The Shed where he'd remain, unharmed, until *"Kidnappers at Hotmail"* had established positive communications with Downing Street. At this point, and as a gesture of goodwill, they'd release him, but with a clear understanding that others would quickly take his place if negotiations broke down.

Eddie Bates abandoned his texting. He looked up, laughed suddenly. 'And what happens if these negotiations break down again, for good? Do we end up killing some poor bugger?'

'Exactly the point I made earlier,' said Vee. 'What's our plan B if they simply ignore us?'

'They won't,' E.W. snapped back. 'No British government has ever experienced this kind of situation before. They have no choice but to take us seriously.'

Rupert forced a tired smile and checked his notes. 'I feel sure the disappearance of the honourable member for Coventry South will convince his parliamentary colleagues that we mean business.' He looked around the table for signs of dissent before moving on to a review of other matters. While the government handed out tax payer's money to bribe illegal immigrants to go home [sometimes before they'd even set foot in the country], Rupert's team had persevered with a more persuasive approach to the problem. But weekly raids on make-shift immigrant camps on the north coast of France had been less effective than expected. More decisive action was needed.

Gerald listened impassively to talk of petrol bombings and how unofficial immigrant camps and surrounding areas were now totally uninhabitable. It was a scorched earth policy but Rupert made it sound like nothing more than a spot of spring cleaning.

Closer to home, in south-east London, they'd shut down three Chinese restaurants. Rupert skirted round the details but revealed that the owners had been running an immigration scam involving Chinese girls on student visas, marrying British men to obtain citizenship. Quickie divorces meant they were then free to marry illegal Chinese immigrants for six figure fees, passing on British citizenship to up to half a dozen Chinese men each in as many years and netting close on a million pounds for themselves in the process.

Like the unofficial immigration camps on the other side of the Channel, the London restaurants were now uninhabitable, the result of what Rupert described as sonar cleansing. It soon became clear that *sonar* was merely the more palatable anagram of *arson*, the word which had dominated a couple of press reports about unexplained blazes at local restaurants.

But unsavoury words like arson had somehow been deleted from Rupert's personal vocabulary, airbrushed from the well-stocked lexicon of his mind, so it wasn't immediately clear to everyone that Rupert's report on *"incentivised exit strategies for unauthorised tenancy"* was inextricably linked to Dizzy's plans for *"kicking Pikey bastards off other people's land".*

The ultimate threat of sonar cleansing was an essential factor in a string of successful negotiations on behalf of a growing list of farmers, private land owners, and local communities. And all of them happy to pay two thousand pounds a time to regain vacant possession of their property.

'It's an historical fact,' said Dizzy. 'Fire gets rid of rats, and the plagues of burglaries, robberies and violence they bring with them.'

Eddie's reaction was ambivalent. His reactions often were when he wanted to test the logic of an argument. He shook his head, let out a huge sigh. 'It all sounds a bit Mafiosi to me. Offers you can't refuse, and all that stuff.'

'It's exactly the opposite,' Vee said quietly but firmly. 'The Mafia is essentially malevolent and corrupt, like a harmful bacteria. We're the antibiotics, a cleansing force to destroy the bacteria infecting our communities.'

Dizzy ran his hand over the fiercely shaved head. 'Never quite thought of us as a dose of streptomycin. But it's not a bad way of putting it.'

'Right now we seem to be the *only* available cure for society's ills,' Vee continued. 'Our justice system merely disguises the symptoms with aspirin and sticking plaster while the disease takes hold and becomes an epidemic. In less than a decade it'll be completely and utterly incurable.'

Her voice trailed off as she finished the sentence and the room fell momentarily silent.

'Justice.' Rupert's pronunciation of the word sounded like a heated blade plunged into cold water. 'It's the heart of the nation,' he said, 'the pulse of a healthy society, the life blood of reason. We must not allow it to become the plaything of indulgent fools.'

And Rupert was right, of course, Gerald knew it, but he couldn't help feeling that things were now moving dangerously fast. He wanted to tell everyone to shut up and be still for a moment, think things through, work out the practicalities, consider all the implications, instead of being swept along on a tide of enthusiasm.

It showed in their faces; all of them, even Eddie Bates. They liked what they'd heard and much vaunted words like *justice* legitimised almost anything carried out in its hallowed name.

Gerald felt a flush of anticipation as he watched Vee cram her notebook and pen into the black leather handbag and slide her chair away from the table. He caught her eye, smiled. 'Can I give you a lift?' he asked casually.

'Kind of you to offer,' she said, rising to her feet. 'But I've got my car outside.'

'Of course.' He slapped his forehead with the flat of his hand. 'How stupid can you get? Wasn't thinking.'

She hesitated as she reached the door, quickly turned, fixed him with emerald eyes. 'Why don't you drop by for a nightcap on your way home?'

He hadn't expected it. The words struggled to reach his lips. 'Thanks, yes,' he stammered. 'Love to.'

'You're on a promise there.' Eddie Bates sidled closer, gave him a playful punch which instantly numbed the muscle in his upper arm. 'Must be the aftershave.'

Gerald shrugged sadly, shook his head. 'I really don't think so. Vee's life's in a bit of a tangle right now.'

'Get it untangled,' Eddie said flatly. 'You haven't got time to bugger about – five hundred Saturdays, top whack.'

Eddie's words rang in Gerald's ears as he drove off. Five hundred Saturdays seemed like a serious underestimate of his life expectancy but, whatever the final tally, he was quite sure he didn't want to waste any of them behind bars.

The front door was open when he arrived at Vee's house. There were packing cases in the hall, still more in the lounge, and clothes in plastic bags hanging from the picture rails.

'Make yourself at home,' she shouted from the top of the stairs. 'Be with you in a minute.'

Gerald shifted a pile of medical books to one side and settled himself on the sofa. 'You've sold the house then,' he called out. 'When are you moving?'

Vee hurried down the stairs and into the room, a bottle of brandy under her arm, a plastic beaker in each hand. 'Sorry,' she panted. 'Couldn't remember where I'd packed the drinks and the brandy glasses are all bubble-wrapped with the rest of the china and glass.'

'Moving house is always chaotic.' Gerald plumped up the cushion next to him, moved along a bit to make more room. 'They say it's as traumatic as divorce and bereavement.'

She sighed, poured the brandy. 'Two out of three's not bad then, is it? My decree absolute came through last week, and I'm out of here for good at the weekend.'

'I'd say that probably warrants a toast,' said Gerald. 'Shall we drink to happier times?'

Vee settled back, grabbed his hand, squeezed. 'Happy days, Gerry.'

For Gerald, who'd always insisted on the correct glass for all occasions, sipping brandy from a beaker was a profanity, like Champagne from a tankard or claret from a tumbler. But, tonight, such sacrilege didn't seem to matter. 'Happy days,' he repeated. 'And lots of them.'

Their beakers touched with the dull, lifeless slap of cheap plastic but with all the grandeur of lead crystal. Vee wrinkled her nose. 'Sorry about the faint aroma of toothpaste,' she whispered. 'Bathroom beakers I'm afraid. Best I could do in the circumstances.'

Gerald sniffed his drink. 'I reckon the Courvoisier will probably overpower the Colgate after the second or third refill. We'll just have to persevere.'

Vee raised her beaker. 'To perseverance.'

'Perseverance,' Gerald repeated. 'We'll certainly need it if we hope to change hearts and minds in Westminster.'

She shook her head, smiled gently. 'That's never going to happen. But we'll sure as hell force them into a few corners.'

'Same thing, surely? Politicians are always more cooperative when they're cornered.'

'I suppose so.' She ran her hand through her hair, swept it from her face. 'They might even get to grips with crime and start protecting law-abiding citizens if they weren't cowering under the weight of human bloody rights legislation.'

Gerald put his arm around her shoulders and pulled her gently towards him. 'The meek shall undoubtedly inherit the earth, Vee, but it'll be a very small plot, six feet under, unless they get mad and fight back.'

'Which, in one little sentence, seems to sum it all up.' She sighed, nestled closer. 'You've gone from meek to messiah in a very short space of time.'

'Messiah? More like messenger. All I seem to do is make announcements or deliver declarations.'

'That's what messiahs are meant to do, isn't it?'

At first he didn't answer, couldn't answer. It was as if someone had thrown a switch in his head, like changing TV channels. The words, when he finally spoke, came suddenly and without warning. 'I'm in love with you,' he announced drily. 'Thought you should know.'

She looked into his eyes, laughed. 'Where did that little outburst come from?'

He shrugged. 'Buggered if I know. Just sort of happened.'

'Well isn't that romantic,' she gasped. 'You make it sound like a sexually transmitted disease.'

Gerald waved his hand. 'Yeah, yeah, I'm sorry. You're absolutely right.' He took his arm from her shoulder, straightened up. 'I simply meant that I hadn't *planned* to say anything.'

'Why not?' she murmured, placing his arm back around her shoulder. 'Didn't you want me to know?'

'I wasn't sure how you'd react.'

'I'm very flattered. But you don't need flattery to get me into bed.'

He winced, gulped the rest of his brandy in a single swig. 'I wasn't trying to get you into bed. Really I wasn't,' he said, rather too earnestly.

'You don't fancy me, then?'

Gerald hadn't prepared himself for this kind of conversation. His eyes widened. 'Of course I fancy you. That's not the point.'

Vee stood up, gently touched her lips with manicured fingers. 'The point, Gerry, is that you talk too much. And, if it makes you feel any better, I accept full responsibility for anything that may happen between us tonight.'

Gerald Arthur Cornfield stopped talking, reached for his plastic beaker, and followed Dr Blythe upstairs.

Chapter Eighteen

A late afternoon sun flickered through the regiment of trees lined up along Park Lane as a white transit van made its way towards Marble Arch. It slowed at Speakers Corner, indicated right, and edged across the one-way system until it was in line with the centre arch of the great marble monument, at which point it accelerated onto a paved pedestrian concourse where it screeched to a stop.

A small group of tourists watched, passive and unmoving, as the rear doors of the van were flung open and two masked men in black tracksuits jumped to the ground. A third man, inside the van, helped them lower a heavy wooden structure onto the concourse.

The driver opened his window and shouted something to the others. They hesitated for a moment, looked across to the park then up towards the traffic approaching from Oxford Street and the Edgware Road before, in a practised performance, they bundled a young man out of the vehicle and over to the structure. His head and hands were quickly secured in a thick, horizontal plank, which opened and shut like an oversized clapper board, while a sheet of white card with black lettering was pinned to the main upright.

And then they were off, along the park's perimeter road in the general direction of Notting Hill, leaving a growing crowd of people staring at a young man in a pillory and a sign which explained his misdemeanour. *"I kick old, defenceless women for fun,"* it said, above a couple of press cuttings which provided the proof.

Nobody paid much attention to the well-dressed, elderly gentleman sitting on a park bench, close to the trees, who waited until two news agency press photographers had taken their pictures before neatly folding his newspaper and heading off down Park Lane towards The Dorchester Hotel. He paused near the central reservation, glanced back towards the sound of a police squad car which had just turned onto the concourse, before making the call on his mobile phone.

'No problems,' he said. 'See you in five minutes.'

Gerald Cornfield passed through the hotel's revolving doors and into the grandiose reception with a jaunty step. He took the lift to the eighth floor, checked his profile in a rose tinted mirror, and made for the penthouse suite where the meeting had been scheduled to take place.

The three men already seated around a baize-covered table had the look of a reluctant audience waiting to be entertained. They glanced impassively at the priceless French baroque which surrounded them as if the room's exquisite elegance had singularly failed to measure up to their superior expectations, and an attentive waitress was banished with the flick of a wrist.

But then, to all intents and purposes, they weren't there; not officially, anyway. The men from the ministries had deigned to hear the pleadings of lesser mortals but, as it had already been made perfectly clear by their heads of departments, that was the upper limit of their commitment.

E.W. took his seat on the opposite side of the table. 'May I present Mr Gerald Cornfield,' he said with a languid gesture towards the door. 'As you've probably been informed, he's directing this particular area of our operations.'

One of the three men, slightly older and obviously senior to the others, looked up, nodded politely. The other two opened beige files and unscrewed the tops of black fountain pens with the parallel precision of formation dancers. One wrote Mr Cornfield's name in royal blue ink while the other consulted his notes.

Gerald slipped off his jacket, draped it around the back of the chair next to E.W. and sat down. 'And your names are?' he asked.

'Unimportant,' E.W. grunted.

The men from Whitehall stared back blankly but said nothing.

'No doubt you're aware of the content of the declaration delivered to number ten by Mr Cornfield's delegation but, as you'll probably be equally aware, there has been no acknowledgement or response.'

The older man tugged at his shirt cuffs. 'I believe that *is* the current position and, indeed, the reason we've agreed to meet with you today.'

'So what's the answer then?' Gerald asked bluntly.

'The matter is to be reviewed in due course.'

'Reviewed,' Gerald repeated. 'Is that it?'

The other man stiffened and took a deep breath. 'I'm afraid that *is* the official position in the matter of your declaration.'

E.W. hunched forward, placed his hands flat on the table. 'You didn't come here just to tell us that, so perhaps we could get to the point?'

'The point is this,' said the other man, betraying no sign of emotion or concern. 'Her Majesty's government *never* negotiates with kidnappers and refuses to be intimated by them.'

E.W.'s eyes narrowed. 'And that has what, exactly, to do with us?'

'Come, come now. Can there be any doubt whatsoever about your empathy and synergy with other, shall we say, more radical elements? You've made no attempt to conceal it but if you expect your representations to Downing Street to be sympathetically reviewed, there must be no further threats or abductions.'

'These radical elements and abductions,' Gerald said, scratching his chin thoughtfully. 'I don't recall seeing anything about them in the papers and it certainly wasn't on the news.'

The other man stared at him from under thick eyebrows. 'Nor shall you Mr Cornfield. Some issues are resolved beyond the glare of public scrutiny. To do otherwise would merely endow them with a credibility they don't deserve.' He paused, permitted himself a weak smile, as if to accentuate his next words. 'It would be a mistake for you to imagine that dark forces are confined to the criminal world,' he said. 'The law courts hold no monopoly on British justice. Do I make myself clear?'

'Perfectly clear.' E.W. unbuttoned his jacket, checked the phantom holster. 'You're telling me the British government is a party to criminal violence... when it feels inclined.'

The other man shook his head. 'You really mustn't put words into my mouth, Major Bevington. I've said no such thing but if that's what you choose to believe, so be it.'

At this point in the conversation, and without warning, the meeting seemed to come to an abrupt close. Nobody said anything but, as if by some strange telepathic agreement, beige files were returned to briefcases, fountain pens slipped back into inside pockets and three men rose to their feet, thanked their hosts, and left.

Gerald poured himself a glass of water. 'I'm not totally sure what that was all about,' he said, settling back in his chair.

'It was a less than subtle warning,' E.W. snorted. 'In plain English, they said we could end up dead in a ditch somewhere if we get too clever and overstep the mark.'

'But that would be ridiculous,' Gerald laughed nervously. 'Surely they'd have us arrested, charge us with abduction, kidnapping, or whatever the hell it is we're meant to have done? Why wouldn't they just throw the book at us.'

E.W. stared out at the city skyline. 'Because that could spectacularly backfire on them and make heroes of us all. We'd end up a bunch of bloody martyrs.'

'I don't think I'd like that much,' said Gerald. 'Dying isn't a very positive career move at my time of life.'

'Only one thing to do, in the circumstances.' E.W. paced the room pondering the options before calling his wife on a mobile phone. 'Be a darling,' he said quietly. 'Tell Rupert it looks as if we shall have to borrow the honourable gentlemen from Coventry South after all. And the sooner the better.'

An ambulance screamed urgently down Park Lane. It might have been a police car, Gerald wasn't altogether sure; they both made an appalling racket. But it was certainly the unmistakeable sound of impending disaster. Get out of the way, it wailed, high speed trouble coming through.

Gerald waited while E.W. finished struggling with a text message before he spoke. 'Dead in a ditch, you said. Are you sure we're not getting to clever, overstepping the mark?'

E.W. shrugged amiably. 'When the enemy rattles his sabre, it's time to toss a grenade.'

'I wonder,' Gerald mused. 'You don't think a bit of passive resistance might be a less dangerous option in the circumstances?'

E.W. rolled his eyes at the grammatical muddle. 'The answer is, of course, Yes – I *don't* think a bit passive resistance might be less dangerous. What you meant to ask, of course, was *do* I think it, in which case the answer would be No,' he said with a smug grin.

'I think we've had this conversation before,' Gerald said, buttoning his jacket. 'I'm not so sure it wasn't when we first met.'

'There you go again. What you mean is you're fairly sure it *was* when we first met.'

But Gerald wasn't paying too much attention to E.W.'s impromptu lecture on English Grammar. An idea had dawdled across his mind, settled itself slap bang in the centre of his consciousness, and was now refusing to budge. By the time he arrived back at Pycroft Cottage it had matured into a full blown stroke of genius.

Chapter Nineteen

Even members of parliament must answer the call of nature, especially after a glass or two of expensive claret. But a brief visit to the gents can sometimes be a dangerous journey, terminating abruptly in the boot of a car, parked in the vicinity of the service entrance to a swish London eatery.

The audacious kidnapping of the honourable member for Coventry South went off unnoticed and without incident – E.W.'s metaphorical grenade tossed into the very heart of Whitehall's sabre rattling territory. And this time the details were unashamedly leaked to the press, giving front page prominence to a previously little known backbencher and the demands of kidnappers who described themselves as activists in the pursuit of justice for *Greyed Britons*.

But MPs, like benefits cheats, parking wardens, and cowboy builders, are not held in high esteem, so while newspapers condemned the honourable member's abduction, the public mood was more supportive.

Speculation was rife. It was rumoured that the kidnappers were members of the opposition, disenchanted with the democratic process. Some claimed there were royal connections, others that it was the work of a religious sect. There was talk of a retired high court judge being at the centre of things and even some mild conjecture about alien abductions.

It went on for a couple of days while Gerald pondered the possibility of dark forces descending on Pycroft Cottage and spiriting him away to some kind of Guantanamo Bay in the Orkneys or Shetlands; perhaps the Isle of Wight. He decided it might be best not to think about E.W.'s *dead in a ditch* scenario, assuring himself that it was no more than a bit of scare mongering by civil service minions.

And it was in this slightly pensive frame of mind that he arrived at the show flat ten minutes ahead of Vee. The oak tree was still there but the country house had been demolished, replaced by twenty-four luxury apartments, with views towards the river and two spaces in the underground car park. Ten of them didn't, in fact, face the river, being more or less in line with the golf club car park but, apart from those on the ground floor, they each had a balcony.

Tennyson Place, it said on the glossy brochure; named after the poet. Apparently he'd had something to do with the area when he was younger; they weren't specific. The prices were less ambiguous and ranged from four hundred thousand to six, but that was the attraction. Pycroft Cottage was on the market, offers around four, and Vee had already sold, leaving her with a handsome five hundred thousand pounds in the bank. Together they could buy a luxury apartment [with river view] and still have a couple of hundred thousand invested.

Gerald hadn't lived in a flat since he was twenty. He'd always preferred something on two floors, where the bedrooms were upstairs and not just off the dining room or next door to the kitchen. Betsy felt the same way. She always said flats weren't natural, only half a house and no garden. They bought Pycroft Cottage soon after their first wedding anniversary and the idea of moving never crossed their minds.

But Vee was an inveterate flat dweller. To her they were compact, convenient, and altogether less permanent than the humdrum responsibility of a house (for which read *home*). Flats were transitory, somewhere to stay for a while until life picked you up and moved you on. It was probably a hang-over from her student days when unencumbered freedom separated the young from a world of adult commitments.

Buying a house in Pixley Green had seemed like a wise move. Both she and her husband saw it as an opportunity to add value to an appreciating asset, confirmation that their marriage had roots. But it only highlighted their differences while demanding their undivided attention. Fix the roof, it whispered; update the kitchen, the bathroom; replace the central heating, the windows. And what about that garden? Lawns to mow, trees to be lopped, hedges to trim.

For Doctor Valerie Blythe, Tennyson Place would be a time machine back to before it all went wrong, a new beginning with a gentle, undemanding man who offered companionship, affection and a welcome element of stability in a wobbly world.

'Gerald Cornfield, isn't it?'

Gerald, who was struggling to make sense of the floor plan dimensions, turned towards the voice.

A well-coiffured woman with deep violet eye shadow and more than her fair share of mascara, smiled expectantly. The badge on the lapel of an immaculate navy jacket said she was Annabelle, Sales Executive. 'I saw you in the papers... Downing Street it was... with a sheepdog.'

'How clever of you to remember my name,' he said, with a sudden flush of pride

'I kept the cuttings... fair play for pensioners and all that.' She brushed her skirt self-consciously with the flat of her hand. 'What's the latest? I mean, have you heard anything more?'

Gerald shook his head. 'Not so far, but we're making progress.'

'Well done anyway,' she trilled, guiding him towards the sales office. 'Did you have any particular flat in mind? Most of them are now completed, although only the show flat is furnished, of course.'

'River view and top floor, I think.' He hesitated, looked around. 'Actually I'm waiting for someone.'

'Please come in and wait, make yourself comfortable.' She cleared some sales brochures from a chair, gestured for him to sit down, before settling herself behind a desk. 'It must take up a lot of your time,' she said. 'All the government lobbying and so on.'

Gerald nodded thoughtfully. 'Changing government policies demands a concerted effort.'

'I do so admire people like you,' she said with a theatrical sigh. 'So dedicated, such resolve. A positive inspiration to others.'

'Others?' His voice sank. 'You don't seriously think I inspired the abduction of that unfortunate MP, do you?'

'Why not?' she said at once. 'Think about it. The kidnappers aren't demanding money or anything, they've simply asked for a fair deal for pensioners. Just as you did.'

'But kidnapping a member of parliament? Wouldn't you say that was a bit extreme?'

She shrugged. 'Not really. It's not as if they're going to kill him or anything, is it? I mean, when all said and done, they're only trying to make the same point as you, but with a touch more drama.' She paused, smiled gently. 'Some folk have even suggested you might've had something to do with it yourself.'

Gerald shook his head. 'Nothing to do with me,' he said, but the flush of guilt rising in his cheeks contradicted him.

'Well whoever it was has nothing to be ashamed of,' she declared reassuringly. 'They should think about kidnapping the rest of them too...useless bunch of articles.' She winked as she reached behind her for a bunch of keys. 'Is it your wife we're waiting for?'

'Partner,' Gerald said, without thinking. And then by way of a retraction; 'Actually she's a doctor.'

But he felt obliged to explain himself. *Partners*, he insisted, were people who shared ownership of a business and had nothing to do with male/female relationships. And, as far as he was concerned, the word had been hijacked, in the same way that *gay* no longer meant brightly coloured, light-hearted, or carefree, and *brilliant* now had little to do with being talented or clever. *Relaxing* holidays, *tasty* meals, *riveting* books, *riotous* parties, *exhilarating* weekends by the sea; each of them reduced to a one-size-fits-all *brilliant*.

Gerald sensed she wasn't particularly interested in his views on word theft. He glanced at his watch. 'She's probably been delayed at the hospital,' he said wearily, at the very moment Vee stepped into the sales office, carrying a copy of Ideal Homes magazine.

'Traffic's terrible,' she gasped. 'Somebody's locked some poor chap in a pillory outside the town hall. Total chaos.'

Annabelle stood up, buttoned her jacket, stepped purposefully round to the front of her desk. 'Same thing happened near Marble Arch a few days back. It was in the papers,' she confided in a tight-lipped whisper. 'So this'll be the *second* one.'

Vee kissed Gerald on both cheeks, mumbled something about it actually being the *fourth* one, but didn't press the point. 'Units eight and ten,' she said, making eye contact with the other woman for the first time. 'We'd like to see both, if that's OK.'

Annabelle checked she had the right keys before leading the way to the lift, with a running commentary on the design highlights of what the brochure pretentiously described as the "Tennyson Place experience".

By five o'clock that afternoon, apartment ten, Tennyson Place, Pixley Green, was formally under offer to Mr Gerald Cornfield and Dr Valerie Blythe, at a fraction below the asking price and with the added benefits of subsidised service charges for the first two years, and a delayed completion, pending the sale of Pycroft Cottage.

An official memorandum of sale put it all into words that left no room for doubt. There it was, in black and white, the future, the next chapter in Mr Cornfield's life... the "Tennyson Place experience". The ridiculous sales slogan made the whole thing sound dangerous, like bungee jumping or hot air ballooning, instead of easy living in a comfortable and secure apartment overlooking a peaceful river.

The Friday Street experience presented more immediate problems. Vee's original plan to move in with a girlfriend, after the sale of her house, wasn't working out and, at Gerald's suggestion, she'd started to transfer some of her things to Pycroft Cottage. But sleeping together in the bed he'd shared with Betsy was out of the question so twin divans had been lashed together in the guest room.

It was a bright, cosy little room but with limited wardrobe space, thanks to Betsy's collection of cotton dresses. Over the years she'd chosen the patterns, bought the materials and run them up herself; two decades of changing hip sizes and hemlines now hanging, limp and lifeless, like faded flowers from a bygone summer, testimony to a life of thrift, self-denial and making-do.

Gerald had never quite plucked-up the courage to banish the last traces of Betsy from his life but now there was no alternative. They had to go. And, besides, they'd be well received at the local charity shop.

But that wasn't quite the end of it. Vee complained about the sour smell of mothballs which lingered inside of the wardrobe like spilled beer on a bar room floor. Her clothes would be better off in the box room, she decreed, draped in plastic bags from a line strung between the pelmet and the doorframe.

And there were difficulties with the bathroom arrangements. Vee was inclined to commandeer it for long periods at a time with a beauty regime most other women carried out at their dressing tables. She devoted a full hour a day to plucking eyebrows, fixing make-up, varnishing nails, fiddling with hair and applying an assortment of sprays and lotions with a dedication Gerald hadn't believed possible. Betsy had never made that much fuss of herself except, perhaps, at Christmas, when she liked to look her very best.

Gerald decided not to think about it and reminded himself that there were two bathrooms and more than enough wardrobe space at the Tennyson Place apartment.

Eddie Bates disagreed. 'There's never enough wardrobe space for a woman,' he announced drily during an evening drink at The Crow. 'If they spot a bit going spare, they'll nip out and buy some clothes to fill it before you've had time to hang up your trousers. It's the same with fridges. They don't feel secure unless it's a lager free zone, chocker block with half a dozen flavours of yogurt and three different varieties of spa water.'

'I must admit, Betsy was a bit of a clothes hoarder,' said Gerald, settling himself on a bar stool and loosening his tie. 'Some of them no longer even fitted her and others she never wore at all.'

'Exactly. They're all the same.' Eddie looked up with one of his cryptic smiles, which usually meant he was about to reveal some highly confidential information. 'I gave it the elbow,' he said

Gerald frowned quizzically. 'Gave what the elbow?'

'Holly. She moved out last weekend... Sunday morning... pastures new and all that crap.'

'I didn't know she'd even moved in. When did all this start?'

'Month or so back.' Eddie stretched his arms above his head, yawned. 'Fact is I'm not cut out for cohabitation.'

Gerald felt obliged to look suitably concerned but knew better than to offer Eddie Bates too much sympathy. 'What went wrong?' he asked coolly.

'My mind couldn't convince my body I'm still twenty-five.' He grabbed Gerald's arm, squeezed. 'It's not a problem, mate, all for the best. Young girl like that needs a young man.'

'But you two got along so well.'

Eddie shook his head. 'Not really. Should have known better than fall for a bird who's never heard of Gerry and the Pacemakers. Fatal attraction, fatal mistake. Won't happen again.'

'And there we were planning to get rich selling wisdom, giving other poor souls the benefit of our vast reservoir of experience,' Gerald snorted. 'It's a wonder we haven't been sued under the flaming Trade Descriptions Act.'

'Hands up, no argument, it wasn't the cleverest thing I've ever done. But the *wish* was stronger than the *wisdom*, end of story.' Eddie laughed suddenly as if he'd just seen the funny side of it all. 'Fact is you can't expect to shoot pool with a piece of rope, can you?'

'George Burns,' said Gerald.

'What about him?'

'It was George Burns who said sex at ninety was like trying to shoot pool with a piece of rope.'

'Dirty old bugger shouldn't have even been *trying* at that age.'

'I've often wondered about E.W.,' Gerald mused. 'Just can't somehow picture him having sex, let alone with someone like Katrina.'

'Don't suppose he does, not anymore. But even when he did, it probably wasn't with women.'

'E.W.? Gay? No way.'

Eddie nodded confidently. 'As a sailor's hornpipe.'

'Don't believe it,' Gerald said flatly. 'He's married.'

'So was Oscar Wilde. Means bugger all, if you'll excuse the pun.'

Gerald's voice sank. 'But why on earth would he marry Katrina if he's the other way inclined?'

'You might just as well ask why Katrina married him.' Eddie's eyebrows lifted a little as he smiled. 'It's what they call a marriage of convenience. He gets respectability, she gets money and security.'

Gerald moved his bar stool closer. 'Hang on a minute, didn't E.W. say Katrina was a wealthy woman when they married? Three or four million, possibly even more, he told us. Do you remember?'

'I most certainly do. And she *was*, of course, wealthy... the second she said *I do*.'

Gerald stared at his friend, looking for signs of the raucous laughter which inevitably followed one of Eddie's tall stories. But there were none. 'So who told you all this?' he asked quietly. 'And what makes you think it's true?'

Eddie shrugged. 'Apparently Rupert and Katrina are an item, have been for a long time. Dizzy reckons E.W. knows all about it, perhaps even condones it.'

'Bloody Hell,' Gerald groaned. 'That's sick.'

'Not according to Dizzy. He says it's all part of a slightly weird matrimonial agreement.'

Gerald sat silently for a moment, nodded. 'Sort of makes sense,' he said. 'I once asked Rupert what type of women he went for. He virtually described Katrina although he never mentioned her by name.'

'And who gives a damn anyway?' said Eddie. 'They're obviously happy with their cosy little threesome, so good luck to them.'

'Ménage a trois,' Gerald murmured. 'Never quite understood the logic of it myself. Two's company, three's a crowd, surely?'

'If you ask me,' said Eddie, checking to see how much money was in his wallet before ordering another round of drinks, 'two's a bit of a crowd, unless the other party happens to be Sophia Loren on a weekend visit.'

'I thought you preferred younger women,' said Gerald. 'Sophia Loren must be six or seven years older than you.'

Eddie turned to face him, leaning on his elbow. 'And you are how many years older than the lovely Dr Blythe?'

'Difficult to say.'

'Then I'll say it for you,' Eddie said with a satisfied smile. 'It's twelve.'

Gerald stared gloomily into his drink, nodded. 'Something like that.'

'So that would be twice the age difference between Sophia and me?'

'But there *is* no Sophia and you, so what difference does it make?'

Eddie laughed. 'None whatsoever mate. But there *is* a Gerald and Vee so don't forget you were already a teenager when she was just a toddler. And that's my final word on the subject.'

'Thank god for that,' Gerald snapped. 'Perhaps, now, we can talk about something else?'

Eddie turned away, glanced around the room as if he might be looking for a familiar face.

Gerald stared in silence at the row of inverted bottles behind the bar, checked his watch a couple of times, sighed.

'Not keeping you up, am I?' Eddie asked.

Gerald ignored the sarcasm and finished his drink. 'Hand on heart,' he said, pushing the empty glass to one side. 'Do you think we've made a difference?'

Eddie looked blank, shook his head. 'Pass. Next question.'

'Oh come on, you *must* have an opinion.'

'On what?'

'Us, for Christ's sake. The Elders, the movement, what our press statements quaintly describe as a group of like-minded people who believe our government has let us down.'

'So far, so good, I suppose,' Eddie said with a doleful shrug of the shoulders. 'At least we're trying.'

Gerald fidgeted on his stool, searching for the words to explain the increasingly complicated muddle which now occupied his mind. 'There's no way round it,' he said after a long silence. 'Someone's got to publicly accept responsibility for what we've all been doing. And that someone is me.'

'Call me old-fashioned, but that sounds like *the* most fucking stupid idea I've ever heard in my entire fucking life.' Eddie raised his arms like a ringmaster introducing the star of the circus. 'Ladies and gentlemen,' he hissed, 'I give you the man who beats the shit out of muggers, vandals, ruffians, thugs, yobs, slobs, and every other arsehole infesting our streets today. He's the man who, single-handedly, kicks pikeys out of other people's fields, keeps illegals out of other people's countries and kidnaps members of our esteemed parliament in a death-defying attempt to cut a better deal for pensioners. A big round of applause, please, for Pixley Green's super-human sub-post master Mister... Gerald... Cornfield.'

'I said I'd accept the responsibility, not take all the credit,' said Gerald. 'Besides there's no evidence to link me with most of it anyway.'

'Then what's the point in sticking your neck out? Better to keep schtum and stay well clear of the Scrubs.'

'Don't worry, I've no intention of going inside.' Gerald hunched forward, stared wistfully at his finger and the pale indentation where his wedding ring had been until a few days earlier. 'No fool like an old fool. Isn't that what they say, Eddie?'

'Tell me about it, mate.'

'On the other hand, old age *does* have its advantages.'

'Oh Christ,' Eddie groaned. 'We're not back to flogging wisdom again, are we?'

'No we're not.' Gerald took a deep breath then let out a long, satisfied sigh. 'I'm afraid we've been missing a trick, ignoring the painfully obvious,' he said. 'While Rupert was turning young thugs into a silent army, silly old farts like us could have become a force to be reckoned with. But it can still be done, I've worked it all out.'

Chapter Twenty

The sweet, cider smell of fallen apples on damp, autumn grass sent a wave of nostalgia through Gerald Cornfield's bones, reminding him of new school terms after lazy summers, championship conkers dangled from knotted strings, football boots with a dubbin shine slung carelessly across the shoulder, and earnest prayers for snow as winter approached.

It was also a reminder of a passing year and an impending birthday which, as always, he'd try his level best to ignore.

But it was an important day; he could feel it in the early morning air, hear it on the breeze which whispered through the open window next to his desk where a beige file, marked *Statistics* lay central to his blotting pad. The figures it contained proved he was right.

Around six million people were members of a trade union at the last count, they said. And the numbers were falling. But there were more than twelve million pensioners during the same period, and the numbers were rising; twice as many pensioners as trade unionists. So, it could be argued, if the unions could hold governments to ransom at the drop of a spanner, pensioners could do much the same thing, but with knobs on.

Strikes, the ultimate sanction and bane of capitalist democracies around the world, could be a deadly weapon for a traditionally powerless section of the community, and Gerald was convinced he knew exactly how to use it, give or take a few adjustments.

Mrs Black placed his morning coffee on the blotter, with a nod towards the beige file. 'Is that the information you wanted then?'

'Its fine,' Gerald murmured without looking up from his diary.

She stood directly in front of his desk, folded her arms the way she always did when she sensed an argument. 'I assume this is all about starting a union or something for OAPs.' She paused for a moment, waiting for a response. 'It wouldn't work,' she declared emphatically.

Gerald looked up momentarily, smiled. 'Absolutely.'

'Most pensioners don't work so they can't strike, can they?' Mrs Black persisted. 'There'd be no point in joining a trade union?'

'My thoughts entirely.' Gerald leaned back in his chair, twisted a pencil between his fingers. 'Pensioners can't withdraw their labour if they are already unemployed. Simple logic.'

'Well then?' She gave another nod towards the file and waited for an explanation.

'I wonder,' Gerald said quietly. 'May *I* ask *you* a question first?'

Mrs Black looked slightly puzzled. 'I suppose so.'

'Why do you keep Detective Sergeant Anderson's contact details in your card index system?'

She shook her head slowly as if she were unsure. 'Do I keep them?' she said. 'I really don't recall.'

'Perhaps you remember how you came by them?'

Mrs Black stared out of the window, her brow furrowed in thought. 'Terribly sorry,' she shrugged, eyes wide. 'I've no idea.'

'Not to worry,' Gerald said with a dismissive flick of his hand. 'It's unimportant.'

She turned to go, but then hesitated. 'I only *ever* have your best interests at heart you know,' she said, glancing first at the file and then at him. 'But I *would* like to know?'

'Well, to begin with, you don't have to be employed to go on strike.' Gerald placed his hand on the beige file as if he might be taking an oath on a holy book. 'Everyone has the right to withdraw their cooperation, make a social nuisance of themselves, providing they don't break the law. You may recall that Mahatma Ghandi used non-cooperation and passive resistance to considerable advantage.'

Mrs Black gave a little gasp of disapproval. 'You're not going to encourage old people to lay down in front of railway trains and buses?'

'Yes,' he answered at once.

'But someone might get hurt, killed even.'

Gerald shook his head, trying to remember how E.W. always explained the grammatical construction. 'I simply meant that the answer to your question was *yes*, I'm *not* going to encourage old people to lay down in front of trains and buses.'

Her eyes narrowed. 'You're starting to sound like the Major,' she said frostily. 'Downright pedantic.'

He waited until she'd left the room and closed the door behind her before checking the word in his Oxford English. **Pedantic.** *adj.* describing a person who is excessively concerned with minor detail or displaying specialist knowledge. **Pedant**/ped-uhnt/*noun*.

It was an acute embarrassment. Gerald was convinced the word meant *stubborn* or *obstinate* but now discovered he'd been confusing *pedantic* with *adamant*, both of which seemed to be apt descriptions of E.W. But his casual browse through the book of words, a few moments of idle curiosity, was interrupted by the telephone.

Rupert's call was brief, his voice subdued. E.W. had been injured, badly injured; knocked down by a car. The driver didn't stop.

Gerald sat, unmoving, trance-like, his eyes fixed on the phone as if it might ring out at any moment with some kind of explanation for what appeared to be a hit-and-run. He glanced down, noticed that his hands were shaking; a faint but visible fluttering through his fingers over which, momentarily at least, he seemed to have little control.

Some issues are resolved beyond the glare of public scrutiny. The words rang in his ears. *Dark forces,* they'd called them. But it was undiluted adrenaline, not fear, that trembled through Gerald's body.

He checked his watch as the clock above the library struck ten, reached for his jacket, and set off towards the lift, a thick beige file under his arm.

'I won't be back today,' he said. 'Try to call you later.'

Mrs Black glanced at her diary, looked up accusingly. 'No meetings scheduled for today.'

'On the contrary,' he replied, 'I've been planning this one for quite some time.'

Traffic was light on the road from the office to the A3 and Gerald reached the car park with eight minutes to spare. It looked as if most of the others had already arrived, spread-out around the perimeter, ready to go. He flashed his headlights twice.

The others signalled back in unison, main beams on for a full minute while Gerald counted them; twenty-four, six short. But it wasn't yet ten thirty, so there was still time for more to arrive.

He fixed the medieval torture device around his left ear. Blue tooth; it certainly felt like *some* kind of tooth was biting into the side of his head and, if reports were to be believed, a frazzled brain was a potential side-effect. But it was the easiest option for telephone communications and, besides, it would all be over in an hour or so.

A convoy of twenty-eight left the car park at exactly ten thirty and turned left on to the A3, headed towards junction ten of the M25 and the start of their motorway orbit around London.

The plan was simple. They'd follow each other down the slip road on to the four lane motorway and form a single line in lane one. Three cars would then move up to occupy lanes two, three and four and the others would gradually fall in behind, creating four lines of seven cars across the width of the motorway well before junction thirteen.

The reality was less simple, and a series of muddled manoeuvres with unyielding lorries and speeding motorbikes took them well past Heathrow Airport and on toward junction sixteen. But then they were ready. Gerald waved a white flag from his car window and the four lane convey slowed to twenty-five miles an hour, creating a yawning gap between the cars and lorries up ahead and a chorus of irate horn blowing from the traffic behind.

Gerald's mobile phone rang out, on cue, at eleven o'clock with a call from the local radio station.

A softly spoken women asked if he was OK to speak and then switched him through to the studio where the hourly news bulletin was already in progress. Someone apologised for the delay and confirmed he'd be on in just a moment.

'It's a sunny autumn morning here on Surrey Sound with temperatures in the twenties.' Jeff, the morning show presenter, warbled his scheduled messages before moving on to the interview. 'But if you're travelling clockwise on the M25 right now, temperatures will be soaring... big time. A fleet of cars has spread out across the motorway and slowed things down to just twenty-five miles an hour.'

He played a few seconds of taped traffic noise and blasting car horns before going on.

'Well, if you're one of the cars dawdling behind this convoy of clowns, you might like to know that they're led by local businessman Gerald Cornfield, who's on the line to me now. Morning Gerald. So what's all this about?'

'We're demonstrating on behalf of Britain's pensioners who, we think, deserve a better deal.'

'And the cars… are they all driven by pensioners?'

'Yes, all twenty-eight of them.'

'Don't you think that's a bit unfair though. I mean it's nothing to do with the drivers stuck behind you. They can't get you a better deal, can they?'

'Quite right. And we'd like to apologise for the inconvenience. But we have to persuade this government to start taking us seriously for a change.'

'So where, exactly, are you now, Gerald?'

'We've just passed the M1 turn-off.'

'Will you be doing a full lap of the motorway?'

'Doubt it. That might be overdoing it.'

'So, the good news… you'll be off the motorway well before this evening's rush hour.'

'Guaranteed.'

'Quick point. What if an ambulance or fire engine needs to get by in a hurry?'

'I understand they regularly use the hard shoulder in emergencies.'

'Finally, then Gerald, will you be messing-up the motorways again anytime soon?'

'Unlikely. We've got a few other ideas to draw attention to the plight of pensioners, so let's wait and see.'

'Well there you have it listeners,' Jeff warbled. 'A rather unusual convoy of slow-moving pensioners, travelling clockwise on the M25 today. Steer clear if you can.'

Gerald opened his window, took a deep breath and prepared himself for the big one; an interview with the Press Association news agency who'd talked about syndicating a story nationwide – and that meant the national press would probably run it.

This time Gerald made the call and was put through to chief reporter Mike Diamond in the news room. Diamond apologised, said he was pressed for time; something about a security alert at Gatwick airport so he might have to cut short the interview. He promised to call back later if things started to kick off, then launched into some questions about the M25 demonstration; how was it going... was it legal... would they do it again? But he seemed more interested in other issues.

'What can you tell me about the abduction of the Coventry MP?' he began. The accent was south London, the tone brusque, the manner indifferent.

'Very little,' said Gerald. 'I wasn't directly involved.'

'Do you know any of the people who *were* involved?'

'Yes.'

'Can you give me a name... some names, perhaps?'

'No, but I have authority to speak on their behalf.'

'Do you condone kidnapping members of parliament?'

'No more than I condone the way successive parliaments have held us all to ransom.'

'In what way... held us to ransom?'

'Well, for a start, they've made common sense a crime and skewed laws to favour the guilty. They've totally ignored the epidemic of street violence, failed to protect our borders and dished-out generous lifestyle benefits to free-loaders with one hand while short-changing generations of pensioners with the other.'

'And how will kidnapping MPs change all that?'

'It's just one of the ways we've tried to focus media attention on our concerns.'

'The others being your little march to number ten, and today's traffic jam on the M25, I assume.'

'Those too, but we've done more than that... much more.'

'Could you just clarify, who are the "we" you refer to?'

'It's a political movement, The Elders.'

'You're their leader?'

'No, but I'm happy to accept responsibility for what we do.'

Diamond paused to check through his notes. 'Would that include sponsoring private street gangs, for example?' he asked.

'We have specially trained security teams, if that's what you mean.'

'It's not what I mean, as I think you know, but let's move on. What about pillories for hoodies? Your idea?'

'I'm afraid not. A lady I happen to know thought that one up.'

'There have been a number of reported confrontations with travellers? Would they be down to you?'

'I'd say any confrontations were down to the travellers concerned. Shouldn't squat on other people's land, should they?'

Diamond cleared his throat. 'I'm a bit confused,' he said with an irritated tone. 'You claim you accept responsibility for *everything* your organisation does but then deny any involvement in the kidnapping of an MP. You tell me you're not the leader of The Elders, that this pillory thing was someone else's idea, and that travellers only have themselves to blame for the recent violence. So everyone else is responsible, but not you.'

'I've never said I was *responsible* for what we've done. I said I was happy to accept *responsibility*, which is quite different.'

'Splitting hairs,' Diamond grunted. 'How do you respond to allegations that you're no more than a bunch of vigilantes, who've taken the law into their own hands?'

'I'd say we're only doing what the law *should* be doing but patently isn't.'

'Looks like you've made TV news,' Diamond interjected. 'Shots from a helicopter coming up now. I hadn't realised there were so many of you.'

Gerald peered through his windscreen; two helicopters hovering to the west of the motorway. A third appeared to be tailing the convoy of cars but keeping its distance. 'Incredible,' he exclaimed. 'Our traffic jam's not much worse than the usual chaos on the M25 yet we seem to warrant three helicopters.'

'It's quite a lot worse than usual,' said Diamond. 'Stretches back to the M23.'

'Probably time for us to leave then. Don't want to outstay our welcome, do we?' Gerald waved his white flag from the car window and the convey accelerated as one. They slipped gradually into a two lane formation as they approached junction twenty-four, and abandoned the motorway for the streets of north-east London.

'What's next?' Diamond asked. 'I assume you've something else planned.'

Gerald swung into a lay-by, switched off his engine, wound the window up. 'Right now I'm going home for a cup of tea. After that I'll ask the nation's pensioners to do what they do best,' he said with a hint of irony. 'I'm talking about fine-tuning the age-old art of moving very, very slowly and cautiously – slow walking, slow talking, slow responses, slow everything.'

'Slow driving on motorways, like this morning?'

'That too. But if enough of us get involved, we could slow-down the entire country – buses, trains, post offices, banks and, of course, the traffic in the high street. Old people could legitimately take five minutes to cross the road, three or more to get on and off public transport, positively ages to find their purses and wallets when they reach the head of a queue. You get the picture?'

'Civil disobedience?'

'Senile dementia! Not a crime yet... is it?'

Diamond's sudden laughter sounded genuine. 'You're a dangerous man Mr Cornfield,' he said. 'I wouldn't be surprised if your snail-paced army might one day hold the whole bloody nation to ransom.'

Gerald pulled the instrument of torture from his left ear and switched on the radio in time for Surrey Sound's midday news. They mentioned the morning traffic chaos and included a snippet from the earlier interview; the bit where Gerald apologised for the inconvenience.

By mid afternoon, the London evening newspaper had picked-up on the Press Association's news wire story about a "snail-paced revolutionary". It was largely complimentary and portrayed him as a champion of the over sixties with plans to mobilise twelve million oldies in a battle for pensioners' rights. Suggestions that he'd masterminded the kidnap of an MP had been denied, it said, along with rumours of his involvement in a vigilante campaign against street crime and anti-social behaviour.

A trimmed-down version of one of the press photographs taken at the Downing Street march accompanied the story, the fuzzy tip of Winston's left ear still just about visible near the edge of the picture. The caption said Gerald Cornfield was a "man on a mission".

The lady in the house opposite Pycroft Cottage gave a little wave from behind slightly parted net curtains as Gerald struggled out of his car and slowly straightened up; not dissimilar, he fancied, to applause for a fighter pilot clambering from the cockpit of a spitfire after a dog fight with the Luftwaffe's finest.

He crossed the small patch of lawn to the front door, turned to acknowledge the wave... but she'd gone.

The acrid smell of burnt toast, a reminder of a hurried breakfast, greeted him in the kitchen where the washing-up was still neatly stacked in the sink along with two wine glasses from the night before. The morning post had been propped up against a half empty coffee pot on the table; a couple of bills, an insurance deal from Saga, and an early birthday card.

Gerald made himself a cup of tea, took the last two digestives from the biscuit tin and settled down to make a few catch-up calls.

Rupert was with Katrina at the hospital. They were still waiting for test results but the positive news was that, despite internal injuries, a fractured collar bone and a broken ankle, E.W.'s condition had improved and he'd regained consciousness. He remembered only parking his car outside the library and crossing the road to the chemist. The rest was a complete blank but witnesses had described a black sports car jumping the traffic lights after hitting an elderly man.

But this wasn't the time to talk about motorway protests on the M25. Gerald promised an update later in the week when they'd all have more time to concentrate on a growing list of outstanding issues.

He was about to ring the office when he noticed the envelope on the shelf above the Aga; a small beige envelope with his name written obliquely across the front in Vee's unmistakeable doctor's scrawl. It was a short letter which began *My Dearest Gerald* and ended with her hoping they'd remain good friends. The bit in the middle didn't really offer a rational explanation; difficult decision, she said, all for the best… and would he mind terribly if she went ahead with Tennyson Place without him.

Gerald felt suddenly vulnerable and exposed, like a small boy who's just discovered a gaping hole in the seat of his trousers and wonders how many people have seen his bum. Vee wasn't the type to keep things to herself; she'd have almost certainly confided in Holly Lockwood, possibly told Katrina Bevington, and that meant Rupert Clark-Hall too. Perhaps even Eddie Bates knew about it.

Eddie's mobile announced that he was unavailable and to please ring the restaurant, but that played a recorded announcement about opening hours, so Gerald rang his home number. Eddie grunted, said he knew nothing about it, but wasn't surprised. Doctors, he philosophised, were no good at relationships thanks to medical school and all that messing about with corpses. Once they'd dissected a few cadavers, laid bare their entrails and innards, the human body somehow lost its all magic and mystique; enough to turn anyone off sex altogether. And, put like that, Gerald had to agree. But it wasn't much consolation for a sudden and demoralising brush off. 'How about a quick drink at The Crow,' he suggested.

'Sorry mate, can't. Gotta be at the restaurant in an hour.'

Gerald's voice sank. 'No problem... still, perhaps I could drop in for a plate of spaghetti and glass of something red.'

'On the house,' said Eddie. 'I may even join you myself.'

Gerald replaced the receiver and listened to the silence; a penetrating silence which seemed to have swept through the house like an icy breeze.

Vee's make-shift clothes line lay in a muddle on the box room floor, cupboards and drawers still open is if she'd left in a hurry. And, in the waste bin, the residue of her life; some tissues smeared with lipstick, an empty perfume bottle, torn-up credit card receipts, a half-eaten packet of mints. He closed the door and went back to the kitchen.

Just before five thirty he called the office, using his mobile phone. Mrs Black was on her way out. She'd left some notes on his desk; nothing too important. It could all wait until the morning.

'Where exactly are you?' she asked.

'Oh, out and about, but headed for home.'

'And will you be home this evening... in case I think of anything important?'

'Probably not,' Gerald said wearily. 'I may drop in for a quick bite of supper at the Casa Roma... have a bit of a natter with Eddie Bates.'

'Have a good evening,' she said. 'Enjoy your meal.'

Gerald felt the rush of adrenaline and a fleeting shiver down his spine as he dialled Dizzy's number. 'I think we have lift-off,' he whispered. 'Tonight, Casa Roma, sometime after eight.'

He sat, perfectly still, staring at the clock on the wall as the silence crept slowly back into the room. Two hours to have a hot bath, shave, polish the black brogues, and take the new black suit from its zip-fronted Savile Row cover. Perhaps a black shirt and tie too; understated but with a subtle hint of menace. And cologne, lots of it, to mark his territory; Knize Ten, from Vienna, the favourite of David Niven and Errol Flynn; a manly, leathery classic and worthy calling card for this special evening.

Gerald stood for a moment in front of the wardrobe mirror, smoothed down his hair with the flat of his hand, and reminded himself to keep his back straight. Then, like a knight fixing a maiden's favour to his lance, he took Betsy's ring from his waistcoat pocket and slipped it back on his finger, with a mumbled but heartfelt apology.

A black cashmere overcoat, draped loosely around his shoulders, billowed and flapped in the October breeze as he strode, with purpose, through the fallen leaves on Friday Street towards a defining moment in his life at the Casa Roma restaurant.

* * *

Eddie Bates leaned back against the bar, facing the door, exchanging witticisms with some diners on a nearby table, a bottle of Chambolle Musigny, opened and ready to drink, on a silver tray behind him.

'And how is our motorway road hog this evening?' he called out, as Gerald handed his coat to a waiter.

Gerald shrugged. 'Not altogether sure. Ask me again later.'

The two men shook hands, patted each other on the back.

Eddie eyed his friend up and down. 'Talk about men in black. Black Y-fronts too, I wouldn't mind betting?'

'Blue and white... striped. And they're boxers.'

'Well, the wine's red,' said Eddie, pouring the best part of a bottle into two balloon glasses. 'Get some down your neck.'

Gerald sipped his drink, thoughtfully, watching him. 'Are you *never* depressed?' he said. 'I mean, surely you must get pissed-off with the world sometimes?'

'Not often. As you know, I get pissed from time to time, but very rarely pissed-off. And I never, ever get suicidal...which is more than I can say for you.'

'I take it you've seen the evening paper then?'

'Couldn't really miss it, could I? All over page three...confessions of a senile delinquent... an open invitation to every PC Plod in the district to stick you behind bars.'

'It's what I was talking about at The Crow... taking responsibility.'

'Taking the rap, more like.' Eddie shook his head angrily. 'The ridiculous thing is you had sod all to do with most of it.'

'That's the whole point,' Gerald insisted. 'I've admitted to nothing more than causing a traffic jam.'

'Splitting hairs.'

Gerald stared into his drink. 'Funny, you're the second person to say that today.'

'Well the other person was dead right,' Eddie grunted. He hesitated for a moment, as if he had something more to say, then reached for a menu and slapped it down on the bar. 'Anyway, I can recommend the lobster.'

'Sounds good to me. Hearty meal for the condemned man, and all that.'

'Nah,' said Eddie. 'They'd have been waiting on your doorstep if they were gonna pull you in today.'

Gerald nodded. 'Makes sense... unless, of course, they knew I wouldn't be at home... that I'd be here, for instance.'

'How would they know that?' Eddie's eyes narrowed. 'Your name's not even in the reservations book.'

Gerald laughed suddenly. 'Even makeshift messiahs need a genuine Judas. And I think I've probably got mine.'

'Somebody's snitched on you?'

'I wouldn't put it like that. I'm sure they've got my best interests at heart.'

'I hope so, for your sake.' Eddie leaned slowly forward, took Gerald's elbow, sniffed at his jacket. 'Is that you I can smell?'

'If you mean the manly aroma of Knize Ten, then yes.'

Eddie took a large gulp of wine, shook his head. 'How about the poncey pong of old poofs? Is that you as well?'

'Lobster, wasn't it?' Gerald said, changing the subject. 'Can I have it cold, with a bit of potato salad?'

'You can have it any way you choose, my son.' Eddie stood up, nodded towards a table for two in the corner. 'Over there do you?'

'A table for four would be better,' said Gerald with a fragile smile. 'I'm expecting some very fond memories to join me for dinner.'

Eddie rolled his eyes and led the way. 'Two cold lobsters, one with potato salad, table ten,' he yelled at nobody in particular. 'And another Chambolle whatsit.'

Gerald sat facing the window. He glanced across the road to a narrow stretch of pavement outside The Jolly Farmer which had been flooded with light as the pub doors swung open and two young girls tottered into silhouette. They wedged chairs against the doors to keep them open and tottered back inside.

'Are they at it *every* night?' Gerald groaned, as the muffled beat grew gradually louder. 'I don't know how you put up with it.'

'We turn up the music in here so our customers have to speak louder,' Eddie said drily. 'That way we drown out the din from across the road... beat them at their own game, so to speak.'

A second bottle of Chambolle Musigny was quaffed with the lobster, prior to the dolcelatte and vintage port, followed by a couple of cognacs with the coffee. And, somewhere in the middle, there were the crepe suzettes floating in more than their fair share of grand marnier.

'I don't suppose you know this,' said Eddie, in a secretive whisper. 'But you're not supposed to drink red wine with fish.'

Gerald leaned forward. 'I've heard that before but I've never quite understood why.'

'Why? Because if you do, it makes you drunk, that's why.'

'That accounts for it,' said Gerald peering out into the street. 'I think I'm seeing double.'

Eddie followed his gaze, hesitated. 'No, you're alright, there's definitely two of them.'

Four large police officers unfolded themselves from two small squad cars, set their caps at a military angle and marched towards the Casa Roma's front door. Two crossed the restaurant to the bar and showed a photograph to one of the waiters, while the others took up a position just inside the door; heads up, arms folded, legs apart, like a couple of genies, recently escaped from their magic lamps.

'I must be more important than I'd thought,' Gerald declared proudly. 'Public enemy number, one by the looks of it.' He rose unsteadily to his feet and headed for the gents, acutely aware that he'd drunk too much. But he smiled at his reflection in the mirror as he washed his hands, combed his hair and tweaked the knot in his tie.

Then, after checking his teeth for traces of an excellent meal, he returned to the table, where an officer stood waiting.

'Gerald Arthur Cornfield?'

Gerald nodded wearily and sat down.

'I have reason to believe you may be able to help us with our enquiries into the abduction of a member of parliament and a series of recent assaults on young people involving replica pillory devices.'

Gerald shrugged but said nothing.

'I'd like you to accompany us to the station, sir?'

'If you insist,' Gerald sighed. 'But I'm not at all sure I'll be much help.'

Eddie Bates drained his brandy glass. 'Is he under arrest then?'

'Did I mention an arrest?' said the officer, with the sudden, pitying smile of higher understanding.

Eddie thought for a second, shook his head.

'Then I think we can assume he's *not* under arrest, can't we sir?'

Gerald leaned back on his chair, thrust his hands into his waistcoat pockets. 'May I ask a question?'

'At the station, sir, if you wouldn't mind.'

'But that's my question,' said Gerald. 'How do we get there now your cars have been nicked?'

All eyes stared into the darkness and the empty space where two police cars had stood only minutes earlier. Two genies abandoned their posts and ran out into the street in a futile gesture of pursuit.

They loitered for a moment at the edge of the curb as if, perhaps, they expected the cars to magically materialise, before acknowledging defeat by calling-in the embarrassing details of a multiple theft of police property.

A barely concealed ripple of laughter spread slowly among the other diners, reaching a crescendo in the vicinity of the bar and culminating in a standing ovation as Gerald took a contemptuous bow before he was led outside to wait for a replacement car.

But it wasn't a car, it was a van; the type used to transport prisoners to jail or police officers to incidents – and this was certainly an incident. The culprits, when apprehended, would be charged with *taking and driving away...* but, until that time, it seemed like a clear-cut case of *taking the Mickey.*

A crowd had gathered outside Pixley Green police station by the time Gerald stepped out of the van and into the glare of TV lights and flashing cameras. They were still there an hour later when Detective Sergeant Anderson finally ran out of questions and Gerald reappeared on the station's granite steps.

'What are your plans Gerry?' somebody shouted.

It was a straightforward question, deserving an honest, uncomplicated answer but Gerald had long-since realised that life is rarely that simple. He buttoned his jacket, straightened-up to his full five feet ten inches, and spoke at length of age, wisdom and a new generation of elders with the unique power to influence the way of the world. He talked about many things but said nothing of harnessing the natural aggression of youth or how a less tolerant attitude to crime and punishment might rebuild confidence in a failing justice system. And there was no mention of military protection for Britain's borders; all that could wait for another time, in a bright new era when liberty and human rights were the just reward for personal responsibility and not simply the sanctuary of the lawless.

Besides, it was close to midnight and it had been a very long day.

A hazy moon rose above the trees as Mr Cornfield crossed the common and headed for home. He gazed up at the night sky for just a moment, blew a secret kiss to Betsy and, with a little wink to God in his heaven, wished himself many happy returns of tomorrow. It may have been the heady mix of lobster and red wine or, perhaps, it was a trick of the light, but just beyond the church spire, and very slightly to the right, he fancied a tiny star winked back.